Claire looked toward the garage's interior

She stopped the car in the driveway, suspended in an instinctive immobility, waiting for a sniff of the predator's scent so she could tell its direction.

I'm acting strangely, she thought. *There's no reason for this feeling.*

She drove on into the garage, unlocked the connecting door to the house and turned on the light before stepping into the kitchen.

Despite the normality of the scene before her, the jumpy feeling remained. Suddenly she felt something, like any angry spider biting at the top of her spine. She whirled around, facing the blackened entry into the dining room, her heart hammering the wall of her chest. She could have sworn she heard a sound from the dining room. Only one way to find out. She would have to go see....

ABOUT THE AUTHOR

M.J. Rodgers is a Washington State native who has recently returned after many years away. And although she has found many parts of the world beautiful and exciting, that old adage ''there's no place like home'' holds fresh truth for her.

Dead Ringer

M.J. Rodgers

Harlequin Books

TORONTO • NEW YORK • LONDON
AMSTERDAM • PARIS • SYDNEY • HAMBURG
STOCKHOLM • ATHENS • TOKYO • MILAN

To my brother, Charles,
a handsome hunk who has
lived the life of a real hero
in many a woman's heart

Harlequin Intrigue edition published March 1991

ISBN 0-373-22157-6

DEAD RINGER

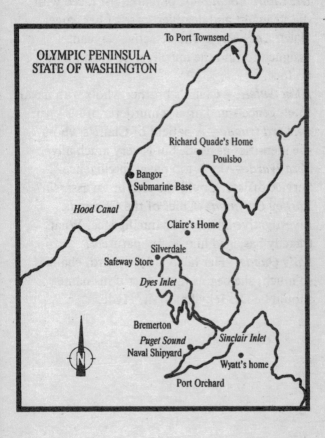

OLYMPIC PENINSULA
STATE OF WASHINGTON

To Port Townsend

Richard Quade's Home

Poulsbo

Bangor
Submarine Base

Hood Canal

Claire's Home

Silverdale

Safeway Store

Dyes Inlet

Bremerton

Puget Sound
Naval Shipyard

Sinclair Inlet

Wyatt's home

Port Orchard

N

CAST OF CHARACTERS

Dr. Claire Boland—A psychologist faced with the strangest and deadliest case of her career.

Wyatt Lockhart—The detective sergeant assigned to find the murderer of the man with no face.

Alan Gillette—Claire's brother who's with naval Intelligence—and after a murderer of his own.

Richard Quade—A patient of Claire's whom she identifies as dead, but is very much alive.

Vera Ward—Alan's top naval Intelligence Service officer. Could she also be an assassin?

Barney Coffman—Chief of the Criminal Investigative Division of Intelligence. What tragedy has aged him so prematurely?

Sally Quade—Her husband, Richard, changes so much, she begins to wonder if his name should be Dr. Jekyll and Mr. Hyde.

Chapter One

He wanted the man to see his face the instant before he killed him, so he could see the shocked expression his victim would have when he found he was looking at himself.

So he hid out of sight, crouched behind the bulk-food section of the Safeway store in Silverdale, Washington, and waited. He had no doubts about his quarry. He had watched him for nearly a year and knew all his habits. The waiting man glanced down at his watch. It was a few minutes before eleven. It wouldn't be long.

The store was virtually deserted, just as it had been this late at night for the last few weeks. The one or two employees who worked as checkers were generally helping with stock. The few customers who arrived weren't interested in fruit or vegetables. The hot August nights sent them to the freezer section. Only his victim headed for the fresh fruit, zeroing in on the cantaloupes. That addiction had decided both the method and place of his death. That afternoon's telephone call had decided the time was tonight.

A whiff of peanuts reached the waiting man's nostrils. He stretched his neck to look into the clear plastic lid of the bulk-food bin he was squatting next to and saw the mounds of fresh roasted peanuts. He lifted the half-moon, plastic cover and reached into the bin for a handful.

His ears reverberated with the crunching sounds of the peanuts between his teeth. He savored the taste even though it brought back memories of the long caged months. He wasn't sure why the two were connected, but he was sure he never got enough peanuts in those days. He never got enough of anything. Remembering past privations stoked his anger and the need for revenge made him impatient for the kill.

CLAIRE BOLAND stepped out of the shower still feeling sticky and hot. She patted her skin with a soft white towel, realizing she had no one to blame for her present discomfort but herself. That pint of Deep Chocolate Häagen-Dazs ice cream she had substituted for dinner had tasted great but now, hours later, the high fat content was pushing her internal thermostat past boiling. She knew better than to eat fatty things in the hot weather, but the thought of ice cream always supplanted her normal good sense with temporary insanity.

She walked into her bedroom and frowned at the rumpled rose-colored sheets thrown haphazardly against the white wicker headboard. Even after a cool shower, she knew going back to bed was out of the question. She'd just continue to toss and turn. Stepping away from the bed, she caught a backward glimpse of her nude body in the full-length, free standing mirror. It was enough to make her wish she had put on her bathrobe.

She had unusually small bones for her five-foot-eight-inch frame and swore she could feel even an extra ounce of adipose tissue. That normally made her conscious of everything she ate. But her subconscious had had the last say tonight, and even more irritating, it was telling her she was hungry again.

Claire's bare feet padded across the giving surface of the living-room carpet, straight toward the firm white tile of the kitchen floor, on a collision course with the refrigerator. She opened it and drank in the funnel of cool air that washed her face, wishing she could climb in. Even with all the windows now open, the trapped heat of the house was stifling.

Cold chicken and some limp lettuce stared at her in all their unappetizing splendor. There was no getting around it. If she wanted something to appease her taste buds, she'd have to make a trip to the store. She walked back to the bedroom and put on a pair of ice-blue cotton slacks and blouse, carefully avoiding a second glance in the mirror.

THE SECONDS INCHED BY for the man who crouched on the floor of the Safeway store next to the bin of fresh peanuts. The detonator felt slippery between his fingers. He rubbed his sweating hands on the rough denim of his blue jeans, never taking his eyes off the aisle where his victim would soon be.

CLAIRE DROVE to the Safeway store with the top of the Allante down. The movement of the car through the still air fanned her cheeks and lifted her long red-gold hair. She sighed in welcome relief at the small respite from the heat.

It was only then she began to wonder what it was she should get. She had never liked food shopping. Jerry had been the one who walked up and down the aisles, finding pleasure in just looking at what was there.

Claire shook her head as though she might be able to shake away the memories. She knew it was futile. In the two years since his death, images of Jerry still frequently crept into her waking thoughts and ran screaming into her nightmares. Flashes of those nightmares made her shiver in the warm night.

The lights of Safeway loomed ahead as she drove down Bucklin Hill Road. She turned right into the parking lot, glancing at the large produce truck parked near the back for unloading. It was while she drove past it that the idea of fresh fruit came to mind. Nothing to prepare. Sweet and nearly fat-free. Her mouth began to water as she thought about everything that was in season.

ANOTHER LOOK at his watch assured the waiting man that only ten minutes had passed, although it seemed more like an hour. He was beginning to wonder whether he had depended too much on habit when the man he had been expecting suddenly turned the corner aisle and headed directly for the fresh cantaloupe bin.

Relief and excitement started the man's pulse racing as his quarry approached not more than ten feet away from his hiding place. He watched as his intended victim picked up one cantaloupe and tested its firmness and then brought it to his nose to smell it. The waiting man had begun to sweat again. It was the wrong cantaloupe! Had all this planning been in vain?

An eternity crawled by as his prey held the cantaloupe in careful evaluation. Then his eyes widened as he caught sight of the much bigger cantaloupe, sitting on top of the pile of fresh fruit. He discarded the smaller globe and eagerly reached for the larger prize. He held it up, obviously admiring its beautiful golden color and the heavy weight of it in his hand. As he brought it to his nose, the man in hiding leaped to his feet and smiled.

He was glad he did. The look of absolute disbelief and terror in his victim's eyes fed something hungry and snarling inside his gut. He was still smiling as he pressed the button on the detonator to explode the bomb inside the cantaloupe.

CLAIRE HEARD a loud booming noise as she entered the Safeway store. For a moment she stopped and listened. When only quiet followed, she decided the noise must have been the produce truck dropping a couple of heavy crates. She dismissed it from her mind and hurried to the left end of the store toward the fresh produce section. She walked past several empty aisles and then a closed photo department and turned right where tables were piled high with fresh ripe fruit. Before she could take another step, a strange haze pierced her eyes and she choked at the sudden pungent smell of smoke.

Her eyes began to water as she made her way down the aisle. She looked up wondering if the haze and odor were coming from the ventilation system. It was while she was still looking at the ceiling that suddenly she tripped over something lying in the middle of the aisle, and the next thing she knew she was falling.

Frantically she grasped at a nearby bin of seedless green grapes. They squished between her fingertips, liquefying into a green slime as she slid down, unable to block her fall. Then there was a flash of movement to her left, not firmly registering on her awareness.

The next thing she knew, she was on the cold vinyl floor, her hand full of squashed grapes, her eyes face-to-face with the mutilated, blackened and gory horror that had once been the face of a human being. The blood froze in her veins.

A gasp more than a cry choked through Claire's lips. She didn't scream. Screaming would have delayed her retreat from the terrifying image before her. A stronger reaction had her body already moving away, pushing her up against the side of the produce trays and to her feet as she still stared, horrified at the carnage and yet transfixed, as though it held her in a cruel hypnotic power.

Backward, ever backward, she stumbled, choking out stunted inarticulate sounds. Only when she was several feet down the aisle was she mercifully able to turn her head away. As she leaned over the potato bin, her body retched uncontrollably, trying to physically remove the emotional butchery slashing at her insides. Unsatisfactory dry heaves was all she could manage.

The physical effort to be sick brought on a pounding headache, and yet amazingly steadied her initial over-whelming panic. She told herself there wasn't anything here that could harm her. The man was dead. It was a man, wasn't it? Her eyes reluctantly returned to the appalling sight on the floor.

From several feet away, she could now see the complete body. Years of training in observation automatically took over. She was surprised how intact the man's body was considering the damage done to the face. No, not just the face. The left hand was also gone.

She tried to swallow. Her throat was too swollen, dry. He was wearing a new pair of blue jeans and an old faded yellow shirt with long sleeves and a large grease stain on the right elbow. His clothing was somehow familiar. An intellectual curiosity, devoid of emotion, pushed her feet forward, as wisps of memory feathered about her.

Her mind was still searching as she looked down at the remaining hand. The thumb was black. An old white scar dug into the back of the hand near the wrist. Then she remembered.

Recognition brought a new wave of horror to numb her brain. She reached sideways, trying to find something firm, something steady to hold on to. Her groping hand knocked oranges to the floor.

Other thoughts and questions scratched at her paralyzed brain. Not wanting to attend to the irritating urgings, she closed her eyes, allowing her mind to rest against the blackness. He was dead. She could do nothing for him now but report his death. She opened her eyes. Everything around her had begun to look like a prop in some B-rated horror movie.

She had to move. She had to get help. The thought pushed her body down the other produce aisle, straight to the closed photo counter at the front end of the store, then left to the checkout stands.

The empty positions spread out before her, chained and still. She hurried down the aisle adjacent to the checkout stands, trying to find a living soul in all this empty expanse and quiet. When she came almost to the end, she realized the first position was open. She stopped and looked around. Where was the checker? Then she heard the voice.

He was singing out of tune as his thin bony body gyrated in front of the stacked boxes of cereal. Small screeches of a popular rock song escaped from the sides of his earphones.

Claire ran down the aisle toward him.

"Help. I need…help," she said. Too late, she realized her voice was too excited, octaves too high.

But she needn't have worried she might frighten the gangly box boy. The bobbing head didn't turn in her direction. The pursed lips kept on with their unintelligible wail. He continued to stack new boxes of Grapenuts cereal. Claire made an effort to swallow but no moisture remained in her throat. She concentrated on moving closer. "Excuse me?"

The young man must have seen the movement out of the corner of his eye because he was startled into dropping a box of cereal. But although he looked at her squarely now, he still did not remove the earphones, so he was unable to hear what she was going to say. Claire realized this and pointed to her ears. It was only then the thought seemed to occur to the teenager to remove the earphones.

"Yeah, sorry. You need something?" he said.

"I don't want to... Is there someone else? A manager?"

"Art's the Assistant Manager. He's doing the checkouts."

"The checkout stands." Claire pointed in back of her. "No one there." She paused to listen to her own words. Were they really so disjointed?

"Must've gone to the back for a minute," he said, staring at the box of cereal in his hand.

Claire could tell this wasn't a young man used to taking the initiative.

"Can you...find...manager?" Claire asked. The words seemed so hard to get out.

"Yeah. I guess so."

He got down from the small stepladder he had been on and led the way to the front of the store. Just as they both turned on the aisle feeding to the checkout stands, a gray-haired man suddenly stepped out from one of the other aisles. Claire jumped, her hand swinging out and knocking over an end display package of Orville Redenbacher's Light buttered popcorn. The box boy bent down to pick it up with a disapproving frown in Claire's direction.

"This lady wants you," the young man said, then immediately put his headphones back on and turned toward his aisle of cereal boxes. Claire's attention switched to the man before her.

He was six-feet, mid-fifties, gray and balding with a large nose and desultory lines crisscrossing nearly every inch of his darkly suntanned face. He wore a very public smile as his heavy hands folded protectively over his ample waistline.

"I'm Arthur Knudsen, assistant manager," he said.

Claire took a breath. "A terrible thing. Dead man. Lying on the floor. No face. Produce department. Get police."

Arthur Knudsen just stared at her.

"You understand? A man. Dead," she said.

Claire knew she wasn't communicating properly. The words weren't making complete sentences. She reached her right hand out to Knudsen as though she might convey her message with it. The eyes before her stared at it and then blinked.

"Who are you?"

"Boland. Claire Boland. He's dead, Mr. Knudsen."

"Someone died? Here?"

His head turned side to side as though looking for the body.

"In the produce department," Claire repeated. "Please. The phone. I'll call."

Disbelief puckered his lined face. "Where is this dead man?"

Claire had no doubt he was counting on her being some crackpot. Nothing to do but show him the evidence. She sighed and led the way.

They stopped a couple of feet from the body. Claire felt another lurch in her stomach at the sight of the remains of what had once been a man's face. But this time she controlled the desire to be sick. She turned quickly as she heard the sharp intake of breath beside her. Knudsen's face sagged ashen before her eyes.

"Shall I call?" she asked.

There was a distinguishable pause before his lips seemed able to form the words. "No, no. You stay here. I'll call. No, better yet, you leave. Get out."

He turned, quickly disappearing toward the back of the store. Had he really said, "Get out"? The shock must have addled his brain. Claire knew she couldn't just walk away after discovering a dead man. The police would have questions. She looked at her watch. It was five after eleven. Until the authorities arrived, at least she could try to keep people from coming into the produce section.

She turned her eyes toward the large round bins of loose nuts, candy and cookies, away from the horror a few feet from her. But her thoughts kept revolving around another death.

Jerry's body had been destroyed too. They had told her not to look, and she had listened. She had wanted to remember Jerry as he had been—whole and full of life. Only tonight she had been supplied with a living color picture to feed the worst of her nightmares. It burned in her brain.

Everything seemed to be getting fuzzy. Her vision tunneled more and more. She felt too weary to fight to clear it.

If she could just lean up against something. She saw the solid countertop in the photo department. Her feet had her there before the conscious decision made its way through her fragmented thoughts. She leaned heavily against the high glass counter's comforting support and closed her eyes. Layers of light and dark registered in alternate rows behind her resting lids like muddy sediments of passing time.

When she next opened her eyes, her vision had expanded to normal. From her position in the photo department, she could see the path someone would take who entered the store. She could also keep an eye on the produce section where the body lay without actually having to continually view the horrible remains. All she could do now was wait. A curious detachment swept her in a weaving wave of light-headedness.

A man and woman came into the store and took a cart. Claire's body tensed. She said a silent prayer they would not come her way. It was answered as the new arrivals steered their cart toward the dairy section.

After what seemed like an eternity to her distorted time sense, two men entered cautiously. One wore the green uniform of a sheriff's deputy, the other a medium-blue business suit. She waved, relieved the wait was over. The man in the business suit nodded at her wave. He said something to the uniformed officer beside him and turned in her direction.

As he quickly closed the distance between them, Claire watched his thick blond hair lift to catch the overhead fluorescent lights. Although at least six-foot-three and powerfully built, he moved easily and purposefully, like a strong, high mountain wind sweeping toward a low pressure valley. When he reached her, she looked up into his green-blue eyes.

"Detective Sergeant Wyatt Lockhart, Sheriff's Department," he said as he flashed his badge at her. His deep voice nestled in her ears, strong and slow, like an unhurried massage.

"Uh...Boland," Claire said, as she held out her hand.

He put his badge away before his large hand took hers. His grip was warm, firm. She knew her hand felt cold and limp in comparison. He was looking directly into her eyes, an absorbing look that seemed to soak up her gaze. A small frown separated his dark blond eyebrows. "Do you know anything about a dead man?"

With some difficulty she tore her eyes away from the whirlpool-like pull of his stare and pointed with her left hand. "The body...over there."

He studied her face a moment more before releasing her hand, moving past her and making his way down the aisle to where the body lay. Claire found herself comforted by this detective sergeant's presence. He exuded a quiet confidence and control. Now she could leave this awful business in professional hands.

She watched him kneel down next to the body. He seemed to be studying the dead man for a long time, but Claire realized it might just be her imagination. Finally he got up and came back to her. Once again she felt his eyes studying her face.

"What do you know about this death, Ms. Boland?"

"I...found the body."

A frown etched Wyatt Lockhart's forehead as he reached into his suit coat pocket for a pad and pencil. "Why didn't you report it?"

She didn't understand his question. "You mean personally?"

Sergeant Lockhart's eyes never left her face. "I mean why didn't you dial 911?"

Claire blinked, realizing she was obviously missing something. "Didn't Arthur Knudsen tell you . . . ?"

"Who's Arthur Knudsen?"

Claire's tunneled vision returned in the swift stroke of his question. She wished there was a place to sit down. Unconsciously she looked around. The throbbing in her head was getting worse. Her hand raised to rub her temple.

"Are you saying...Knudsen...no call...?" Her thoughts and voice faded away.

"We got an anonymous call, a male voice telling us a dead man could be found here, but that was all. Now at the risk of repeating myself, who is this Arthur Knudsen?"

Claire tried to marshal her thoughts. "Assistant manager. I went to find . . . He said he'd call."

"How long ago was that?"

Claire looked at her watch again. Could it really be only ten minutes after eleven? She stared in disbelief.

"Ms. Boland? Did you hear my question?"

"About five minutes."

Wyatt nodded. "That's about when we got the call."

"But why didn't he . . . ?" Her thoughts and voice were again fading. She wasn't really asking the sergeant the question. She was voicing her own puzzlement. He seemed to understand that and didn't pursue her half question.

"Where did Knudsen go to make this call?"

Claire's hand waved toward the back of the store. It ended up pointing at the approaching uniformed deputy she had seen earlier at the entrance. He stopped in front of Wyatt.

"I found two stock boys in the back and another one near the cereal display," he said. "There's a couple shopping on the other side of the store. No one seems to know anything. The stock boys said there was also an assistant manger around somewhere, but I haven't found him. I see you located the body."

Wyatt nodded. "Male, white, late twenties, about five-ten, stocky, curly black hair. We'll need as many crime scene investigators as you can find. And get a hold of John Sanders."

"The bomb technician?"

"Yes. Looks like someone blew this guy's face off. And while you're making the calls, wake up the pathologist. I want the body examined at the scene this time and not in the mortuary."

Fighting an encroaching dizziness, Claire worked to keep her eyes open as another man joined Wyatt and the uniformed deputy. The newcomer was thirtyish, pudgy, had masses of curly red hair and pale pasty skin. Claire was thinking that he looked like the Pillsbury Dough boy with a Ronald McDonald's wig.

Wyatt turned to him and smiled. "Hi, Tom. Glad you came along. We don't often get to be the first on the scene."

Tom nodded back. "Well, my excuse is that I was out for a drive and heard the call come in on the radio. But this is the neighborhood where I live. What were you doing at the Silverdale precinct this late?"

Wyatt shrugged. "I was just cleaning up the paperwork on a burglary when this call came in. The on-duty detective was out following up on a liquor store robbery, so I thought I'd take the call. Just as well. They would have had to get us in on the act anyway."

Claire was beginning to get dizzy from the enormous effort to concentrate on the words the men were speaking. She had stepped back to lean up against the counter in the photo shop. Now that the situation was in capable hands, she could feel a definite loosening of the hold she had kept on herself.

"Murder?" Tom asked, as he glanced over at the body.

Wyatt nodded. "Certainly appears to be. Secure this area for the crime scene investigators. Round up all the employees you can find and get their statements. If they saw anything at all, bring them down to Port Orchard. Find the assistant manger, Arthur Knudsen. I definitely want him in for a talk."

Tom was nodding. "I'll close the store for a few hours. We don't want customers walking in and out while our teams are trying to do—"

Wyatt turned from Tom and quickly moved toward Claire. She was leaning heavily on the counter, cold sweat seeping through her pores as waves of dizziness flooded through her. Before she knew it, he was at her side, his strong arm around her, propping her up. The warmth of his supporting arm and the genuine concern in his deep voice were instantly steadying.

"Are you going to pass out on me, Ms. Boland?"

She tried to smile, but her jaw wouldn't cooperate. "I'm trying my best not to, Sergeant Lockhart."

He took a firmer grip around her shoulders and smiled. "How about some ice for the back of your neck?"

The thought of ice at the back of her neck sent a new chill through Claire's body. She looked up at the tall blond sergeant and shook her head. "I'm in shock. I should be kept warm."

The slightly slurred words sounded strange and foreign in her ears, as though someone else had said them. She found it curious how part of her knew what was wrong and could explain it so clinically while the rest of her mind floundered in a swirling abyss.

The next thing she knew Wyatt was taking off his suit coat and wrapping it around her shoulders. "Maybe this will help. Lord knows I've been looking for an excuse to take it off."

The lingering warmth from his body inside the coat surrounded her in surprising comfort. The awful, cold waves of dizziness began to subside. Suddenly her sense of smell seemed to return as she detected the pleasant fragrance of Old Spice clinging to the fabric of his coat. She couldn't believe it had been only twenty minutes before that she had come out of a shower still feeling too warm. It seemed like another lifetime.

"Thank you," she said as she looked up to find his concerned eyes still watching her.

"Come on, Ms. Boland. We're going to take a turn around the block. Maybe we can help you walk off some of that shock."

Claire wouldn't have dreamed of arguing. She wanted to be as far away from that nightmare in the produce section as she could get. And she couldn't think of a better escort.

With his strong arm back around her for support, Wyatt led Claire out into the warm midsummer night.

THE KILLER stepped up to the telephone on the other end of the Safeway entrance and put the detonator in his pocket. Then he dropped a quarter in the slot and dialed the number he had memorized. It was answered almost immediately, as if the person on the other end of the line had been waiting. The man in the jeans and light yellow shirt spoke quickly.

"Stage two is complete. Ride the bicycle in tomorrow and tie it up where we discussed. Stage three will take place around noon."

He didn't wait for a response, but hung up the phone and started toward the truck. He halted and ducked back into the shadows as the woman with the red-gold hair suddenly came out of the Safeway store with a tall blond man.

He couldn't be sure, but he thought she had seen him in that instant she tripped over the body. He would have liked to have stayed around to hear what he could, but he knew he had to be leaving. And he certainly couldn't chance her seeing him a second time.

They walked away and he once again started for the dark blue pickup truck. As he thought about it, he realized it might not even matter if she had seen him the first time. Silverdale wasn't that small a town. Chances are she had never met Richard Quade. He gave her retreating back one last look before opening the driver's side of the pickup.

He positioned himself behind the wheel and took a moment to become familiar with the dashboard instruments. As he started the ignition, a doubt surfaced to claim his thoughts. What if she had met Richard Quade? He frowned momentarily and then shrugged. If she had, she would be wishing she hadn't after he got through with her.

Chapter Two

Wyatt guided Claire out of the air-conditioned store into the still, warm night air. He matched his long stride to her shorter one, heading them in the direction of Dyes Inlet, where he knew the tide was in and reasoned the air from the water might provide a little fresh breeze.

As his arm encircled her slim frame, he inhaled the light, enticing fragrance emanating from her skin. He found he was also having a hard time keeping his eyes off the reddish-gold of her long hair as it danced around her shoulders under the summer night sky like hundreds of soft glowing fireflies.

"You're not a native, are you?" Wyatt asked. He was sure if she had been in Silverdale long, he wouldn't have missed her.

She took a moment to respond. "No."

Speech apparently was still difficult for her so he decided to carry the conversation for them both. "Well I've lived here all my life. Attended Olympic College. Took the ferry over to the University of Seattle every day to complete my degree. Only been out of state twice and each time I couldn't wait to get back.

"You see, I'm not one of those people who takes where I live for granted and is always looking for something better. I'm always discovering new things right here. Like tonight. Smell that air. It's so clean and sweet you can taste it."

He talked for several minutes about the beauty of the Olympic Mountains and the profusion of natural rhododendrons in the spring and foxgloves in the summer. Then he related a childhood memory of wild deer coming to the door of his parents' home and the time he ran for two miles beside a red fox through a coastal forest of dense fir trees. The more he talked, the more even her breathing became. Gradually her shoulders straightened within his supporting arm.

She was steady on her feet now. When they reached the bridge above Dyes Inlet, a block from the Safeway store, Wyatt stopped and gently turned her toward him. "Any better?"

She nodded under the streetlight. Her voice was deeper, steadier. "Much, thank you. I'm sorry. I'm usually not so delicate, and I'm definitely not the fainting kind."

Reluctantly he let his hands drop to his sides. "Considering what you saw tonight, I'd say you've done exceptionally well."

She smiled up at him as the water beneath them lapped complacently against its shiny, rocky shore. Faint tenacious halos of summer light still lit the western sky in a stalwart struggle against the blackness of night. Watching the deep blue of her eyes, Wyatt struggled internally to force his thoughts back to the very serious and deadly business at hand.

"If you feel up to it, I'd like to get your statement while things are still clear in your mind. Would here be all right?"

Her voice was definitely crisper and deeper as she responded. "Yes, of course. I'm ready. To begin with I—"

Wyatt put up a hand to halt what Claire was about to say. He reached into his pocket for a tape recorder. "Mind if I run this?"

Claire nodded. Wyatt placed the recorder in his dress shirt pocket and turned it on. He pulled out a notepad and pen.

"The interview will go more quickly and be better organized if you just respond to my specific questions. First, I'll need your complete name, address, that sort of thing."

"Claire Boland. 655 Cedar Lane, Silverdale."

Wyatt was making notes. "Telephone?"

"555-6807."

"Age? Marital status?"

"Thirty-one." A small pause. "Widow."

Wyatt couldn't read her expression in the subdued light, but her answer had sounded sad. He found himself having to resist an urge to put his arm around her again.

"Children?"

Another pause. "No."

"What do you do for a living?"

"I'm a psychologist."

Wyatt dropped his pen. As he bent to retrieve it, he looked unseeing into the blue-black waters below them. *A psychologist?* He had the sudden mental image of himself riding up on a white charger to save her as she pulled out a sword at the last minute to slay the dragon herself. He found it a disappointing scenario.

"Sergeant Lockhart?"

Wyatt raised himself to his feet once again. Carefully avoiding her face, he concentrated on the faintly lit horizon stretching before them serene and still as he mentally left the Middle Ages and advanced to the end of the twentieth century.

"Where is your office, Dr. Boland?"

He felt her watching his averted face for a moment before answering. "On Byron Street, off of Silverdale Way."

"How long have you been practicing here?"

"I moved from San Francisco to Silverdale two years ago."

"What brought you to the Safeway store this evening?"

She shrugged. "Just groceries."

"Do you normally do your shopping this late at night?"

"No. I just got hungry and decided to drive to the store."

"What time did you reach the Safeway market?"

"Around eleven. My home is just ten minutes away by car."

"Describe your exact movements when you entered the market."

"Well, I decided I only wanted some fresh fruit so I didn't stop to get a cart. I headed toward the produce section."

"Did you see anyone? Hear anything?"

"No checkers or other shoppers were around. I do remember hearing a loud booming sound. I thought it came from the produce truck that was unloading at the rear of the store."

"When did you hear this loud boom?"

"At the moment I entered the store. I couldn't really tell from what direction it was coming. I didn't give it much thought. I headed directly for the fruits and vegetables. I saw no one."

"And when you reached the produce section?"

"There was a strong smell of smoke, like something burning. It was very unpleasant, and there was a light haze in the air. I looked up to see where it might be coming from and that's when I tripped and fell over the body."

Wyatt was beginning to understand her earlier shock even more. "You fell over the body?"

Claire nodded. "The body was lying in front of me. What was left of the face was about a foot away."

He could tell from the diminishing volume of her voice that she was still shaken up. With her renewed distress, he found himself moving closer to her and his voice becoming softer.

"What did you do then?"

"I got up and went for help."

He listened to her details of talking with the box boy and assistant manger without further interruptions.

"And that's when Arthur Knudsen left me in the produce section and told me he would call the police," she finished.

Wyatt turned off the tape recorder. "Thank you for your cooperation, Dr. Boland. I'll have your statement typed. Come to the Port Orchard office tomorrow, and you can sign it."

Surprise riddled Claire's voice. "That's all?"

Wyatt was taken back by her tone. "Well, yes. Since you just happened on the scene and since you didn't know the dead man...."

"But I did know him."

Wyatt was sure he had heard wrong. He looked over at Claire's face, her eyes large and deep in the pale light. "What?"

"I knew the dead man. I recognized him."

Wyatt's voice was full of disbelief. "How? His face was gone."

Claire nodded. "Yes, his face and his left hand. I recognized his clothing and right hand as those of an afternoon patient."

Although still feeling skeptical, Wyatt turned the tape recorder back on. "What about the man was familiar, Dr. Boland? I didn't notice anything distinctive about his clothing."

Claire's voice rose as though attempting to overcome the disbelief in Wyatt's. "Not distinctive, but recognizable. New jeans and a faded yellow, long-sleeve shirt with a prominent grease stain on his right sleeve. His right thumb was black, no doubt from a severe trauma to the area beneath the nail and there was an inch-long white scar on his right wrist."

The preciseness of her words caused Wyatt to rethink his assumption that she had to be wrong. "Describe him."

"Twenty-eight, five-ten, stocky, curly black hair, full matching beard, pug nose, light brown eyes."

Wyatt squinted at the confidence in her words. "You're sure?"

"I'm sure. His name was Richard Quade.

"Where can I find this Richard Quade's family?"

"His address was 66 Beach Street in Poulsbo. I could get you his telephone number from my office records."

"No need to," Wyatt said. "I'll find it in the directory. What did this man come to see you about?"

Claire shook her head. "I'm sorry, but such information is privileged under the doctor-patient relationship."

Wyatt frowned. "The man's dead."

"Yes, but even the fact that he was a patient of mine is considered confidential. I've only told you because it was necessary to explain how I knew him."

Wyatt shrugged. "All right, for now we'll leave the issue of Richard Quade's treatment. Anything else you wish to add?"

"I can't think of anything. Am I free to go?"

Wyatt realized she suddenly seemed preoccupied and eager to be on her way. She held her head and her slim shoulders straight and erect giving him the impression she had made a decision of some sort.

"If you're not feeling well enough I could drive...."

"You've been very kind, Sergeant, but I'm feeling fine now."

Claire took off Wyatt's suit coat and handed it back to him. As he took it from her, her hand brushed his like a soft caress. He felt his pulse quicken at her touch and tried to catch her eye to see what it might tell him, but her head was averted.

"My car is right over there," she said.

Wyatt followed the point of Claire's hand toward her car. He did not mask his surprise. "The red Allante convertible?"

She nodded, noticing his startled reaction to her car. Wyatt watched her walk toward it thinking that she must have a lucrative practice to afford such an expensive automobile.

As she got in and drove away, he scratched his chin. Expensive or not, it wasn't a car that seemed to fit her reserved manner. He was frowning as he walked to the telephone booth.

CLAIRE DIDN'T drive home. She headed automatically toward her office. There was something she wanted to listen to.

But even her preoccupation with her current quest could not fade the image of the tall blond detective's last look, his green-blue eyes the color of an unsettled sea. She was used to men looking at her with interest. She wasn't used to looking back with interest, but she had tonight.

Despite the horrible death of Richard Quade and all the questions it surfaced, she had felt inexplicably drawn to the handsome sergeant. His sharing of his love for his Washington home, his masculine scent, the deepness of his voice, the feel of his arm around her had all heightened her awareness of him as an extremely attractive and desirable man. And when their hands had brushed, an old, almost forgotten excitement had risen within her.

She had quelled it, of course. Her profession had given her years of practice in controlling her emotions, or at least the outward manifestations of them. But he was very handsome and . . . disarming. Somehow he had slipped past her shield of detachment tonight. It must have been because of the shock.

With difficulty, she put thoughts of Wyatt Lockhart out of her mind as she reached the deserted parking lot surrounding her small office building. She parked and hurried up the open wooden staircase, unlocking the entry door and then the interior door into her office. She flipped on the lights and within less than a minute, the cassette tape was playing on her recorder as she sat back in her leather chair, feet propped up on the edge of her large oak desk.

Clear visual images swarmed her memory. As his voice replayed on her tape, she saw Richard Quade once again enter her office that afternoon, right hand in his jeans, his left hand painting abstract pictures of his words on a canvas of air. She had immediately recognized he was left-handed.

Her patients always told her so much by their actions, sometimes even more than by their words. Everything was part of the symphony of feeling being played before her senses.

Human beings communicated endlessly, effortlessly, often wordlessly, and mostly unconsciously. But Richard Quade had a lot of words to contribute, too. She listened to the taped session.

"I've never been to a psychologist before. But at this point I don't really know where else to go, what else to do."

His tone had been deep, gruff, self-disparaging. But his inability to focus on any one object, his relentless pacing, had communicated his deep fear that she might not be able to help. Claire felt that Richard Quade had come to the end of his rope and she was it. More than once his left hand had reached into his shirt pocket for the pack of cigarettes there, only to come away empty-handed as he reread her No Smoking sign.

Since she knew he couldn't rely on smoking to relax him, Claire had sought to put him at ease with her voice and manner. "Do you want to sit down? You might be more comfortable."

"No."

"How can I help you?"

He had paused then and looked away from her, out the window where his eyes focused on some internal picture. "I've been getting calls."

Richard Quade said "calls" in a way that hinted of menace.

"Something is threatening you?"

He had looked at her then with something like hope. "Yes. Exactly. *Something. Something* has been calling me."

He had emphasized the word something as though until that moment he had not been able to put a label on his fears.

"How does this something call you?" Claire asked.

His tone had become impatient, as though the answer should have been obvious. His hand fingered the open pack of cigarettes. "When it dials my number, of course."

"On your home telephone?"

"Yes. But at work, too. Only once, but he called there."

"You said 'he.' Is this something a man?"

Richard Quade had not seemed to know how to answer that question. He had walked around the room in confusion. "Once he was. Now he is…" His voice had trailed off.

"What is he now?"

"Now he's dead," Richard had said, but his voice held more hope than conviction.

The words had surprised Claire, but she had long ago learned to take anything a patient said without outward approval or censure.

"Who was he when he was alive?"

Richard Quade looked uneasy. "I . . . can't tell you."

That wasn't unusual. Often patients refused to tell her things that were too painful for them to hear. It was as though until they said the words out loud, they could still refuse to believe at some level. She tried another approach.

"Was he someone close to you?"

"No. I met him by chance last summer. On the Hood Canal."

"Did you like him?" Claire said.

"Yeah. He was friendly, seemed interested in me. It had been a long time since someone had shown an interest in me. Of course, I realize that was because we looked . . ."

Richard had stopped and swallowed as though he might be able to get rid of his last words. He apparently hadn't meant to say them. When Claire didn't press him about it, he seemed to feel safe enough to go on.

"He'd rented a boat. We went fishing. God, I hadn't been fishing since I was a kid."

His right hand had come out of his pocket then, opened and joined the left in the painting of his air pictures. That was when she had noticed the blackened right thumb, the scar on the back of the hand, the grease spot that waved like a dark flag on his sleeve.

"We caught this one big fish. This size, would you believe? Never did find out what it was. We were going to ask when we got back to shore, but . . ."

Claire waited but Richard's happy recollection of the fishing trip had been interrupted by another memory. She could tell it was a very dark one, a memory that brought the fear back into his eyes.

Claire probed gently. "Was this man older, younger?"

"My age."

"How long did you know him?"

"Two days," Richard said.

"And did he die right after that?"

Richard Quade had stopped pacing. "How did you know?"

"Just a guess. How did he die, Richard?"

"We'd been drinking pretty heavily. A breeze had come up that night on the Hood Canal. The mainsail broke loose and swung around catching him at the back of the head. He went down like a rock."

Claire waited, but Richard Quade had stopped talking and started pacing again. "What did you do?"

"I tried to revive him. He had no heartbeat, no pulse. I waited until morning and then I . . . buried him."

"Buried him?"

"In the water."

"You didn't tell the authorities about his death?"

A strange look now. Guarded. "No."

"And this voice that calls you on the telephone, mostly at your home, you think it's this man's voice?"

"Yes."

"Do you recognize the voice?" Claire asked.

"I didn't, at first."

"Then how do you know—"

"He told me who he was."

"I see. Did he tell you why he was calling you?"

Richard Quade's eyes had stared at the floor in front of him as though they were looking at a pot of boiling water into which he expected to be thrown. "He told me he knew I had killed him."

Claire had kept her voice even and calm. "Why would he say that, Richard?"

"He described exactly how I had dumped him overboard. He even knew the trouble I had because at one point his pants' pocket had gotten caught on a hook and I had to tear it loose before I could slip him over the rail. He said he had come back to kill me."

Claire could tell Richard believed the threat could be carried out. That belief was dangerous. She tried to defuse it. "But you told me you didn't kill this man."

"I . . . don't remember killing him."

"But you had a reason to?" she said.

Doubt pierced his eyes shut. Then the words escaped in a rush, as though they had been penned up. "I don't remember thinking it. But after it happened and I realized what it could mean, I was glad he was dead. God help me."

"Were there other boats on the Hood Canal that morning?"

"I guess. I didn't much notice."

"Has this dead man spoken to anyone else?"

Richard looked at her with bruised eyes. "Of course not. Damn it, he's dead! I buried him! You think I don't know what this is? You think I don't know I'm losing my mind? Why do you think I came to you anyway?"

Claire had kept her voice calm and matter-of-fact. "Because you want me to stop the telephone calls."

Richard's expressive hands dropped to his sides in surrender and relief. "Yes."

She had gotten up then, circled the desk and leaned on its edge in front of him. "Tell me exactly what this dead man says on these telephone calls."

He looked up at her face just a few feet from his and seemed to read something in her eyes. "You can stop these calls?"

She smiled at him. "Of course."

The relief had oozed out of his pores like hard sweat. He leaned over, felt for the chair next to him and sank into it as his rubber legs gave way. Claire returned behind her desk and sat down.

"When did you start receiving these calls?"

"Last Monday night. Exactly a week ago."

"What did the voice say?"

"At first he just laughed. Asked me if I was surprised he could come back from the dead. I thought it was an old friend, out of touch for a while, playing around. I asked who he was."

"And he told you he was this dead man?" Claire asked.

"Yes."

"And you didn't think it might be someone's idea of a sick joke? Someone who knew you had met the man?"

"It's no joke. I've never told anyone about him before."

"Not even your wife?" Claire said.

"No. Never her."

"Could someone have seen you drop the body overboard?"

"No. The things he said . . . only he would know them."

"What's his name, Richard?"

The man's face shut down suddenly. "I can't tell you."

Claire realized that this man's secret was killing him. But at the moment, he seemed almost more willing to face death than to disclose it. She could not press him. Not now.

"What did you say after he told you who he was?" Claire asked.

"I . . . didn't say anything. He laughed and told me he'd be calling again. Then he hung up."

"Were you at home?"

"Yes. It was about eight. Sally, my wife, was cleaning up the dishes. She told me later she hadn't heard the phone ring. The twins were in bed."

"When did he call you next?"

"The next night. Eight-thirty this time."

"What did he say on the second call?"

"He laughed and asked me if I knew who it was. I said yes. He told me I shouldn't have killed him. I swear to you, Dr. Boland, it wasn't until then I realized I had. I mean consciously, that is."

"What else did he say?" Claire said.

Richard Quade squirmed in his chair. Claire waited until she was sure he wouldn't or couldn't answer.

"Did he call you every night after that?" she said.

"No. He missed one. Last Friday he called me at work. Said the same stuff as before."

"This information sheet you filled out for me says you work at the Puget Sound Naval Shipyard?"

"Yes. I'm a mechanic. I was in the shop when he called."

"Can you tell me any more of his words?" Claire asked.

"No. They . . . referred to him."

"Did they include threats to kill you?" Claire asked.

"Not at first. He kept telling me to do the right thing, to go to the Hood Canal and jump in."

"He wanted you to commit suicide?"

Richard nodded.

"When was the first time he threatened to kill you?"

"Last night. Sunday. He said since I couldn't make up my mind to do the right thing, he was going to have to do it for me. That's when I decided to look you up in the telephone directory and make an appointment for today. I had to do something. I can't live with this anymore. It's driving me crazy, or else I already am."

His eyes were haunted. Claire got up and came around to the front of the desk again. "You're not crazy, Richard. You're faced with a threat to your life. You have a strong will to live. That's why you're fighting back. Now this is important. I don't want you to answer the phone again until I tell you."

"Not talk on the phone?"

"Place calls, but have someone screen your incoming calls. If anyone refuses to give his name, don't talk with him."

Richard's voice was relieved. "It's so simple. Why didn't I think of it? He won't be able to get to me!"

Claire knew it was this man's belief in his ability to stop the calls that would actually stop them. She touched his arm.

"I told you we could stop the telephone calls. That's how we'll do it. I think you must also be ready in case this man tries to contact you in another way when he's thwarted from using the phone."

"You think he'll try to contact me? How?" Richard asked.

"We probably won't know unless he tries. Don't worry. No matter how he tries to get to you, we'll fight him. And we'll win."

He looked directly at her face then. It was the first time since they started the interview. That was when she saw the deep terror in his eyes.

"Do you believe in ghosts?" he asked.

"No."

"But these calls. This man—"

"I believe this man is real," Claire said.

"You don't think he's just in my head?"

Claire deepened her grasp on Richard's arm. "Everything is in our heads. We have no perception, no understanding of this world without our heads. And that's our strength because what the mind can conceive, it can master. We'll master this, Richard. Together."

She had reached over her desk then to retrieve her card. She handed it to Richard Quade.

"Keep my number with you. If he tries to contact you, call me immediately. If I don't answer personally, leave a message on my answering machine. I check it frequently and will get back to you soon. At night call this number printed here. It's my home phone. Can you come back to see me tomorrow afternoon at four-thirty?"

Richard Quade had risen and taken her card.

"Yes. I'll come. I feel better, Dr. Boland. This is such a relief. I don't know what to say."

It was a vulnerable moment for Richard. He was ready to give. Claire's voice slipped through his dropped shield to grab what she could. "Tell me who he is."

He looked at her in agony as he mouthed the words she had succeeded in dragging to his lips. "Richard Quade," he said and then he silently left her office.

CLAIRE'S MIND returned to the present, to the stark light of the fluorescent bulbs of her office that tried to keep the early morning blackness from rushing through the windows. She turned off the tape and leaned back again in her chair. That final name had stunned her more than all the rest of Richard Quade's story.

When he had first started to speak, she had thought Richard Quade was suffering from a repressed terror. She thought he subconsciously believed he'd killed this man and must be punished for it, hence the voice on the telephone who spoke to no one else.

But if Richard Quade thought it was himself who was threatening his life, then the case had to be something quite different. Could it be one of multiple personality, two personalities inhabiting the same body, struggling for ultimate control?

Multiple personality disorders were rare, only about one-hundred and forty surfacing in the psychological case histories since the first reported in 1817. Was this one? It was unlikely, but on the other hand, what else could explain a man getting threats from himself?

If that was so, it had turned into a life-and-death struggle. On a fishing trip a year ago, the second personality had communicated with the original one. They became aware of each other. Soon afterward the second personality had apparently vanished, leaving the first with the impression it had died.

Now, the second personality was resurfacing. Only this time it wanted to kill rather than cohabitate. But why did it call itself Richard Quade? In all her reading she had never heard about a case of multiple personality where both had the same name. The individual personalities always maintained different names as well as different personalities. One went with the other.

Could this be another dimension to the psychological phenomena? If this was a case of multiple personality, it might end up being a new chapter in the textbook. She had looked forward eagerly to the next afternoon's session.

Only now she would never know the truth. Richard Quade was dead, his body and any and all personalities that had inhabited it.

She lowered her long slim legs from their position on the desktop, finding she had a very strong case of pins and needles. As she massaged the circulation back into her calves, she felt sadness. She had liked Richard Quade. She had wanted so much to help him and now their chance was lost.

The pendulum from a small old-fashioned clock ticked rhythmically on her desk. At times she found it soothing. This morning it was irritating. She was tired. It was time to go home.

As she put away the cassette tape and turned out the light, an unsettling thought raked through her mind. Had the second Richard Quade personality been insane? Had he murdered his rival for the body he coveted, not realizing it meant his death, too?

Chapter Three

Sergeant Wyatt Lockhart knocked at the thin wood door of the Quade residence in Poulsbo with a short hard rap. He listened but heard no footsteps. He searched along the wall for a door bell on the darkened porch. When he found it, he pressed it twice, quickly.

After a minute he heard some scuffing noises. Then a woman's voice asked who was there. He identified himself.

The porch light came on as the door opened to a young woman with light, blinking eyes and short, pale blond hair. She hugged a thick yellow bathrobe to her thin frame.

"Did you say Sheriff's office?" she asked. Her yawn was pronounced and displayed all the fillings in her back teeth.

Wyatt brought out his badge. "Yes. I'm Detective Sergeant Lockhart from the Sheriff's office. Are you Mrs. Richard Quade?"

"Yes. What's wrong?" She seemed to be waking up a little.

"I've been trying to reach you by telephone, Mrs. Quade."

The woman looked guilty. "I unplugged the phones earlier this evening. What did you want to talk to me about?"

Before Wyatt could answer, a gruff male voice called out from somewhere behind the woman. "Who in the hell is it at this time of night?"

Mrs. Quade looked apologetically at Wyatt as she answered. "It's the Sheriff's Department, honey."

Before Wyatt had time to speculate on who Mrs. Quade could be calling "honey," a stocky, full-bearded man with light brown eyes and black curly hair, wearing pajamas, came to stand next to the woman. From the description Claire had given him, Wyatt Lockhart knew he was looking at Richard Quade. Unlike his wife, Richard Quade didn't seem to have any sleep in his eyes, only irritation. His voice confirmed that emotion.

"What the hell do you want?"

"Are you Richard Quade?" Wyatt asked.

"Yeah, I'm Quade."

"Mr. Quade, are you the only Richard Quade at this address?"

"Yeah. What's this all about?"

Wyatt shook his head. "A man was killed tonight who resembled you, Mr. Quade. Since we haven't identified him yet, I thought I'd best come by to be sure it wasn't you. I would have called, but I couldn't get through on the phone. Please accept my apologies."

Richard Quade glowered at him. Wyatt didn't like the look, but he could understand that being awakened made just about anyone grouchy. He turned away and headed toward his car.

As he got behind the wheel, thoughts of Claire Boland came forcibly to mind. Her misidentification of Quade must have been from the shock of her experience. He didn't really blame her, but he blamed himself for going to the Quade residence before an official identification. Stupid move. Still, she had been so sure it was Quade, she had convinced him.

He drove back to his regular office at the Port Orchard precinct to check out for the night. Tom Watson, his chunky, red headed detective, met him at the door and followed him into his office.

"I see you're still up," Wyatt said.

All of Tom's chins smiled. "What the hell. I knew you needed your best detective on this one. And I've just proven it by getting a tentative identification on the man with no face."

Wyatt took off his suit coat and hung it over the back of his office chair. "You did? But how? I checked the body. There wasn't a wallet, just a five-dollar bill in his jeans. Only other thing was a set of keys that had fallen from his pocket onto the floor."

Tom was nodding. "That's all I needed. Once I eliminated the employee cars in the parking lot, I checked out the only unidentified one. Keys fit. It was a stolen vehicle. Found a wallet in the glove compartment with this expired driver's license. Belongs to Roger Thayer, a resident of Carson City, Nevada. I'm having the lab boys tow the car in."

Wyatt sat down behind his desk as he took the expired driver's license from his detective. He looked at the poor quality photograph. For just a moment he thought there was something familiar about the face, something around the eyes, but he couldn't place it so he shrugged it aside.

"Good work, Tom. Get them to dust the car for prints. Let's match up the right thumb print to the guy's license. I'd like to get a complete set of prints from the body's remaining right hand off to Carson City at first light. The Sheriff there may be able to tell us more about this Roger Thayer. How did he die?"

"Lab work will take a while. But John says it looks as though the guy picked up a cantaloupe and the thing exploded in his face."

"It was set to go off?"

Tom nodded. "Maybe. Except John says he couldn't find anything big enough for a timing mechanism. Weird, huh?"

Wyatt didn't answer. He was sitting and thinking, his right index finger rubbing against his chin.

"How do you pick out a ripe cantaloupe, Tom?"

"Search me. My wife does that sort of thing."

Wyatt looked at his companion and shook his head. "You're a chauvinist. Give Nancy a break sometimes and offer to do the shopping. You might even learn something."

Tom grinned, as though knowing he'd been set up to ask his next question. "Okay, Mr. Expert. How do you pick out a ripe cantaloupe?"

"First you feel it to see if it's firm. Squishy ones are on their way to spoiling. If it's too hard, it was picked too soon. Those are the ones that look more green than golden. Then you smell the cantaloupe to see if it's fresh. A fresh ripe one has a faint juicy odor."

"Okay, so what has that got to do with our murder victim?" Tom asked.

"Elementary, my dear Watson. Our man was smelling the cantaloupe when he got it."

Tom's chunky face lit up with a smile. "Oh, I see. Somehow while he was smelling it, he detonated the explosive placed inside the fruit?"

Wyatt nodded. "Might have shaken it up just enough. And it also tells us something else."

"What's that?" Tom said.

"Our victim was left-handed. Otherwise, it would have been his right hand that was blown off."

"Yes I see."

"Is John checking the other fruit?"

Tom nodded. "We had it carted out in a truck. It's going to take a while, though. John's going to need some help."

"I'll get him some tomorrow." Wyatt checked his watch. "I mean later today. Did you find the assistant manager?"

Tom shook his head. "A stock boy gave us Arthur Knudsen's address and telephone number but they're fictitious and he's not listed in the directory."

"How long has Knudsen been working at the store?" Wyatt asked.

"About six months."

"What's his normal shift?"

"Five to one. He left work two hours before quitting time."

Wyatt continued to rub his chin. "Suspicious to say the least. Anyone else on the suspect list so far?"

Tom pushed some curly red hair off his forehead. "What about the looker who supposedly found the body? What's her name?"

"Dr. Claire Boland."

"Could she and Knudsen be in on this thing together?"

Wyatt shook his head. "She's not the type."

Tom Watson eyed his superior knowingly. "You mean she's too pretty to be, don't you?"

"No, of course not," Wyatt said too quickly.

Tom smiled. "With all that long red-gold hair and those deep blue eyes, I'd say she's at least a nine-and-a-half."

Wyatt squirmed in his chair. "I'm not saying she isn't. But it isn't her looks that have convinced me she's innocent. It's the fact that she waited for us while Knudsen took off."

Tom studied Wyatt for a moment. "I watched the way you caught her when she was about to collapse in the store. Neither the deputy nor I anticipated her condition. But you'd been watching her, hadn't you?"

Wyatt's voice sounded defensive to his ears. "You saw the body. The woman had been through quite a shock."

Tom shook his head. "You can't fool me, Wyatt. I know the signs. When I met my Nancy, I couldn't keep my eyes off her, either. Why don't you just come right out and admit it. The lady is beautiful and fragile—just the kind that brings out your suppressed streak of Sir Galahad."

Wyatt shook his head at his detective, irritated that Tom appeared to know him so well. "Remember our first directive—never get personally involved with a witness in a case."

"I remember. But you didn't let it stand in your way of pursuing Jennifer."

Wyatt exhaled in obvious disgust. "Yes and what a mistake that turned out to be. Jennifer alone proves the importance of the department's point about noninvolvement."

Tom shrugged. "Sorry, Wyatt. Didn't mean to rub salt into an old wound."

Wyatt shrugged his broad shoulders as he sat down at his desk. "It's not bleeding anymore, Tom. But the scar serves as a reminder not to be so eager to repeat one's mistakes.

Now what do you say we get back to trying to solve this murder and just forget about how beautiful our witness may be.''

RICHARD QUADE LAY on the den's sofa staring up at the ceiling. He thought this would be the time for him to get some sleep, but something was very wrong. How could the Sheriff's office know to come here? He stroked his beard thoughtfully as he went over every movement of his evening's plan.

It should have been foolproof. No one had seen him come into the Safeway Store; no one had seen him leave. There was just that woman with the long red-gold hair. She must have seen his face when she tripped over the body.

Well whatever she thought she saw, she was obviously getting it mixed up in her mind. That was just as well. As long as her impressions were fuzzy, what she told the Sheriff's office would not end up leading to him. He was safe now. And after tomorrow he would look up this woman and ensure he'd be safe for good.

CLAIRE SLEPT IN until nine-thirty Tuesday morning. She slid out of bed and sleepily put some bread into the toaster, before going in to brush her teeth. Out of habit, she switched on the radio news.

The Center for Science and International Affairs was urging Congress and the President to require the use of PALs on Naval weapons.

Claire's interest was instantly peaked. Just the other day, at least two of her patients had discussed this PAL acronym. They had described it as a device designed to prevent unauthorized arming of nuclear weapons. Army and Air Force weapon systems had these control devices, but Naval weapons were free of them. That freedom was bothering the CSIA and other academics.

Claire listened as a spokesman quoted from an article, which stated that after the leaders of the two superpowers,

"The third most powerful man in the world is a commander of a Trident submarine. Suppose one of them decides, out of what he believes to be a higher patriotism, to activate a thermonuclear bomb. Psychologists cannot guarantee that any individual will not be seized at some point by a totally irrational idea or by an aberration."

Claire nodded her head at that observation, but she was unclear about her feelings concerning the issue. Many of her patients worked either at the Bangor Submarine Base where the Trident subs were home ported or at the Puget Sound Naval Shipyard where vessels with nuclear weapons were home based. Most were against these PALs—even afraid of them. It proved a stressful issue.

When the report was over, she put the toothbrush in her mouth only to take it out again when the local news immediately gained her attention. She switched off the faucet and listened intently.

"On the local Washington State scene, the body of a man was found in a grocery store in Silverdale late last night. He has been identified by the Kitsap County Sheriff as Roger Thayer, a former resident of Carson City, Nevada. No further details have been released. However, an assistant manager at the grocery store is being sought for questioning in the death. In other news..."

Claire switched off the radio and headed for the telephone. She got out her directory and found the listing for the Silverdale Precinct. The phone rang only once before a woman identifying herself as a deputy answered. Claire asked for Sergeant Lockhart.

"Sergeant Lockhart works out of our detective unit in Port Orchard. I'll be happy to give you that number," the woman said.

Claire wrote it down and instantly redialed. However, her second request also went unfulfilled, this time by a male deputy.

"I'm sorry, but Sergeant Lockhart isn't expected in until later this morning. He took some late calls last night. Can somebody else help you?"

"I hope so. I need to confirm the identity of a man found dead in the Silverdale Safeway store last evening. Sergeant Lockhart was working on the case."

"No problem. I can get that information for you." Claire waited uneasily. "He's been identified as Roger Thayer from Carson City, Nevada."

"You're sure?"

"Yes, ma'am. We confirmed with Nevada this morning."

Claire murmured a thank-you and hung up the phone.

"But I recognized the man," she said aloud. "I'm sure it was Richard Quade!"

Her mind clearly replayed the image of the clothing, the marks on the hand. They had been there, hadn't they? A sick, sinking feeling pulled at her stomach.

She stumbled back into the bathroom and finished brushing her teeth. She braided her long hair and circled it around her head, all the time carefully avoiding her own eyes in the mirror.

She was in her office within thirty minutes without conscious memory of putting on clothes, eating or driving a car. Her mind had filled with excavated doubts. They closed in on her like old relics from a cursed tomb. She listened to her messages and checked her calendar. Her first appointment was due in five minutes.

She sat back in her chair and gave herself a pep talk. Her perceptions were good. She could trust them. She flipped through her list of patient numbers until she found Richard Quade's. She reached for the telephone and punched out his number. A woman's voice answered on the second ring.

"Is Richard Quade there?"

"No."

"Is this Mrs. Quade?"

"Yes. Who's calling?"

"Mrs. Quade, this is Dr. Boland."

The voice on the other end of the line sounded immediately concerned. "Doctor? Is something wrong?"

"No. Nothing's wrong. I'm a counselor, not a medical doctor. Richard came to see me yesterday and we scheduled another appointment for today. I'm calling to confirm the time for that appointment."

"He's at work. He didn't say anything this morning about being home late because of an appointment. He might have forgotten. Perhaps you'd best call him at work. I can get the number for you."

The woman's words ripped right through the fabric of Claire's calm, exposing her doubts once again. She forced herself to answer.

"I have the number, Mrs. Quade. Thank you."

Claire hung up and put her head in her shaking hands. If Richard Quade had left for work that morning, he could hardly have been lying dead with his face blown off last night in Safeway's produce section. Her confidence began to fade.

Jerry's face flashed into her mind—the handsome face full of life that she had thought she knew and loved so well. Then his other side emerged—the imagined white face devoid of everything save death that had come to haunt her the moment she had been told of his suicide.

For the thousandth time she asked herself how she could have missed the signs in her own husband. She and Jerry and her brother, Alan, had grown up together in San Francisco, been inseparable until she had had to say goodbye to them both when they went to the Naval Academy.

But even schooling had proved only a temporary separation. Jerry and Alan had come back to her in San Francisco, both choosing to work in Naval Intelligence Service there. She had earned her shingle by then and had begun practice. Then Jerry's parents had died and Alan and she had mourned with him. Within the next year she and Jerry had been married.

Their marriage felt so natural, so right. Alan remained part of their lives, continuing his close friendship with Jerry. It seemed the three of them would be together forever. Then one crisp cold December day, without warning, seemingly without reason, Jerry took his life.

He had been on assignment. The next thing she knew she was being visited by a superior in his command at the Naval Intelligence Service. He solemnly advised her Jerry Boland had committed suicide involving explosive material, the specifics of which he could not discuss.

Jerry's suicide had hit Claire hard, too hard. She had refused to believe at first, but gradually she had to accept the truth. She had not only lost her husband on that day but also her belief in her psychological training, because she had seen no warning signs to his suicide. None whatsoever.

For almost two years she had fought to regain the lost ground, gradually rebuilding confidence in her perceptions. But now the case of Richard Quade was bringing all the doubts back. Once again she was beginning to mistrust what she knew to be true.

The buzzer from the waiting room went off, jolting her back to the present. She looked at her watch. Her patient was on time. She had to put aside the resurfacing doubts. She couldn't lose all the ground she had gained in the last two years. Not if she hoped to maintain her own sanity.

WYATT LOCKHART LOOKED over the reports from the crime scene crew but couldn't concentrate on the words. He was obviously still feeling the effects of a long night. However, his eyes opened wide as they read the pathologist's report of distinctive marks on the body.

There it was. The scar on the right wrist, the blackened thumbnail. Claire Boland must have seen the marks and just thought they looked the same as those on her afternoon patient. It was understandable; she had been quite shaken.

An unbidden memory of the feel of her soft shoulders surfaced unexpectedly. He wondered when she would come in to sign her statement and found himself straightening his tie at the thought.

He decided he needed another cup of coffee. He got up, stretched and meandered over to the machine. John Sanders, the charge and explosive expert, was already pouring himself a cup.

"Save me some, John. It was a long night for us all."

John's nod was punctuated with a yawn as he moved aside.

"What have you found?" Wyatt asked, filling up his cup.

John scratched his balding head and adjusted his glasses. It was always his preamble to rendering a decision.

"This is an interesting case," he said. "First time I ever came across a lethal cantaloupe."

"So the explosive was in the fruit?"

"You got it. Center had been scooped out and replaced with black powder explosive. Potassium perchlorate, sulfur, charcoal—simple, low-power stuff. Placed in cellophane to keep it dry."

"Like something a high-school student might make?" Wyatt's tone was mocking, but John's response was straight.

"Actually, I made some of the stuff in high-school chemistry lab once, only I used potassium nitrate in place of the potassium perchlorate. It's not difficult, all you have to do is—"

"Spare me, John. I got a C in chemistry. Just tell me how the stuff went off."

John once again scratched the shiny dome of his head and adjusted his glasses.

"This is the interesting part. Whoever put that black powder in the cantaloupe used a chemical sealant to close the edges of the tampered fruit and, when it was time, ignited the powder by a fancy, remote, radio-frequency-controlled sensor."

"A remote detonation?"

John nodded.

"Does that rule out the high-school students?" Wyatt asked.

John sipped some coffee before answering. "I would say so. That small igniter was very sophisticated, very sensitive. I'd lay odds it activates on one special frequency only and from a distance of probably fifteen, twenty feet."

"So you're saying that the guy who planted this stuff had to be somewhere in the vicinity to activate the blast?"

John nodded. "Absolutely."

"What about regular radio waves transmitting in the vicinity of the sensor? Could they have triggered it prematurely?"

"Doubt it. But I won't know until I can check on the exact frequency activating it. It's going to take time. Which reminds me," he said as he put his coffee cup down, "I'd best get to it. I'll let you know."

Wyatt watched John walk away, feeling restless. He knew he should return to his desk to begin the meticulous investigative work required to get results. But intruding on his resolve were a pair of deep blue eyes and a head of red-gold hair.

He recognized the signs. Her distress and beauty had reached a part of him generally inaccessible since Jennifer's cold dismissal of their marriage. Still, even memories of his ex-wife weren't enough to dampen his desire to see the psychologist again. He sauntered over to the reception area and told the deputy on duty to be sure to let him know when Claire Boland arrived.

RICHARD QUADE LOOKED up as the Puget Sound Naval Shipyard's lunch whistle blew, his eyes narrowing against the glaring sun. He kept beneath the bus's hood, casting his face down when anyone passed by, moving screwdrivers and wrenches with deft hands.

Shipyard employees scurried around, heading toward one of the four gates to grab a bite to eat at a nearby McDonald's. Nobody took any notice of the extra intra-yard bus pulled off to the side of Building 456 or of the man in machinist's overalls leaning against its engine. If they noticed anything it was only the sign displayed at the back of the bus's window: Puget Sound 1891-1991, 100 Years Centennial Celebration.

But Richard Quade noticed everything. It was almost ten past when he saw the tall uniformed figure come out of Building 850 across the street. He waited for the second man in uniform to emerge. He did a moment later, pausing to drop coins into the newspaper stand for a copy of the *Post Intelligencier*. He had a straighter carriage than the first man, a more authoritative walk.

Richard Quade watched both men as they approached the bicycle rack on their way toward an automobile parked in the second stall. The sign above the parking position read, Shipyard Commander Only, in gold letters on a blue background.

Quade reached down behind the front headlight of the bus and removed the small square box with the raised red center. He turned the device in the direction of the two men. Step by step they approached the rack of bicycles in front of Building 850, and with each step Richard's finger moved closer toward the button. When they were just alongside, he pressed the detonator.

ALAN GILLETTE of the Naval Intelligence Service headquarters at Mare Island Naval Shipyard in Vallejo, California, took the emergency call from the Puget Sound Naval Shipyard at two-thirty on Tuesday afternoon. His tanned face drained of all color as he listened to the news. Then his solid compact frame bolted out of its chair as his deep blue eyes widened in shock. His response was precise and to the point, reflecting his natural thought process. "I'll be on the next plane."

Alan grabbed his perpetually packed suitcase. His only stop on the way to the gate was the southwest corner of Building 521, the Mare Island Shipyard Commander's office.

"Sir, there's been an unexplained explosion in front of Captain Kent's office at Puget Sound. The Captain is unhurt, but others, yet to be identified, are dead. Reports are sketchy. I'm flying up to take command of security."

Alan was in his car and heading toward the airport when he thought about his sister, Claire. For the last two years he had made up one excuse after another as to why he couldn't go to Washington to see her. Now it looked as though his excuses had just run out.

Chapter Four

Claire looked at her watch. Two-thirty. She was free until her appointment with Richard Quade at four-thirty. It was time to make a visit to the detective unit of the Kitsap County Sheriff's Department. She got into her red Allante convertible, donning dark sunglasses and a white bolero-style hat to shade her head from the hot afternoon sun.

She didn't want to admit it to herself, but she was looking forward to seeing Wyatt Lockhart again. Spoiling that meeting and nearly everything so far this day, however, was her misidentification of the dead man.

The morning sessions with her patients had been conducted under a growing unease. More than once her mind had wandered back to the produce department at the Safeway store and the body she had found. There had to be an answer for what she thought she saw. She just prayed the answer wouldn't be that she lost her ability to perceive reality.

It took her just about twenty minutes to reach the Port Orchard facility for the Sheriff Department's detective unit. She was immediately shown to Wyatt's office.

He stood up as she entered. Claire smiled, feeling a bit self-conscious as his green-blue eyes followed her every movement into the chair opposite his desk.

He sat down after she did and handed her two typed pages containing her statement of the night before. Claire felt embarrassed as she came to her identification of the dead man.

"You can change it," Wyatt said, seeming to read her mind.

Claire's sigh was small. "It's what I told you last night."

Wyatt's voice was crisp, but not sharp. "You were upset. You'd had a nasty shock. Perhaps things are clearer to you now."

He was giving her the benefit of the doubt. She appreciated his effort plus the fact he hadn't reproached her for the false identification. She put down the typed statement.

"Sergeant, I apologize. I really thought he was Richard Quade."

He watched her for a moment with those unsettling green-blue eyes and then flashed an unexpected smile. "We all make mistakes. You can use my pen to cross out anything you wish."

Claire wondered fleetingly what it would be like to bathe for an extended moment in one of those devastating smiles. She tried to shake away the thought as she used the offered pen to sign the unchanged statement. She handed both back to him.

His smile had faded. "I don't understand. You know you were wrong. Why don't you just cross off the part that pertains to the identity of Richard Quade?"

"Because right or wrong, this describes what I saw."

Wyatt looked at her as though she was some rare bird that had come to perch in his office. He picked up her signed statement and placed it in a case folder. "Did you know Roger Thayer?"

"No. He was the dead man, wasn't he?"

Wyatt nodded. "You identified his clothing and the distinctive marks on his right hand quite accurately. Why did you think they belonged to Richard Quade?"

"Because when Richard Quade visited my office Monday afternoon, he was wearing new jeans and an old, faded yellow shirt with a large grease mark on the right sleeve. The thumb on his right hand had been blackened beneath the nail. It looked like the type of injury that might occur if one missed a hammer stroke and hit the thumb instead. There was an inch-long, white scar on the back of his hand near his wrist."

As she saw the disbelief in Wyatt's eyes, she quietly wondered if she had imagined the whole thing. That old familiar sickness began to clutch at her stomach again.

"You said his thumb looked like it had been hit with a hammer. Couldn't it have gotten black from being caught in a door?"

Claire nodded. "It's possible."

"Then why did you mention a hammer injury?"

"Because I've gotten a similar blackened thumb from missing the nail with my hammer and hitting my thumb instead. Since Quade is left-handed, it seemed likely that his right hand was holding a nail in place while his left hand was swinging the hammer and—"

"How do you know Richard Quade is left-handed?" Wyatt asked.

Claire could see his eyes squinted slightly as though he was trying to bring something into clearer focus. "Well I guess as anyone might know. I observed which hand he favored when we met."

Wyatt steepled his hands. "What hand do I favor?"

She knew he was testing her. "Your right. Your watch is on your left wrist. You write your notes with your right hand and it's the one you use to rub or scratch your chin when you're thinking."

A small smile played about his lips for a moment. "And what percentage of the population is left-handed, do you suppose?"

Claire didn't know if Wyatt's question was directed at her, but she decided to answer it anyway. "Less than ten percent, and left-handedness is an inherited trait, like eye color or hair color."

Wyatt was quiet for a moment as he digested her words.

Claire leaned forward in her chair. "Why are you interested in this, Sergeant?"

"The victim was left-handed, too."

Claire frowned. "Who was Roger Thayer?"

Wyatt didn't seem surprised at her interest. "A year ago he escaped from the Nevada State Penitentiary."

"An escaped convict? What was his crime?" she asked.

"He was serving time for attempted murder and armed robbery. His sister is flying over from Carson City tomorrow. She's arranged for a simple funeral Thursday morning."

"A funeral here?" Claire asked.

Wyatt was looking down at the case folder on his desk. "Uh, huh. Looks like Roger Thayer wasn't very popular in Carson City. Funeral services will be at Millbrook Chapel at nine."

Claire made a mental note of the information before asking her next question. "Who do you think killed him?"

Wyatt looked at her a moment without speaking. "What do you know about Arthur Knudsen?"

Claire once again sat back in her chair. "I never saw him before last night. Why do you ask?"

"Do you know nobody has seen him since you talked with him?"

Claire once again leaned forward. "Arthur Knudsen's disappeared? You suspect him?"

Wyatt was watching her. He once again ignored her question. "Death by explosion is pretty unusual. Not a method an average murderer selects. Takes a different kind of mind to get its jollies from watching flesh being blown apart. A real sick mind."

Claire's palms were getting uncomfortably moist. She rubbed them against the light linen fabric of her suit skirt. "Are you saying you think this murderer is a psychopath?"

"Can you offer another explanation? This sick mind stuffs cantaloupes with explosives and waits until some unsuspecting shopper just happens to pick it up and then he sets off the charge."

The image seemed wrong to Claire. "Is this your opinion?"

"It's the opinion of the Chief. Personally, I'm more inclined to follow up on the missing assistant manager. Of course he could be a psychopath. Which toss of the coin would you call?''

Claire thought over his question. "I'd get a new coin."

Wyatt stretched back in his leather chair with a fluid grace that emphasized the muscular frame within his tailored suit. "You don't buy either theory?"

Claire shifted her weight in her chair, trying to keep her mind on the man's words and not the way his powerful body filled out his clothes. "If this is a psychopath you're up against, I doubt he's a random killer."

Wyatt frowned. "Why not?"

"If Roger Thayer was the victim of a random killer, he would have been one of many people shopping on a crowded Saturday afternoon and picking up exploding fruit. As it is, I doubt any other fruit in the store had been tampered with."

Wyatt eyed her speculatively. "You're right. We didn't find any other tampered fruit. Why did you assume that? Why couldn't this murder be like the Tylenol poisonings years ago?"

Claire shook her head. "Because the situations are different. The Tylenol poisoners wanted to be miles away when their victims died. Such a person gains power from imagining himself as joining forces with fate to select a random victim. But a minute ago you said this murderer wanted to watch the explosion. That means he was at the scene. That also tells me it was someone who wanted to be sure the right person was being exploded."

Claire could tell by Wyatt's sudden shift forward that what she was saying interested him. His next question underlined that impression. "He was after Roger Thayer?"

"My guess would be yes," she said.

From the changing expression on Wyatt's face, Claire realized she had used the wrong terminology. "Your guess?" he repeated.

"It's an educated one, Sergeant." Claire felt increasingly irritated that she cared what this man thought of her opinions.

Wyatt shrugged and leaned back again. "In any case Knudsen is probably our man. He was on the scene and he disappeared right after the body was found."

Claire shook her head. "I don't think so. Knudsen was shocked and badly shaken. I don't know why he's missing, but it isn't because he killed Roger Thayer."

Wyatt's look was amused. "You read his mind, Doctor?"

Claire kept her voice even. "I read his face, Sergeant."

"You were mistaken when you identified Roger Thayer as Richard Quade. Perhaps you're also mistaken about reading Knudsen's face?"

He had uncomfortably hit the nail on the head. Could she really depend on her senses anymore? The sudden fear that she might not be able to prompted her next words.

"Yes, I was wrong about Richard Quade. Frankly, being wrong concerns me more than you can know. My work involves my sensing people accurately. My failure to do so is most...disturbing."

Wyatt read her distress and once again felt it pulling him to come to her aid. "Is there something I can do?" he asked before he could restrain himself.

"Let me work with you on this case. Maybe I can learn why I was wrong. It's most important I reconcile this sensory distortion. In return, I would offer any behavior interpretation—"

Wyatt got up and began to pace. "The Department does not hire psychologists to—"

"You wouldn't be hiring me," Claire interrupted. "I would be volunteering my services to assist, in any way you deem of use."

He watched her eyes, steady and strong. He could refuse her eyes but not the small quiver she was unsuccessfully trying to control at the bottom of her lip.

You're a foolish romantic, he told himself as he looked away from her watching eyes, afraid he might betray himself. "Perhaps we could reach an understanding. I'll think about it."

Claire let out a trapped breath. "Thank you, Sergeant."

Wyatt heard the genuine gratitude in her voice and tried to ignore the pleasure it gave him. "The Chief of Detectives will have to approve your official status. I'll need to convince him. If you don't think Knudsen killed Thayer, who would you say did?"

Claire wished she had a better answer. "I don't know."

Wyatt didn't look disappointed. "Your honesty is in your favor. I won't work with someone who tries to bluff me. But I also won't work with someone who goes off on her own. If I decide to use you as a consultant, I will demand you keep nothing from me. Is that clear?"

"As long as it doesn't compromise a patient-doctor communication," Claire said.

Wyatt turned back to study her. She wanted to work on the case but not at any price. He could respect that. "Even if I don't agree to make you a part of this investigation, you're going to the funeral, aren't you?"

Claire was a little disconcerted by Wyatt's question. She mentally stepped back from a direct reply. "Isn't that why you gave me the place and time for the services?"

Her answer seemed to amuse him. "You would have asked if I hadn't offered, wouldn't you?"

He said he wanted honesty. Claire smiled as she gave it to him. "Absolutely."

His eyes caressed her face then and her breath caught as she felt his attraction for her. Suddenly, his eyes looked away and he seemed to collect himself as though he had remembered something unpleasant. Aware she was evoking such conflicting emotions in the tall handsome sergeant pushed Claire's own heart to a quicker beat.

Being so easily swayed by Claire's distress and smiles irritated Wyatt. This was precisely the way he had fallen for Jennifer. Her apparent vulnerability had caused him to rush in to offer his help and heart. Only later she had discarded both without a qualm.

When he spoke his voice carried a faint hint of his remembered disillusionment. "Well, Dr. Boland, why are you going to the funeral of a man you claim to have never met?"

Faced with the direct question, Claire found she wasn't sure. "I thought there might be something about Thayer that could help me to sort out why I thought he was Richard Quade."

Wyatt heard the hesitation in her voice. "What is it you think you might learn? Or is there something you haven't told me?"

Claire felt irritation at her defensive role. "You have my statement. You know everything I do."

Wyatt paced toward her. Now he was almost sure there was something she wasn't telling him. "Actually, Doctor, all I really know is that you and Roger Thayer were alone in the produce department Monday night and now he's dead."

"We were not alone!" Claire had said the words quickly, feeling a bit intimidated by the physical advance of the sergeant's tall frame. Now as she realized what she said was true, some fleeting, shadowy image was trying to come into focus.

Wyatt stopped directly in front of the chair she sat in, forcing her to stretch her neck upward to see him. His tone was tough. "Who else was there?"

His demand broke in to scatter Claire's elusive memory. Irritated with her failed attempt and with the sudden inquisition tactics of Sergeant Lockhart, she jumped to her feet and stretched her five-foot-eight-inch frame as tall as she could. Unfortunately, even with three-inch heels and her hat on, she barely made it to the sergeant's chin. That fact only fed her irritation.

"Stop badgering me! I don't know who killed him. I want to help you find the murderer. The trouble with you is...is..."

Looking up into those sparkling green-blue eyes, Claire suddenly couldn't think of a thing wrong with him so in absolute frustration and confusion she turned and stomped out of his office.

Wyatt watched Claire leave, excited by the strength of her emotions and the resurgence of his own feelings at her presence. She looked so sophisticated today. She had immediately given him the impression of a cool detached woman. He hadn't liked that image.

But he liked the impression he had just gotten of her. Despite her profession and education, their conversation told him she had her doubts and insecurities just like anybody else. It was a comforting discovery.

Of course he hadn't meant to badger her. But he really thought there was something she wasn't telling him. He had tried to get her to release it by employing a direct assault. Unfortunately it had backfired and made her angry. He didn't want to upset her. He admired her firmness in letting her statement stand. Such a decision spoke of someone who took strong responsibility for her actions.

He thought there was merit in her ideas concerning the murderer of Roger Thayer, too. Should he try to convince the Chief to make her part of the investigative team?

He rubbed his forehead with both his hands, trying to summon a logical thought process but finding only the memory of the deep blue sparks he had caused to flare in her eyes and wondering what other emotions he might be capable of igniting there.

His pleasurable thoughts were interrupted by a knock on his open door. He looked up to see Tom Watson pausing in the doorway.

"Roger Thayer's mother is on the phone," his detective said. "She's very emotional. Says Thayer was her adopted child and she disowned him ever since he killed his father at the age of eleven."

"He killed his father?" Wyatt repeated.

"Cute kid, huh? I thought you might handle her better."

Wyatt shook his head. "Handling sensitive conversations with emotional women does not appear to be my forte this morning, Tom. But transfer her to my line and I'll give it a try."

CLAIRE CHECKED her watch. It was after five. No use waiting anymore. Richard Quade was obviously not going to show for his appointment. She felt disappointed and worried. What had made him change his mind?

As she gathered up her purse and keys, she decided to try calling him at the Shipyard. After eight rings she hung up. Everyone had obviously left for the day. She might as well, too. She was heading toward the door when the phone rang. She hurried back to her desk and picked it up, hoping it would be Richard Quade.

"So how's my favorite sister?" a familiar voice asked.

Claire couldn't feel disappointed. "Alan! I'm so glad to hear your voice. It's been months since we talked."

"I know, babe. And I don't have much time now. Can I come by for dinner tonight?"

"Dinner? You're in Washington?"

"Arrived this afternoon at the Seattle Tacoma Airport, or as the taxi driver corrected me, SEATAC. So what about dinner?"

"Of course, Alan. Eight okay?"

"Great. Love you. Bye."

Before Claire had a chance to say goodbye, Alan hung up. She shook her head as she replaced the receiver. That was just like him, always on the run. He and Jerry had been so much alike that way. Once again with thoughts of Jerry, the cloud descended over Claire's spirits.

While she was putting the key in her own door, she heard Dave Reyes, the gastroenterologist whose office was directly opposite hers, locking up. They were the only tenants of the small office building. She flashed him a smile and received a big one in return.

Dave had one of the nicest dispositions Claire had known. He also had one of those great faces that always exuded goodwill.

"So, Claire, not working late tonight, I see. Why don't you come have dinner with Marj and me? The kids are staying over at a friend's house, so it should be somewhat civilized."

"Thanks, but my brother's in town and coming to dinner."

"Well good. Or is it? You look kind of down. Been a rough day?" he asked.

She looked at her friend and let out a long controlled sigh. "You're very observant. I think it was last night that did me in. I'm getting too old to upset my sleeping patterns. Makes me a zombie for days afterward."

They went out the front door together and began to negotiate the several painted wooden stairs taking them down to street level.

Dave's expression was inquisitive. "I hope the late night was the result of a hot date?"

Claire shook her head. She didn't want to share her unpleasant experience. She offered a purged version. "It was too hot to sleep so I came back to the office to review one of my sessions from yesterday. Unfortunately my patient missed his appointment today."

"Was it Richard Quade who stood you up?"

Claire stared at Dave in total bafflement. "How did you know?"

"Don't worry, it's nothing spooky," he said. "I saw him going into your office yesterday is all. He's been a patient of mine for the past year. I recommended he see you last week. I knew he needed someone to talk to."

"Why do you say that, Dave?"

"He's a nervous man, kind that's always looking over his shoulder. I've felt sorry for him. I can poke at the internal organs, but I know some of my patients would benefit more from a poke in the mind. I hope you can help him."

"Not if he doesn't come back. What is he seeing you for?"

"High blood pressure. I've got him on moderate medication. He exercises and eats lots of fruits and vegetables. Now, if I could just get him to quit smoking. Or maybe you could. Hey, that's an idea. We could start working on patients as a team."

Claire knew Dave wasn't serious. She smiled as they headed for their cars and his voice became more excited.

"What a great team we'd make. I've got several hypochondriacs I'd dearly love to get rid, uh, refer to you. As a bonus, since you don't have any office personnel, I'll even share my receptionist."

Remembering Dave's receptionist, Claire shook her head. "Sorry. Deal's off. Nobody would come to see me with that sourpuss face sitting in my outer office. One look from her and even the Terminator would run."

Dave's smile was broad, even proud. "Yeah. But boy does she get the patients to pay on time!"

Claire laughed and said goodbye to Dave, definitely feeling lighter for the conversation. The radio came on when she started the engine on the Allante. The national news was focused again on the use of PALs to control Naval nuclear weapon deployment.

Claire listened as a Pentagon spokesperson assured that inadvertent and unauthorized launches from Navy ships were currently prevented by electrical and mechanical interlocks, rigid team procedures and tight physical security.

Claire didn't know what to believe and was secretly glad the decision wasn't up to her. Being forced to make decisions in situations with insufficient data was the way most of her patients caught and nourished their neuroses.

The idea of nourishment reminded Claire of dinner. But the sudden queasiness in her stomach made her skip the turn-in for Safeway. She continued down Silverdale Way toward Mark-it Foods. She was almost there when the local news concerning the death of Roger Thayer came on to say the Sheriff had no new leads in the case.

Her misidentification of the dead man as Richard Quade came back in full force. If only she had seen him today, she might have been able to figure out what had confused her. She couldn't force him to see her. And if this other personality had taken over, what then?

It was a sudden whim. She didn't get them often, but when she did, she seldom failed to pursue them. She turned the wheel quickly and headed for the address in Poulsbo she had memorized.

The young thin blond woman who answered Claire's knock a few minutes later looked at her tentatively. "Yes?"

"Mrs. Quade?"

"I'm Sally Quade."

"I'm Dr. Claire Boland. I spoke with you this morning?"

The cloud lifted from the pale eyes. "Oh, yes. Please come in, Dr. Boland. Rich isn't home, yet. I thought he was with you."

Claire watched Sally bring out the burning cigarette she had been holding behind her back. "He never showed for our appointment. That's why I'm here. I wanted to make sure he was okay."

Sally nodded as she led the way into a bright kitchen. Claire's nose picked up smells from the big cooking pot on the range.

Sally Quade beckoned her to one of the kitchen chairs. "You didn't reach him at the Shipyard to remind him of the appointment?"

"No." Claire didn't mention she hadn't tried.

The cloud was back in Sally Quade's eyes. "I can't imagine what's keeping him. Perhaps he stopped at the store."

Claire had a perverse need to ask her next question. "Didn't he go grocery shopping late last night?"

Sally looked at her a bit strangely. "Just for a couple of things, but I wasn't thinking of a grocery store. I meant he might have stopped at a hardware store for tools or something."

"Is this normal for him? I don't mean stopping after work for tools. I mean going to the grocery store late at night?"

Sally shrugged. "I guess, during summer. He's got this thing for fresh fruit. Buys it daily. He doesn't like the crowds right after work so he waits until just before bedtime. Did you see him there last night? Is that how you knew?"

Maybe that was it. Maybe she had seen Richard Quade there. Maybe in her horrible experience, she had imagined the man on the floor to be him because she had just seen him in the store. A sudden image of Richard Quade's face flashed before her eyes. Where did that memory come from?

Claire tried to ignore the nervous perspiration that had broken out on her forehead and upper lip. She concentrated on keeping her voice as even as possible.

"Sally, I believe Richard is in trouble. Has anything happened lately? Anything that has upset him?"

Sally lit another cigarette. She still had half of one burning in the ashtray. She didn't seem to notice.

"Excuse me a minute. The girls are playing in the backyard. I want to check on them."

Sally got up, moved over to the kitchen sink and glanced out the window. She seemed satisfied at what she saw, turning back to face into the room. But she avoided looking at Claire.

"It's hot in here. I heard it was ninety today. I'll turn on the fan," she said, as she reached over to do so.

The sudden breeze detached a long strand of red-gold hair from Claire's braids and blew it across her face. She felt its touch like an annoying fly. She knew Sally was deciding whether to discuss her husband. Everything about her posture and mannerisms was hesitant and even a little fearful. Claire tried some reassurance.

"Sally, I want to help."

The thin blond woman returned to her chair across from Claire. Her hand was shaking as she brought the cigarette to her mouth.

"It all seemed to begin about a year ago. Rich goes out sailing by himself for a week on his vacation each year. Gives him time to really relax, think, he says."

Sally looked down at the second cigarette burning in the ashtray. A frown slashed across her face. She put out the smoking butt quickly before she continued.

"He did his normal thing last year, rented a boat, went fishing along the Hood Canal. But this time, he had an accident."

Sally paused to deeply inhale her cigarette. She exhaled the smoke as though reluctant to let it escape her lungs.

"An accident?" Claire prompted.

Sally nodded. "It was the mainsail. It swung around and struck his head, knocking him unconscious. He lay on the deck of the sailboat for hours, maybe even a day. When he finally came to, he found his way home. But he had been hurt and . . . changed."

Sally had stopped talking. She was listening. Suddenly, she jumped and headed for the sink. Claire heard the front door open and a man's heavy footsteps. Richard Quade strode through the entry hall straight into the kitchen. Before he got there, Sally Quade had washed the cigarette evidence down the drain.

Richard Quade didn't even look in Claire's direction. He was focused on his wife as he walked over to pass a kiss near her cheek.

Sally's voice quivered. "You're late. Is everything okay?"

"Yeah, fine. There was an unexplained explosion on the Shipyard today. Shook up the brass. Place was flooded with Shipyard police. They rounded us up and took us to this big auditorium to be questioned. Gave us the third degree. Really stupid. Like they expected somebody to confess or something."

Claire was studying Richard's movements, voice. He stroked his beard with his left hand. His fingers were short and stubby as she remembered, but the mannerism was new. She couldn't help but glance at his right hand. His thumbnail was not blackened. She could see no scar on his wrist.

So she had imagined it. The familiar sick feeling crawled at her insides followed by something like despair regurgitating up her throat. She forced herself to look at Richard Quade, to accept the reality before her. Physically, he looked exactly the same as he had Monday afternoon in her office; and yet her senses almost reeled at the obvious differences in his every movement.

Claire tried to make sense out of what she had learned from Sally Quade and what she was now seeing. The Richard Quade she met Monday had told her it was the "other" Richard Quade who had been hit on the head, the one who had been "dead" the last year. But Sally Quade's version of the story implied it was the Richard Quade she had been living with the last year who had suffered the head injury.

The stories didn't match.

Could the head injury have been the trigger for the release of the second Richard Quade personality? If so, it was logical for the man she had met in her office to have associated the injury with the disappearance of the second Richard Quade. But it didn't make any sense for the Richard Quade she had met to have told his wife he was the one who had been hit. Why had he done so?

Richard Quade hadn't looked at Claire yet. He was still watching his wife's worried eyes. Sally Quade was trying not to look scared. "I'm glad you're all right. The doctor has—"

Richard Quade interrupted his wife as his nostrils flared. "I smell cigarettes. Damn it, Sally, I've told you to do your smoking outside. Now how am I supposed to enjoy dinner with the air all fouled up with that filth?"

Richard Quade was complaining of cigarette smoke? This was a new Richard Quade, indeed. Claire decided this was the moment for asserting her presence. She stood and extended her hand.

"Sally let me wait for you, Richard. I became concerned when you didn't make our appointment. Perhaps if you have a few minutes before dinner, you might want to talk now?"

Richard Quade turned to Claire with pronounced suspicion and hostility etched in his harsh look. "Who in the hell are you?"

Claire had no chance to react. Sally Quade had jumped back suddenly from her husband and was screaming.

"Oh no! Dear God, it's happening again!"

Chapter Five

Wyatt left a message on Claire's answering machine. He tried to busy himself with paperwork while he waited for her to call. The minutes passed very slowly.

The Chief hadn't liked the idea of making Claire a part of the investigation team since she had found the body. But Wyatt had finally convinced him. Her need to work on the case had ended up being the determining factor in Wyatt's mind.

He could still remember the small quiver of her lower lip, the sigh of relief when he told her he would consider her offer. And now he wanted to talk with her so he could tell her. He just couldn't help being a sucker for the role of rescuer.

After looking at his watch for the tenth time, he decided to give it up. Then he had a thought. She hadn't gotten any fresh fruit the night before. Why not surprise her by bringing some fruit over to her place around dinnertime?

After a moment or two of consideration, he decided it was the best idea he'd had all day and went home to shower and change.

SPECIAL AGENT ALAN GILLETTE of the Naval Intelligence Service shook his neatly-cropped light-brown hair in disappointment at the reports he was reading. He looked up at the very tall, large-boned dark young woman standing at attention in front of him. Vera Ward's face could have been chiseled out of marble. Alan was beginning to hope his six-month-old decision to give her command over NIS security at the Puget Sound Naval Shipyard had been a good one.

"These don't tell me much, Vera."

"I don't know much, sir," she said.

Alan's blue eyes deepened. "Why not?"

"The Shipyard's Criminal Investigation Division didn't give the case to me until nearly two hours after the explosion. That's when I had all the Yard employees brought in for questioning and gave them strict instructions on silence. That's also when I called you."

"You should have gone to the CID, not waited for them to come to you. Your people must have known about the damn explosion."

"We went on security alert at once, closing the Yard. But no one knew it was an explosion at first. The Fire Department, the corpsman from the dispensary and the Shipyard uniformed police were first on the scene. When CID got into the act, even they were not immediately aware the situation required NIS involvement."

Alan threw the report on his desk as he got up to pace. He could imagine the chaos. He knew he couldn't really blame Vera.

"So the two victims of the explosion were the captain's driver and the visiting commander from the Pentagon?"

"Yes, sir."

"Didn't the Shipyard's uniformed police even recognize the explosion had taken place near the captain's parking space? Didn't anyone miss the car?"

"They did, sir. But debris was scattered over a large area. Pinpointing the origin of the blast site has been difficult. And the visiting Pentagon commander had signed out the car. Everyone assumed he was being driven to the airport to catch his plane."

Alan nodded. "But actually the visiting commander and the driver never got into the car. Is that right?"

"Yes, sir."

Alan recircled his desk and sat down. "What was this Pentagon commander doing here?"

"He had come to talk with the captain about the President's visit next week. As you know, sir, the White House is supporting the Naval Command in resisting efforts to force Permissive Action Links, PALs as they're called. Are you familiar with them, sir?"

"Yes. The PAL prevents a vessel's commander from using a nuclear weapon until a civil authority 'enables' the weapon by providing the proper arming code. But your report says this Pentagon commander was at the NIS office earlier. What was he doing here?"

The woman, still standing at absolute attention, paused. "He had stopped by to see me, sir."

Alan picked up the papers he had tossed a moment before. "He's listed in your report as Commander Antonio Corson. You knew him?"

"We worked together when I served on the admiral's staff at the Pentagon. You may remember, that's where I was assigned before assuming my position here."

Alan rubbed the back of his neck as he looked for even a tiny crack in her marble mask. There wasn't one.

"Why did you leave your job at the Pentagon?"

"A personal matter, sir."

Alan shook his head. "Nothing is personal to me, Vera. Why did you leave your job at the Pentagon?"

"It involved a difference of opinion, sir."

"Yours and who else's?"

Her jaw tensed slightly. "Sir, it started when the Center for Science and International Affairs first started pushing for Naval ships to be equipped with PALs. I was in graduate school at MIT then and came to believe that the control of nuclear weapons in this manner was desirable. Later, when I assumed my position on the admiral's staff, my views were found to be . . . an embarrassment."

"To whom?"

"To the Admiral, sir. To Tony. To the rest of the staff."

"Tony? You mean Commander Antonio Corson?"

"Yes, sir."

"So they forced you out?"

"No, sir. Tony wouldn't let them. He insisted I be given a fitness report that would not jeopardize my promotional opportunities."

"You could have had a very fine career there. Why did you choose to express your views and rock the boat?"

The pause was much longer before she answered this time. "They are my views, sir. I believe in them. I also believe I have the right to express them."

"Was Corson in favor of PALs?" Alan said.

"No, sir."

"What kind of a man was he?"

"Very thorough, sir. He insisted on accompanying the crew of the nuclear-powered aircraft carrier Nimitz on one of its cruises just so he could access command personnel. His reports back to the Admiral confirmed the Navy's contention that sufficient safeguards were already built into a nuclear-weapon launch sequence. PALs were categorically rejected."

"But he didn't convince you?"

"No, sir."

"Did Antonio Corson lessen the impact of your leaving because of a personal relationship you had?"

A small pause. "Yes, sir."

She held up well, Alan thought. Commander Corson probably had been her lover at one time for him to have intervened on her behalf with the admiral. But standing there being questioned about his death, she stood cool and calm. Of course, she might not have really cared. It was always so hard to tell with her.

"Vera, get moving on this investigation. Check on everyone at this Shipyard. Since it was the captain's car that was blown up, consider the possibility that Captain Kent was the intended target and not this visiting commander."

"Yes, sir. But according to preliminary reports, Commander Corson was out in plain view when the explosion occurred. It would be difficult to have mistaken him for Captain Kent. There is . . . was little physical resemblance between the two men."

Alan nodded. "Your point is well taken, but there's every reason to play it safe."

"Yes, sir. I've gone to our special protection procedures for Captain Kent. Do you think we should close the Shipyard?"

Alan shook his head. "The aircraft carrier Nimitz is in dry dock being prepared for refueling. The President is due next week. We can't let an assassin close down an entire Shipyard. Proceed with business as usual, but go to stage D for security."

"Yes, sir."

"Good. Barney Coffman, Chief of CID, is waiting outside. You've read his report. Use it as a stepping stone for your own investigation. Send him in now and get busy with some answers."

"Yes, sir." She no sooner left the office than a tall gaunt man in his early fifties with lots of gray in his brown hair entered and smiled at Alan, extending his hand.

"Alan! It's good to see you again."

Alan grasped Coffman's large bony hand, amazed at how fast the man had aged in the intervening two years since they had met.

"Finding you in charge of CID at Puget Sound came as a surprise, Barney. I thought you were up for Squad Supervisor at the FBI? How did you get the job here?"

Barney smiled as he released Alan's hand and took a seat. "It wasn't easy. I had to screw up a lot."

Both men laughed. "Come on, Barney. Tell me what happened to get you to leave the Bureau. I thought it was like your family."

Something dark and sad passed through Barney's watery-brown eyes. "Nothing can replace family, Alan. My wife's dead. Passed away six months ago."

Alan shook his head. "I'm sorry, Barney. I hadn't heard. I seem to remember you have a son?"

Barney's eyes were hollow. "Not anymore."

Alan heard the man's pain. "I didn't know."

"I didn't expect you to. Just wanted to explain. Larry's death broke her heart, you see. And after she was gone, well there was no one left. I needed a change of scene. I moved here just a few months ago when I heard about the opening in the Criminal Investigation Division.''

Alan knew the man's family meant a lot to him. He remembered visiting Barney at his office in the J. Edgar Hoover Building in Washington, D.C. and seeing his desk cluttered with pictures of his wife and son. No wonder the ravages of age had descended on him so soon. Alan tried to inject a more positive atmosphere.

"Well for my sake, I'm glad you're here. Your investigative record at the Bureau was tops.''

Barney looked uncomfortable at the praise. Alan quickly moved forward. "Your report indicates that despite your men's efforts to check identification and get statements from everyone within the Shipyard, nothing turned up. How do you explain that?''

Barney's gaunt frame moved uneasily in his chair. "You must understand, Alan, we had no eye witnesses. The Shipyard's uniformed police surrounded the area first and sent for medical assistance. Only then did they call my office. The assassin of the Pentagon commander could have easily left with the remote control device before the order was made to seal off the area.''

"You said the Pentagon commander's life. Do you believe he was singled out to be killed?''

"No, not really. I think it was a random terrorist act. Very few people on the Shipyard even knew the commander was here.''

Alan leaned closer. "You've heard the news about the battle over the installation of PALs on Naval nuclear weapons?''

Barney shrugged. "It's been in the news.''

"Commander Corson was a representative of the Pentagon, Barney, a direct emissary from Admiral Frost, the chief opponent of these PALs. Could there be a connection with his death and the fight taking place in Washington?''

Barney didn't look concerned. "I guess it's possible.''

Alan looked down at his report. "You said 'remote control device' a minute ago when you referred to the explosion. Nothing about a remote control device is in this preliminary report."

"Here's an update," Barney said as he passed a paper to Alan. "I just came from the laboratory. The bomb was not attached to the Captain's car as we first thought. It was a plastic explosive cleverly molded into a bicycle frame bar. When the two men passed by the bicycle rack, the remote trigger was activated."

"A bicycle? Someone parked a booby-trapped bicycle and then blew the bicycle up when the intended victim got near enough?"

"Yes. Someone with a good knowledge of explosives."

"And with access to this Shipyard," Alan said.

Barney nodded. "Which is why my people are rechecking the background of every employee on the Yard. We're looking for a knowledge of explosives. And also tomorrow, I'm instituting new security procedures to ban the use of bicycles inside the Yard."

"Leave the background investigations to Vera Ward and her team. NIS has jurisdiction over this case now."

The look in his watery-brown eyes sharpened as Barney Coffman leaned forward in his chair. "Alan, don't cut me out of the investigation. Vera Ward is . . ." The man's voice faded.

Alan frowned. "Vera Ward is what?"

Barney Coffman shook his head. "When you mentioned PALs, you got me to thinking. That FBI check I did for you on Vera before you would let her take over NIS operations at the Shipyard revealed that the real reason she left her Pentagon staff job was because she was a little too verbose in her support of PALs."

It disconcerted Alan to find out that Barney had known this about Vera and had not included it in his FBI report seven months earlier. It wouldn't have made any difference in his appointment of Vera, but it made a difference in his confidence in Barney.

"Why didn't you tell me this before?" Alan asked.

Barney shrugged. "It was a side issue, then. It had nothing to do with her performance. I didn't want to be unfair."

Barney leaned toward him. "But now I feel I had to tell you because of this unexplained death of Commander Corson. After all, Vera was one of the last people to see Commander Corson alive. I've got to tell you I'm not sure where her loyalties might lie."

Alan thought over Barney's words then shook his head. "You can't have it both ways, Barney. Either you believe this bomber chose a random victim or he's some kind of nut opposed to Naval command in a weapon-launch situation. Which is it?"

Barney leaned back in his chair and shrugged. "I just think we should explore all the possibilities."

Alan rose and extended his hand. "We will. But I won't withdraw my support of Vera because of different beliefs or vague innuendoes. If I expect her to do the job, I owe her my trust. Now let's try to keep an open mind about this thing until we've got some solid proof as to what's going on. Deal?"

Barney shrugged and got to his feet, clasping Alan's hand in a halfhearted shake. "Okay. Want to go get some beers?"

"Another time, Barney. I've got to brief Captain Kent and then I have a very important dinner appointment."

Barney paused before making for the door. "Where is the Captain? I called his office earlier and they said he had left."

"He's home while NIS rechecks his office to be sure there are no booby traps waiting. The assassin has struck once, he might very well try again."

CLAIRE OPENED her door and just stood there for a moment, staring at her brother in pleasure. Then she grabbed him in a serious hug.

"Alan, you look wonderful. It's been years too long."

Alan said what they were both thinking. "Two years. The last time was Jerry's funeral."

Claire relinquished her hold on him and stepped back. She had tears in her eyes. "Well all I can say is that rapid promotion certainly agrees with you. Come on in. Dinner is almost ready.''

Alan began to follow her into the kitchen, but paused en route to look around. ''You've fixed up Grandmother's place very nicely, but don't you feel isolated here in the woods?''

''Spoken like a true city boy. No, a nice family lives about two blocks away. We visit all the time. They're off on vacation this week. I know things have been busy for you, but you should have taken time before this to come visit your only sister.''

He watched her quietly for a moment as she resumed her salad tossing. ''You're right, Claire. I should have come before now.''

Claire looked up when she heard the apologetic tone in his voice and smiled. ''I wasn't serious, Alan. I know you've been up to your earlobes in work. Besides, the airplanes fly both ways. I should have come to see you.''

Alan searched her face. ''But you never would have, would you?''

Claire turned away. She was frowning as she ground the fresh pepper over the lettuce. ''No, I can't go back.''

She felt Alan's hand on her shoulder. It was a warm grip, a steadying hold. It made Claire feel a little teary, but she controlled herself.

''Here. You put this salad bowl on the dining-room table. I'll get the rest of our dinner.''

Alan returned from the dining room shaking his head. ''Well, Claire, I recognize most of the furniture, but I've got to tell you somehow it looks more comfortable here. Our high rises in San Francisco always seemed...''

''So much more cosmopolitan? Sophisticated? Less in tune with the muted tones and casual furniture I always insisted on buying?''

Alan nodded. ''Exactly. Funny, I never thought about it before. The apartment was Jerry's pick. He was the flamboyant one, always seeking what was daring and new. Even with the spectacular view, that place wasn't quite what you felt comfortable in, was it?''

Claire shrugged as she busied her fingers with stirring the vegetables. She concentrated on keeping her tone light. "It was where he was. That was all that mattered."

Alan was so quiet, Claire glanced over at his face. He looked strange, almost guilty, like he shouldn't have brought up the subject. She gave his arm a squeeze. "It's okay."

Alan's returning smile was strained. "I knew you were strong enough not to fall apart, to work your way through his loss. I'm proud of you."

Claire looked back at the pot of steaming vegetables, not feeling very proud. She and Alan had never talked about Jerry's reason for suicide. Brother and sister had shared tears together at the funeral, but in their occasional letters and telephone conversations over the past two years, it seemed as though they both deliberately avoided the one topic that had probably been most on their minds. Why had her husband and his best friend killed himself?

With all her excavated doubts over the Roger Thayer murder, Claire didn't think now was the time to pursue that painful subject. She deliberately refocused her thoughts. "If you'll get the hot rolls out of the oven, I'll manage the steamed vegetables and broiled salmon fillets. But I warn you to save room for the fresh strawberries for dessert."

Alan licked his lips. Claire laughed, feeling the tension release. They didn't talk through dinner, but toward the end, Claire found herself curious. "How long are you going to be here?"

"I'm not sure."

Alan leaned back in his chair, his large, well kept hands ending up in his pants' pocket. Claire had noticed they generally did when her brother had something he was keeping a secret. "What's up?"

"Just routine stuff."

Claire shook her head. "I'm not buying it, Alan. We both know your position is too exalted now to take care of the routine stuff. What's going on?"

He watched the concern in her eyes. It felt good to be with her again. And yet the disquiet was never very far away. He pushed it aside momentarily as he decided how to answer her question.

"Two men died at the Puget Sound Naval Shipyard today."

Claire shook her head. "Dreadful. By an explosion?"

Alan came out of his chair. "Where did you hear that?"

Claire hurried to explain, surprised at Alan's sharp tone. "A patient missed his appointment with me this afternoon because he was detained and questioned at the Shipyard."

Alan moved away from the table and began to pace in obvious agitation. "They were supposed to say nothing."

Claire rose and came to stand next to him. "He had to explain to his wife why he was late. I just happened to overhear."

Alan faced her. "He said nothing about anyone being killed?"

"No," Claire said. "I made the connection because he mentioned being questioned about an explosion and you mentioned the deaths."

Alan shook his head and exhaled wearily. "I guess spouses have to get told something. Sorry to mess up your appointment schedule."

Hearing Alan's voice return to normal, Claire smiled and turned to clear the dishes. "It's okay. He probably wouldn't have showed anyway. As it was, he threw me out of his house tonight."

Alan frowned. "A patient threw you out of his house?"

"Figuratively speaking, of course. All he really did was to tell me to get out and never come back."

Alan's frown deepened. "Who is this guy?"

Claire's response was interrupted by the doorbell.

"Expecting anyone?" Alan asked. Claire shook her head. "Then let me get it," he said turning to do so.

WYATT STOOD on Claire's doorstep, holding a basket of fruit and a surprised expression when a man opened the door.

"Yes?" the man with the light brown hair asked. He was compactly built and neat as a pin, possessing the sophisticated quiet good looks that Wyatt realized probably appealed to a lot of women. And although Wyatt knew he had never met him before, there was something familiar about the deep blue of his eyes. He swallowed a taste of disappointment before he spoke in his most official tone.

"I'm Sergeant Lockhart, Kitsap County Sheriff's Department. Is Dr. Claire Boland at home?"

Alan looked at the basket of fruit and then at Wyatt and stepped aside to give him room to enter.

"Yes, come in. I'm Alan Gillette," he said holding out this hand. "Claire's in the dining room clearing up the dishes." Alan raised his voice and called in that direction. "Claire? The law's here bearing gifts."

Wyatt took Alan's offered hand and found a firm grip to match his own. If this man was Claire's romantic interest, she at least seemed to have selected well. That fact didn't make Wyatt at all happy. Obviously this visit was an ill-timed one. But there was no turning back now. He followed Alan into the dining room where a few scattered dishes still lined the tablecloth. Claire emerged almost immediately from the kitchen.

She looked surprised. Wyatt didn't know what else to do, so he just held out the basket of fruit he had brought. "I thought you might want some fruit since you weren't able to get any last night."

Claire stepped forward. Wyatt could feel Alan's eyes watching and could have sworn the man was stifling a smile. Claire looked slightly flushed as she took the basket of fruit. "Thank you, Sergeant. It was very thoughtful. We were just going to have some coffee. Will you join us?"

Wyatt was saying no and backing up toward the door when Alan grabbed hold of his arm and almost dragged him back to the table.

"Of course he'll stay, if for no other reason than to explain to me what was going on last night that prevented you from getting any fruit, Claire."

Wyatt couldn't read any jealousy, irritation or anything but good-natured humor in Alan's voice. If he was a romantic interest of Claire's, he was a remarkably easygoing one. Before he knew it, Wyatt found himself sitting at the dining-room table with coffee and sliced strawberries topped with whipped cream.

"Well, who's going to explain?" Alan asked. "Will it be you, Claire, or Sergeant Lockhart…that sounds rather too formal. What's your first name, Sergeant?"

"Wyatt."

"Call me Alan. I've had enough experience in the military to learn to resent an address of 'mister.' Calling someone by their last name is equally as bad. I'll put up with it at work, but when it's time to relax, I like to feel I can dismiss those barriers. Been in law enforcement long?"

Wyatt liked Gillette's open manner. Still, he detected a confidence and a sharp intellect behind the easy conversation. The man was more than he projected. Wyatt wondered how much more.

"I joined the Sheriff's Department after college, twelve years ago. You said something about being in the military?"

Alan shrugged as though talking about himself was boring. "I'm presently doing some work at the Shipyard in Bremerton." He turned toward Claire. "What did you and Wyatt get involved in last night that interfered with your getting some fruit?"

Wyatt could see Alan's eyes watched Claire closely as an amused smile curled his lips.

"Try to behave, Alan. I went out to the grocery store and fell over a dead man."

Claire's scolding tone of Alan was playful, intimate. Wyatt felt suddenly like an outsider. He shifted uncomfortably in his chair. He should have known she'd be involved with someone.

Alan sat forward, the smile wiped from his face. "What?"

Claire nodded. "You heard right. I fell over a dead man, literally, in the Silverdale Safeway store."

Alan frowned. "How did the man die?"

"He was murdered," Wyatt said, quickly. "I came by tonight to ask Dr. Boland not to discuss the details of that murder until the investigation has been concluded."

Alan looked from Wyatt to Claire. He reached out a hand to grasp her arm. Wyatt noted with a pang the proprietary way in which Alan's eyes searched Claire's face. His genuine care for her was obvious. "Was one of your patients involved?"

She looked at Alan and frowned. "No. I only thought so."

Alan wasn't satisfied. "You're being evasive. That's not a trait that comes naturally to you, Claire. What's bothering you?"

Claire sighed in obvious discomfort. Wyatt sensed she was having a hard time finding the right words to put the man off. He felt a strong desire to come to her aid. He turned to Alan.

"Claire is an important witness and I hope you will respect her unwillingness to discuss the matter. Now I must be going."

Wyatt got up quickly and walked directly to the entry. Claire caught up with him just as he reached the front door. "Sergeant?"

He turned at her call, relieved to see Alan had not followed her. As she came to stand before him, he inhaled her light perfume.

"Thank you for coming tonight," she said. "You had already left your office this evening when I returned your earlier call."

Wyatt looked over her head at the paneling in the entry hall as though it was a fascinating piece of work. "Dr. Boland, I didn't mean to badger you this afternoon. I was only trying to get at the truth. I thought there might be something—"

Claire shrugged, not waiting for him to finish. "It doesn't matter. Have you had an opportunity to consider my offer?"

Wyatt glanced at the expectation in her eyes. "Yes. My chief thinks your help might be of importance in this case."

"And how do you feel about it, Sergeant?"

Her eyes were searching his in the dim light of her entry. He found himself wanting to reach out to touch the wayward, red-gold strand of hair lying across her cheek. Then he remembered Alan Gillette in the next room and cleared his throat.

"Call me Wyatt."

She smiled at the message in his words and put her hand in his. "Thank you, Wyatt. This means a great deal to me. I won't forget."

He felt the squeeze of her hand and resisted a strong impulse to lean down to kiss her smiling, upturned face. He knew if he stayed much longer, all those insistent impulses might start taking over so he quickly turned and left.

As he got into his old Chevy Blazer, he looked back at the closed door to her home, finding there were two things back there still bothering him. One was her red Allante convertible parked in the driveway, and the other was the sophisticated good looks of Alan Gillette parked in her dining room.

WHEN CLAIRE returned to the dining room she sat down heavily in her chair and sighed. Alan was leaning back in his chair and studying her. "Tired?"

"A little. That murder business kept me up late."

"And the sergeant?"

Claire looked over at the mischief in her brother's eyes. "You can be a brat at times, Alan Gillette."

Alan smiled. "Since cave days, Claire, men have been showing their affection by bringing food to their women. It's an ancient, ingrained ritual stemming no doubt from man's need to prove to his desired mate that he could obtain nourishment for them both as an inducement for her to accept him."

Claire was beginning to smile. "Alan, what does this little piece of dubious ancient history have to do with anything?"

Alan's face wore a satisfied smirk. "Subconscious drives made Wyatt bring that basket of fruit to you tonight."

Claire smiled at her brother. "Subconscious drives? Who's the psychologist here, anyway."

"It doesn't take a psychologist to figure out the guy could have just called to tell you not to discuss the murder."

Claire shrugged. "He also wanted to tell me his chief had approved of my lending some psychological assistance on the case."

Alan's voice was lightly sarcastic. "Oh right. That part would have been very difficult to say over the phone."

Claire made a face at him as she began gathering the dishes.

Alan just smiled in return. "I'll lay you odds it's really our sergeant who approves of you two working together. Do I detect a bit of excitement on your part, too?"

Claire looked up. "Let it go, Alan. Sergeant Lockhart and I only know each other courtesy of a particularly grisly murder. As a matter of fact, occasionally I get this impression that he associates me with something that bothers him."

"Something that bothers him?" Alan repeated.

She shook her head. "I can't be sure, but I think something about me may remind him of someone unpleasant from his past. And if that's really the case, I know how strong past disappointments can control current behavior."

Alan frowned at her. "You're thinking of Jerry, aren't you? You're not free of his memory?"

Claire sighed. "I'm a psychologist, Alan. I'll never be free of the knowledge that I neither saw his pain nor could help him resolve it."

"But, Claire, maybe the suicide was a spur of the moment thing? Maybe Jerry never showed—"

Claire interrupted. "Suicide is not something a healthy individual all of a sudden decides to do. A person walking toward the door of suicide leaves footprints along the way. If a wife who's also a psychologist can't see them then..."

Claire's voice trailed away as the pain showed on her face. Alan came over to put an arm around her shoulders. It was as he feared. Claire did not understand Jerry's suicide. How could she? Only he had hoped with time she would be able to accept, to forget. But the time had passed and she hadn't.

Still what could he do? He was sworn to secrecy. Fear of seeing her like this was precisely the reason he had avoided her company the last two years. He knew his duty and his love for her would conflict.

He schooled his voice to project his most authoritative tone as his arm gave her a tight squeeze. "If Dr. Claire Boland didn't see the signs, it was because they weren't there."

Claire smiled at her brother, thankful for his belief even if she couldn't share it.

Alan returned her smile. "As a matter of fact, you're so good sometimes I think it's a shame you're so damn logical."

His words startled Claire. "What makes logic regrettable?"

"Well when you know something will never work, it prohibits you from ever giving it a chance. I think it's been the scientists who didn't know how dumb they were who have made the most advances by bumbling blind luck. You should try it sometime."

Claire eyed him sharply. "And I suppose you're going to tell me that's how you conduct your business affairs?"

Alan smirked. "Not my business, but certainly my affairs."

Claire shook her head. "You should be ashamed of yourself, Alan Gillette."

Alan looked anything but ashamed as he grinned and started for the door. "No doubt. I'm going to have to call it a night, babe. Meet me for lunch tomorrow at the Sea Galley in Bremerton. Shipyard folks say its decent. You can catch me up on the last two years."

"I'd love to have lunch with you, but I'm afraid you'll be disappointed with my recent history. Surviving it has been my most significant attainment."

Alan was just about to open the door when he hesitated and turned back to Claire. For a moment she thought he was going to say something, but then his hands descended into his pockets and he just mumbled good-night.

RICHARD QUADE SLAMMED the telephone book against the door to the garage with a loud slapping sound. Damn it! That psychologist was in the same office building as the doctor!

Somehow he had slipped up. He thought Roger Thayer was going to see his regular doctor, that Reyes chump, when he went into those offices on Byron Street the day before. But he must have made a visit to that psychologist instead. What a stupid mistake!

He should have followed him into the building. After an entire year of careful surveillance and planning, he had screwed up.

Richard Quade began to pace. He had to think. If only he knew what the guy had told this psychologist. It had to have been something pretty startling to have caused the woman to show up at his home tonight. He hadn't even recognized her at first. Dressed in a suit and with her hair up, she had looked quite different.

Damn the woman! The last telephone call to Thayer had been a mistake. Describing the scene he had witnessed of the body being dumped overboard had obviously pushed the guy too far.

Well, it was too late now to worry about. The idiot had probably gone to that psychologist and spilled everything about who he was and what he had done. And she was the one in the grocery store Monday night, too. Of all the rotten luck. He thought she might have seen him. But what if it was something about Roger Thayer she recognized? What had she told the police? What did she know?

Damn it! He mustn't let his imagination go too far. If she had seen him and told the police, he would have been questioned at least, and he wasn't. So, if she knew, she hadn't told. Yet.

Well, if she was so hot to have an appointment with him, he'd see she got one. Tomorrow. He couldn't depend on her keeping quiet forever. He'd have to silence her. For good.

Dr. Claire Boland was one mistake he could erase.

Chapter Six

When Claire got to her office Wednesday morning, she activated her answering machine. She had two messages. The first was from Wyatt. From the time on the call, she realized the message had been left late the afternoon before.

She smiled at the thought of the tall sergeant's arrival at her home the previous night. She hadn't missed the way he looked at her or how he came to her aid when Alan was questioning her too closely.

But what she had told Alan was true. She could see Wyatt battled the attraction he had for her because of some previous association. It was probably just as well. The last thing she needed while trying to regain her emotional bearings was a distracting romantic interest.

Still, she couldn't deny she found Wyatt very attractive and his internal conflict over her very exciting. She was woman enough to be pleased he couldn't dismiss her too easily.

All thoughts of Wyatt vanished, however, as Claire listened to her next recorded message. It was timed late last night and was from Richard Quade. He apologized for being upset the night before and asked her to call him at his number at the Shipyard. Claire immediately reached for the phone.

Someone else answered. She tried to give the person her name, but they put the phone down to get Richard before she could.

"This is Quade."

"Richard?"

"Yeah. Who's this?"

"This is Dr. Boland. Your message said you wanted to see me?"

"Oh, yeah. I'm really sorry about last night, Doc. I wasn't myself. I really flew off the handle. Just shows you how much I need your help. You'll see me again?"

Claire's hope returned. "Of course. When can you come in?"

"Uh, how about late this afternoon?"

Claire checked her appointment calendar. "My latest appointment time is at four-fifteen. Can you make it?"

"Four-fifteen will be fine. I can cut out a little early."

"Have the telephone calls stopped?" Claire asked.

"Telephone? Oh, yes, the calls. They've stopped. No more threats. Thanks, Doc. See you this afternoon."

Claire hung up the phone thinking she should be reassured, but she wasn't. This Richard Quade knew about her, unlike the one who had become so angry at her presence in his home the night before. And yet, this Richard Quade didn't sound like the first Richard Quade who had come into her office two days before. The man who had been so terrified at the telephone calls was not the same man who had just dismissed them so casually.

The more she talked with the very changeable Richard Quade, the less she seemed to know. Her perceptions told her he was a different person. Could she trust them?

Sadly she put her head in her hands. She thought again about the month following Jerry's death when she lay in the dark through the long nights, trying to understand why she never saw the torment her husband must have been feeling. How had she failed him?

No answer had come to her then and none came to her now. She lifted her head. She had to keep busy. Work had pulled her out of her depression two years before. It would forestall another now. Perhaps the afternoon session with Richard Quade would help to clarify her perceptions. She was looking forward to it.

"CARSON CITY HAS FAXED all the information they have on Thayer," Tom told Wyatt when he bounded into his office around ten. "They're checking on all his known associates and calling around to interview them. I faxed a picture of Arthur Knudsen to them so they can ask if he was known to Thayer."

"Any leads to Knudsen's whereabouts?" Wyatt asked.

Tom shook his head. "He didn't make friends with any of the other employees at Safeway. Each says the same thing. Arthur Knudsen kept to himself and talked only about business."

Wyatt frowned. "What about the local agencies?"

"He owns no property in the state. He has neither a Washington State driver's license nor a car registration. None of the banks show him with an account."

"How did he cash his paychecks?" Wyatt asked.

"Store did it for him when he did his weekly shopping. It's like the guy doesn't exist outside that store."

"Or was trying not to leave any traces," Wyatt said. "Don't give up. Circulate his picture among the merchants at the Silverdale Mall. Maybe somebody remembers seeing him there."

Tom nodded.

Wyatt opened the file on his desk and took a moment to review his notes. "Did you follow up on what Thayer's mother told me yesterday about his being adopted?"

"I'm having to get a court order to gain access to his natural parents' names," Tom said. "It's going to take a while."

"Well, keep at it. There's a motive for this murder somewhere. Someone hated this man enough to blow off his face."

Tom frowned. "You've ruled out a random killing?"

Wyatt nodded. "Claire thinks it unlikely."

A smile was beginning to form on Tom's lips. "Claire?"

Tom was interrupted and both men were startled at a sudden banging on Wyatt's door. Tom reached over to open the door, exposing a short dark-haired woman with a determined look standing on the other side. She didn't give either of them a chance to speak.

"I'm Doris Thayer. I demand to know what you're doing to find my brother's killer!"

RICHARD QUADE WATCHED Claire get into her car and drive away. Wherever she was going to eat, it must be some distance. It didn't really matter. All he needed was a minute or two.

He glanced around cautiously, finding the small parking lot was empty. He had left his truck around the corner. Dr. Reyes and his receptionist had left a few minutes before. The building should be deserted. He would do his work, undisturbed.

He slowly climbed the front steps and opened the outside door. He quickly stepped in, out of view of the street. The floor directory to the small one-story building was simple. Dr. Boland's office was on the right and Dr. Reyes's was on the left. He moved across the carpet to the right office and grasped the knob. He turned it and then turned it again. It was locked.

His anger surfaced readily. Damn the woman! How was he going to get in? Then he saw the planter.

It was a large corn plant, nearly six-feet high, bending toward the light of the front windows, dividing the hallway between the two offices. The planter base was roomy—a foot-and-a-half across. He dug his fingers deep into the fertilized earth. A moist pungent smell filled his nostrils.

He scooped the earth, digging a small grave. Then he took the package hidden in an inside pocket of his light jacket and buried it. He felt suddenly sad that the large corn plant had to die. Sometimes he thought the world would be better with far fewer people and far more plants. He was sure it would be better without Dr. Claire Boland.

ALAN AND CLAIRE ATE their lunch in thoughtful silence. She waited until the dessert tray was being passed before asking the question that had been in her mind.

"What is it, Alan? What's wrong?"

He stopped his unconscious study of the tablecloth and looked up at her, blinking. "I'm sorry. I know I'm rotten company. I probably should have called and canceled our lunch date, but I didn't want to miss the opportunity of seeing you today."

"Can you tell me what's bothering you? I can be a good listener, and I know how to keep a confidence."

Alan shook his head. "I trust you, Claire. Completely. You know that. But as you also know, I don't have the kind of job that can be discussed."

Claire did know. It had been Jerry's job, too, one chocked full of intelligence secrets vital to the National Defense, not to be shared with anyone, including spouses. So many of her and Jerry's nights together over dinner had been quiet ones, just like this luncheon.

Had those long spans of silence begun the separation of their real communication? Should she have insisted on discussing their feelings and not assumed Jerry's mind was on business? Would it have made a difference? She had asked herself these same questions over and over. She never got an answer.

"What are you thinking, Claire?"

Claire shook her head almost sadly. "Just about Jerry."

Alan's pained look made her reach over to touch his arm. "It's just that you and he always seemed to approach the job in much the same manner. 'Damn the torpedoes, full speed ahead.'"

Alan looked more uneasy. "I think you'll find I've changed. A bit of doubt and worry do creep in with experience."

Claire watched Alan raise his arm to signal the waiter for another iced tea. A vivid memory crossed her eyes. She saw him again at twelve years old with his arm around Jerry as they talked about taking on the world together when they grew older. They had been so confident, so sure of themselves.

"Claire?"

"What? I'm sorry. My mind wandered."

"I asked if you wanted some more iced tea?" Alan said.

"Yes, please."

Claire accepted the second glass from the waiter and remained silent until he had moved on. Despite what Alan said about not talking, she knew sharing would do him some good.

"There hasn't been anything in the news concerning the Shipyard explosion. I assume you're keeping that information under wraps until your investigation is complete?"

Alan nodded. "Your assumption's right. I know I can count on your discretion. The news media got wind of it somehow, though. We've been swamped with calls for verification. We've given them an alternate story, but at the moment they seem hesitant to run it. Obviously your patient and others like him have said things they shouldn't."

"You haven't identified who's responsible?"

"No, damn it, not even a clue, and we don't even know if or when he'll strike again. That's the worst part."

Claire heard the vehemence in Alan's voice. She squirted a fresh lemon slice into the golden brown liquid of her iced tea.

"Is this the case of a killer who just happened to pick a Naval shipyard to commit his crime, or is this the case of a killer who is committing his crime because he's on a Naval shipyard?" she asked.

Alan watched her stirring the lemon through her drink, the ice cubes pinging against the side of her glass. "NIS has taken over because we believe it to be the latter."

Claire put down her spoon. "Then you don't think you've got a murderer who might kill when he's off the Shipyard as well?"

Alan eyed her speculatively. "What are you getting at?"

She shook her head. "Nothing really. Just a wild idea. Killing a victim by explosion is not a normal method as someone reminded me recently, and the man I found murdered was—''

"Excuse me, sir. Are you Alan Gillette?" the waiter said.

"Yes. What is it?" Alan said.

"An urgent telephone call. If you'll step over here please?"

Claire had no opportunity to complete her sentence. Alan left immediately for his call and when he returned to the table, his face told her something distressing had happened.

"I'm sorry. I've got to get back to the Shipyard. I'll call you later if I may?"

"Of course. Whenever you can," she said.

He placed the money to cover their lunch on the table, took a last sip of iced tea and quickly leaned over to kiss her cheek. As he straightened up, he smiled down on her, but the expression in his eyes told her he was already miles away.

She watched him leave the restaurant, thinking again about the similarities between him and Jerry. Alan was right. He had changed. He hadn't been one to worry and doubt before. But she could now see they were emotions that had become familiar to him.

Claire sipped her iced tea. Did he see her as changed, too? Time had healed her pain, but after two years, her confidence could still be shred by the resurfaced distrust of her perceptions. Doubt and worry had become her companions also. And more and more she was beginning to realize how lonely life was with just their company.

CLAIRE WALKED up the stairs to her office with her next patient. For the next hour she was immersed in his problems. She was so caught up in their conversation that they went fifteen minutes over the allotted time. It didn't matter to Claire. She didn't have an appointment that next hour.

But when she opened the door to let her patient exit, she was very surprised to see Arthur Knudsen pacing in her waiting room. He was unshaven and disheveled and his clothes were badly crumpled. He deliberately turned his face away until her patient left. Then he rushed up to Claire.

"I had to come to see you. I've been calling every few minutes over the last hour. All I've gotten was your answering machine. Please, I must talk to you."

For a split second Claire thought of making some excuse and going into her office to call Wyatt. But Knudsen's anxious fearful face told her if she tried it, he probably wouldn't be there when she returned. She knew she was taking a chance, but perhaps it would be best to hear what he had to say before she made an attempt to contact the Sheriff's office.

"All right, Arthur. Come in."

He followed her into her office and closed the door behind them. His eyes were wild. He didn't look as though he had slept in the last two days. His voice was a whimpering demand.

"You must go to the police and tell them you discovered the body on Monday night. You must not mention me at all. I must not be involved."

Claire clearly saw and heard his desperation. She purposely kept her voice calm and even. "Arthur, I'm sorry but what you ask is impossible. I waited for the authorities Monday night and gave my statement to them then. They know I discovered the body and they know you went to call the Sheriff's office. And you did call them, didn't you?"

Knudsen sank despondently into a chair. "I shouldn't have done it. I should have just left. But I wasn't able to think at first. By the time I realized what I was involved in, it was too late."

Claire walked over to Knudsen's chair. "Arthur, why don't you go to the Sheriff and just explain—"

His head rose and he sneered at her. "It's your fault! I told you to go home! If you had gone, they never would have known I saw anything." Suddenly, the anger in his voice turned into a sob. "Why couldn't you have just gone home?"

Claire was used to dealing with people overcome by emotion. But Knudsen's rapidly changing moods from anger to self-pity were both irrational and unpredictable. He was obviously very unstable. She tried to think how best to approach him and decided some reassurance might help.

"I know you didn't kill that man in the Safeway store, Arthur. When the Sheriff's office checks the evidence, they'll realize it, too. If you'll just talk to them—"

Knudsen sprung out of his chair. His sudden move caused Claire to jump back. He shouted at her. "Talk to them? Are you crazy? They're looking for me! They'll lock me up! I can't go through that again. Never!"

His eyes were filled with terror. Claire could tell the man before her had lost his mental balance. His wild look told her he was plummeting away from her or anyone's reach into some internal abyss.

Her voice reached out to him. "Arthur, what can I do?"

Knudsen ignored her question, as though he hadn't heard it. He stumbled over to the window, tearing the drape back as though he already felt closed in. "I won't let them get me."

Claire chilled at his vehemence. Suddenly she was afraid to be in the same room with the unpredictable man. He was so obviously terror-stricken and irrational, he might be capable of anything.

Slowly she tried to back up toward the door. Unfortunately she bumped against her desk on the way, upsetting the pendulum clock ticking there. It landed with a loud thump.

Knudsen whirled around at the sound, looking at her as though she was the enemy. His silent anger reached across the room, clawing at her skin. Claire knew she had begun to shake. She tried to keep her voice calm and even.

"Arthur, let me try to help you. Talk to me about this fear. Explain it to me so that I'll understand."

His jowly face contorted as his voice sneered out his pain. "You psychologists never understand. Oh, you say you do, but you can't. You can't understand what it's like to be buried alive!"

"Buried alive?" Claire repeated as she continued to back up toward the door. She didn't know what was going on in Knudsen's head, but obviously the demons he was fighting had no basis in current reality. His eyes seemed locked on some internal image, horrible and frightening. "What is scaring you, Arthur?"

Knudsen watched Claire in a shocked fear. His face went white and she could see his hands had begun to shake.

"Leave me alone! Get out of my head! I shouldn't have come here. You can't help me. Oh, God, no one can help me!"

With the verbalization of the words, Arthur Knudsen seemed to focus even more strongly on some unspeakable terror he was reliving. His eyes darted around the room frantically. "I won't go back! I won't let them lock me up!"

Claire choked a frightened scream as Knudsen lunged at the desk. She soon realized she wasn't his goal, however. Instead he pushed her to the floor and grabbed the silver letter opener that sat on the corner. In absolute horror she watched helplessly as he dug it into his wrist.

"WE DEACTIVATED the bomb," Barney said the moment Alan stepped from the fifth-floor elevator doors. "Like I told you over the phone, my men found it in time."

Alan's stomach knotted tightly as he looked at the small metal lunchbox with the wires disconnected from the sticks of dynamite.

"You found this right here under the model of the U. S. Battleship Oregon?"

Barney nodded.

Alan looked past the model of the battleship encased in its protective glass to the teak wood and glass entry doors of the Shipyard Commander's office, not fifteen feet away. He felt frustrated and angry. "Damn it. It's got to be a Shipyard employee."

Barney shook his head. "Not necessarily, Alan. Someone could be getting on the yard by posing as a repairman for a computer or reproduction machine. At least the captain was in no real danger since he was at his yearly physical today. Only workers who just happened to be in these offices would have been at risk."

Alan was shaking his head. "Just like Commander Corson 'just happened' to be walking by that bicycle rack? No, I don't think so. Whoever is doing this is more clever and focused than that. But who or what is he or she really after?" Alan asked, mostly of himself.

Barney shrugged. "Maybe it's the captain who's been targeted. Both devices seemed aimed for him."

Alan nodded as he turned to look at the CID Chief. "How did your men find this one, Barney?"

"I've put my criminal investigators on overtime walking the Shipyard, watching out for anything suspicious. It was while on one of these walkthroughs that the bomb was spotted. We can't be sure there aren't more, Alan. You realize that of course?"

Alan sighed. "Of course. But I've alerted the Marines to do a thorough search and called out an additional company. I want the employees rounded up again and questioned. That should be Vera's job. Which reminds me, where is she?"

Barney shrugged. "When I called to notify her of what my investigators found, no one answered the phone."

Alan turned to Barney in stunned disbelief. "Nobody answered the phone at NIS headquarters?"

THE MOMENT the ambulance had reached Harrison Memorial hospital with Claire and Arthur Knudsen, who was sedated, she got out of the back and literally ran into a waiting physician. He assured her he already knew about the suicide attempt as the paramedics wheeled Knudsen through the emergency-room doors. The flurry of activity disappeared suddenly behind the doors under the white letters, Ambulance Personnel Only.

Claire found herself alone on the street side, her own image reflecting back at her from the glass doors, the echoes of the ambulance siren still vibrating in her ears. She turned to her right to the Emergency Department entrance and went in. She went to the public telephone and found the Port Orchard number for the Sheriff's Detective offices and punched it in. The crisp voice of a deputy answered.

"Sergeant Lockhart's not in. Can someone else help?"

"Please contact the sergeant. Tell him Knudsen just tried to commit suicide. Ask him to meet Dr. Boland in the waiting room at Harrison Memorial Hospital."

She hung up the phone, not waiting for an acknowledgment. As she paced despondently across the brown carpet of the waiting room, she berated herself. She should have read the man's irrational state sooner. His suicide attempt was her fault.

Locked in the cage of her perceived defeat, she didn't even notice when Wyatt strode into the room. He stood beside her and had begun speaking before she even turned in his direction.

"What? I'm sorry, I didn't hear what you said."

Wyatt's eyes were studying her face. "I said I got your message. An emergency-room nurse just informed me they're still working on him. How did it happen?"

Claire exhaled heavily as though trying to rid herself of a lingering weight. "Knudsen became uncontrollably upset. He reached for the letter opener. I couldn't stop him."

Claire knew she was shaking. She tried to control the worst of it by clasping her hands together. She felt Wyatt suddenly by her side. His arm went around her shoulders, warm and comforting. His words were spoken gently. "You saw the wounds. Is he going to make it?"

She shook her head. "I don't know. There was a lot of blood. I don't know if he went deep enough. The letter opener wasn't very sharp. He kept..."

Claire put her face in her hands, trying to blot out the image. A moment later she became aware of Wyatt's arm tightening around her and his voice, infinitely gentle, urging her to sit down on one of the brown vinyl waiting-room chairs. She sank into it, keeping her eyes closed, letting her mind go blank.

His arm felt strong and steadying and she was grateful for its touch. Even the scent of his Old Spice fragrance seemed familiar and soothing. She didn't know how long she sat with head bent, mindlessly complacent, but when she finally opened her eyes, the awful blood-chilling images were replaced by the concerned look in his green-blue eyes.

She sat up. His arm was still around her and he was smiling. "Feeling better?" he asked.

His presence and warm acceptance of her emotional upset made everything more palatable. She nodded in answer to his question and smiled. "Thank you. You're very good at this."

Wyatt's eyes sparkled. "Holding you in my arms?"

His words were said warmly and intimately. Their meaning startled her into a more upright position. "I meant—"

He was still smiling as he leisurely brushed a red-gold curl off her forehead and interrupted what she was about to say. "I know what you meant, Claire."

Her name sounded special when he said it. As she began to realize he was lightly flirting with her, she felt a warm rush that momentarily left her breathless. She wasn't sure what she was going to say next, but in any case he didn't give her a chance to say it. He got up to get her some water.

"Drink this. I don't know why having something to drink helps, but I think strong emotion dehydrates the body or something. You probably understand that better than I."

She took the cup from his hand and drank the entire contents. As she was handing it back to him, she realized he was watching her closely. "Thank you," she said, feeling the warmth climb up her neck again at the sustained contact with his eyes.

Finally he looked away and sat down next to her again, this time at a discreet distance. "Ready to tell me about it now?"

She nodded. "Arthur Knudsen showed up at my office around three-thirty. He said he had to talk with me."

Wyatt spoke his words calmly, but their meaning was specific. "Why didn't you call me?"

Claire tried to keep the defensiveness out of her response. "He was standing right in front of me. There wasn't any way I could get to a phone and call you without him vanishing again. I thought the best thing I could do was to listen to what he had to say and try to get him to come to you himself.''

A small irritation laced Wyatt's next words. "The guy's obviously a candidate for loony-tunes. Couldn't you see that?''

Claire inhaled, fighting for emotional strength. "I realized he was extremely upset, yes. But I thought he might be rational enough to talk about what was bothering him.''

"Okay, you listened. What did he have to say?''

"He came to ask me to lie about his having seen Roger Thayer's body in Safeway on Monday night. Naturally, I told him I couldn't.''

"So he did kill Thayer?''

Claire shook her head. "No, I don't think it was that. Knudsen was in an irrational emotional state. After two days of indulging some deep fear, he had convinced himself if he talked with the Sheriff's office, he would be locked up.''

Wyatt shook his head. "Listen to what you're saying. The man came to you to ask you to lie for him because he knew if we got him in custody, we'd lock him up for Thayer's murder. When you refused to lie for him, he tries to commit suicide. If that isn't a guilty conscience, I don't know what is.''

Claire sat up straighter as she shook her head. "On the surface, I know your conclusions sound logical. But I believe other factors are causing Knudsen's present irrational behavior. From my brief discussion with him, I think it has roots in some past trauma, which the death of Roger Thayer has reopened.''

Wyatt heard the conviction in her words. However, he was wary. She had also believed Richard Quade was Roger Thayer. He decided to probe deeper.

"He'd rather die than be questioned by the police?''

She shook her head. "It's not the questioning. He seems to have an inordinate fear of being locked up. He spoke of it in terms of being buried alive. Those were his very words.''

"Why should he think we'd lock him up?" Wyatt asked. "If he's innocent and had come forward on the night of Thayer's murder, he could have given us his statement then and be done with it. No, he's got to be hiding something. What is it?"

"Wyatt, I know his actions seem bizarre. Most actions associated with unreasoning fears are bizarre. But I do believe such fear is at the basis of Knudsen's behavior."

"How long did you speak with him?"

"A few minutes," Claire said.

"And you were able to diagnose a major earlier trauma leading to such an unreasoning fear that quickly?"

Claire fought against a moment of uncertainty. "I know we were together only briefly, but he manifested that fear quite clearly in his words and actions. I can't be certain, of course. An in-depth psychological evaluation would take a long time."

Wyatt paused for a moment to consider her words and Claire was distracted when two reporters stopped at the emergency-room's reception desk and asked for Knudsen's doctor. The nurse was doing her best to turn them away.

Claire looked at Wyatt in surprise. "The media knows?"

Wyatt shrugged. "We've had a bulletin out for Knudsen. Every journalist for miles is no doubt monitoring our calls. They'll probably all be descending on the hospital soon."

Claire sighed. "I don't want to be here."

"Don't worry. We've never released your name to the press. Come on. Let's take a walk and get some air."

She nodded as she rose with him and proceeded to walk out the waiting-room doors to the ambulance entrance.

No sooner had she passed through the glass doors, however, when her attention was suddenly diverted by the loud screech of an approaching siren. It cut abruptly as the ambulance turned into the emergency entrance and stopped a few feet in front of her.

With somewhat detached curiosity, she watched as the doors opened and a new victim was rolled from the back of the vehicle. However, all detachment fled when Claire took one look at the man's face on the stretcher. Her mind jolted in an agony of recognition. She ran forward.

"Dave! Dave!"

Dr. David Reyes didn't answer her.

Chapter Seven

Wyatt watched Claire turn to the paramedic at the side of the stretcher, her voice a harsh croak. "What's wrong with him?"

The paramedic was busy rolling the stretcher from the ambulance. He barely looked in her direction as he answered. "If you mean this guy, the building he was in exploded. The receptionist is still in the ambulance. She's a DOA. He's got a chance, though. Got lucky. Must have dropped something under his desk. We found him under it. Saved his life by protecting him when the wall blew apart."

Wyatt stepped forward quickly as he saw Claire's knees give out when they rolled Dave through the emergency medical doors. He put his arms around her to steady her against him.

"It's all right. I've got you," he said in her ear.

He all but carried her back into the waiting room, depositing her carefully on the closest chair. He didn't remove his arms, but held her to him tightly, wondering whether she wasn't a prime candidate for emergency-room treatment herself from the way she was trembling against him.

Feeling her fragility in his arms, he felt something strong and decisive crushing his emotional barriers. Gradually her trembling stopped and her breathing seemed to come easier. She also seemed to be fighting to sit up straight. Somewhat reluctantly he released his tight hold to give her more flexibility.

"I'm sorry, Wyatt. This seems to be becoming a habit."

"What's that?"

"My needing your support."

He smiled at her. "You won't find me complaining. However, I can't help thinking that perhaps we could devise more pleasant reasons for your ending up in my arms?"

She had to smile up at him in spite of everything as she eased herself out of his arms. "You've been very supportive, figuratively and literally."

Wyatt sat back. "To Serve and Protect is our motto, remember. Who was that man they just brought in?"

"Dr. Dave Reyes. We have offices in the same building."

Wyatt turned more fully toward her, his heart increasing to an erratic beat. "*Your* building was the one involved in the explosion?"

Until he had said the words, he could tell Claire hadn't fully taken in the impact of what had just happened. She might have been in that building. She might have been killed. Those thoughts now showed clearly on her face.

"I'll take you home in a minute. I just need to call in a deputy to watch Mr. Knudsen and see which detective got the nudge on this latest murder."

Claire's face was white. "Latest murder?"

"Think it through, Claire. Someone just blew up your building. Somewhat coincidental, wouldn't you say?"

Claire's eyes were wide in shocked understanding.

Wyatt gave her shoulders a little shake. "Claire, I don't want to leave you but I have to. I've got to make those calls now. You'll be okay here for a few minutes?"

She nodded.

Wyatt got up and headed toward the door to use his car phone. He paused to look back at her. She was very quiet, very still and pale. With an effort he turned his eyes away so he could begin to concentrate on what needed to be done.

Claire rested her head on the chair's back and tried to think.

Roger Thayer had been killed by an explosion on Monday. Two men at the Puget Sound Naval Shipyard had been

killed by an explosion Tuesday. And Dave's receptionist had
been killed and Dave badly injured by an explosion today.

Three days, three explosions. These couldn't be coincidences. She had to talk to someone. Since she couldn't tell
Wyatt about the explosions at the Shipyard, it had to be
Alan. She reached into her change purse for a quarter and
went back to the public phone. A woman answered Alan's
line. Claire identified herself.

"This is Special Agent Ward, Dr. Boland. Mr. Gillette is
unavailable at this time. May I help?"

"No, I must talk to Alan. I'm his sister. Can you leave
him a message to call me? It's important."

"Certainly. He has your number?"

Just in case he didn't have them at the shipyard, Claire
gave her office and home numbers. It was only when she
hung up the phone that she remembered her office number
wouldn't be of use anymore. She put her palm flush against
the wall and leaned her head against the cool surface, newly
stunned at the thought. Her watch face flashed four-forty-
five. Suddenly she remembered her appointment with
Richard Quade.

"Oh, no," she said aloud.

Wyatt strode up to her at that moment. "What is it?"

She waved her hand aimlessly in the air. "I had a patient
due at four-fifteen."

Wyatt shrugged. "Is that who you were calling just
now?"

She shook her head, not wanting to reveal who her patient was or the fact that she had just tried to reach Alan.
"I've got to call Dave's wife. Marj will have to be told."

Wyatt took her arm and began to lead her back to the
seats in the waiting room. "A deputy at the station knows
the doctor and his wife. He's already gone to pick her up. A
police officer to watch Knudsen will be here soon. Then I'll
take you home."

Claire shook her head. "I appreciate the thought, but I
can't leave until I hear how they are."

As they reached the waiting-room chairs, Wyatt released
her arm and they both sat down. There was nothing re-

served in the warmth of his words. "It's you I'm concerned
about, Claire. Wouldn't it make more sense for you to go
home and get some rest?"

She looked away from the open regard in his eyes, feeling the strength of his concern. A part of her wanted to in-
dulge in the excited feeling that attention was generating.
But another part retreated, unsure and hesitant.

Deliberately submerging her disturbing array of emerg-
ing emotions, Claire focused her attention on a young
Oriental woman holding a tiny baby who was just entering
the waiting area. She headed directly for the emergency-
room receptionist.

Wyatt shrugged, his voice sounding disappointed. "I'll
need you to make another statement concerning this suicide attempt by Knudsen. I'll also need a statement concerning—"

Claire was only half listening. A familiar name spoken at
the reception desk caused her to interrupt what Wyatt was
saying.

"Wyatt, that woman over there just said, 'Knudsen.'"
Claire was on her feet and starting for the desk. Wyatt
wasn't far behind.

"I Mrs. Knu...son," the young woman kept repeating
as she waved a piece of paper in her hand.

Wyatt took the paper. "It's a marriage license, dated a
year ago. Looks like this is Knudsen's wife, all right."

He handed the paper back. "Mrs. Knudsen, do you speak
English?"

Whatever she said back wasn't in English. A young
Oriental nurse suddenly appeared in the corridor and ran up
to the young mother, speaking quickly and fervently.

Wyatt tried to get the attention of the nurse. "What's
going on? Do you know this woman?"

The young nurse turned in his direction. "She is my
neighbor. Her husband has been missing. She has been very
worried. I called to tell her he is here. She doesn't speak
English."

They were interrupted by the doctor who had taken
Arthur Knudsen into emergency surgery.

"He's going to make it."

Claire's immediate relief was overshadowed by the words of a feminine voice behind her. She turned to see a young, plump, brown-haired woman with two small children. "I'm Mrs. Knudsen. I understand my husband is here?"

Claire stared at this new woman and then turned to look back at the other one. Two Mrs. Knudsens?

ALAN WALKED into Vera Ward's office and slammed the door behind him. She literally jumped to attention.

"Vera, where have you been? Do you know what's been found on the fifth floor of Building 850 in the hallway outside of the commander's office?"

"Yes, sir. I was informed a few minutes ago, sir."

"Well why weren't you out there?"

"I was on the phone, sir."

Alan finally became aware that something was wrong. The hard ice mask she normally wore so well was beginning to melt around the edges. "Vera, what's happened?"

"Sir, Admiral Frost is expecting you in Washington, D. C. immediately. A special military transport is waiting for you at the airport. The helicopter has just arrived to fly you to your connecting flight. May we talk on the way?"

Vera's dark eyes carried an unspoken plea Alan read loud and clear. It forestalled anything else he was about to say. He nodded and stepped aside for her to lead the way. She picked up a folder from her desk and walked stiffly out of her office.

Once they had reached the makeshift helicopter pad where a chopper was waiting, Alan turned to Vera before taking the final few steps that would place him aboard. "What do you have to tell me?"

"Sir, this folder contains a complete report. In it you'll see we've found bugs in Captain Kent's office and in all of our NIS offices on the Yard. Before your return I shall have the bugs cleared and a complete check made on all communication facilities. But be advised, sir, that at this moment, we must consider our entire operation compromised."

RICHARD QUADE LISTENED to the evening radio news bulletin regarding the "collapse" of an office building in Silverdale, which took the life of a woman and seriously injured a man. Their names were being held pending notification of family.

He smiled as he turned off the radio and headed toward the garage. Now that his little mistake had been erased, he could concentrate on getting to the important business he had come to do. His contact had called to verify that phase three had gone off without a hitch. Two more phases, and their jobs would be complete.

As he opened the garage door, however, he stiffened. The twins were playing on the floor. One of the girls was just picking up the bomb shaped like a toy airplane.

"SO, THE EXPLOSIVE that was used in Dr. Boland's building was not the same kind of explosive used to kill Roger Thayer?" Wyatt asked as soon as he read the preliminary report.

John Sanders rubbed his head and adjusted his glasses. "The Thayer murder was black powder. This office explosive was high-powered gelatin dynamite. It nearly leveled the building."

Wyatt walked around his office scratching his chin. He turned back to John. "Any similarities?"

John shrugged. "This explosion was triggered by a timing device. Went off around four-fifteen. The Thayer explosion, as you'll remember, was a remote, radio-frequency trigger. If it's the same guy, he knows his explosives. That's all I can tell you now."

"And what can you tell me later?" Wyatt asked.

"Well if there's a third explosion, it would tell us—"

Wyatt was impatient. "What are you suggesting, John? We have to wait until somebody else is blown up before we can go after this maniac?" He turned to Tom. "Was it the same murderer?"

Tom moved uneasily in his chair. "We have no physical evidence to tie the two murders together. There wasn't anything left after the office explosion. I talked to everybody in the homes and offices around the Byron address for three square blocks. Nobody saw anything suspicious. We won't know if the hair we found on Thayer's clothing was his or somebody else's until Seattle gets back to us."

Wyatt exhaled. "And when will that be?"

Tom fidgeted some more in his chair at Wyatt's frustrated tone. "Three, four weeks. If we don't have a suspect, you know they drag their feet."

"We have a suspect. Get me a court order to collect a hair sample from Knudsen. Send it to Seattle. Have them compare it with those on Roger Thayer's body."

"What's our probable cause?" Tom asked.

"He fled the scene of the crime, he went into hiding and he's tried to commit suicide."

Tom shrugged. "But couldn't that be because of the two wives?"

Wyatt's look wasn't tolerant. "If he had cooperated with us, we probably never would have found out about the two wives. And you can bet that a man who uses women that way isn't going to suddenly get remorseful and try to commit suicide because he's been found out."

"So you think he was afraid of being caught for killing Thayer?"

Wyatt ground his teeth. "You got any other ideas? The Sheriff's office in Carson City, Nevada, has tracked down all Thayer's prison associates. They're either still doing time or otherwise accounted for. We're getting zilch from the patients of the medical doctor and the psychologist. And if these two explosions are tied in, it was only Knudsen on the scene both times."

"Wasn't Claire Boland also there both times?" Tom asked.

Wyatt felt himself getting very annoyed at the suggestion. "She wasn't the one who disappeared before we arrived or later slashed her wrists and had to be rushed to the hospital."

"Good point. But what's the motivation? Why would Knudsen have killed him?"

"Maybe Thayer found out about the bigamy," Wyatt said. "Maybe he threatened Knudsen and Knudsen decided to shut him up. I'd be interested in seeing what Nevada says about a possible earlier association between Thayer and Knudsen."

Tom nodded. "Those reports will be in early tomorrow."

"Check them first thing, Tom. I'll be getting in late. I've got a funeral to go to."

"Somebody die?" Tom Watson asked.

"Yeah, Roger Thayer," Wyatt said.

"Oh, that funeral. Are you going to see who shows up?"

Wyatt shook his head. "I'm going to talk to Thayer's sister again. This time perhaps I can get her to answer some questions. By the way, did you remember to send over a unit to pick up Claire Boland at Harrison Memorial Hospital?"

"Yes. Which reminds me, I couldn't find her statement concerning Knudsen."

Wyatt shrugged. "I haven't gotten it yet. She was too worried about her friend at the hospital. I'll stop by her place tonight and get the details."

Tom looked at his boss knowingly. His voice held good-natured sarcasm. "Much better surroundings. I'm certainly glad to hear you're adhering to our first directive so well."

Wyatt didn't respond, not minding being kidded about his changed attitude toward Claire now that he had an out. "Actually since *Dr. Boland* is performing as a psychological consultant on this case, her status as witness has been upgraded to that of colleague. And, as I recall, there are no directives against fraternizing with one's colleagues, are there?"

Tom Watson shook his head in defeat.

CLAIRE APPROACHED her car, still parked in the lot next to the charred remains of what had once been her office. Fortunately the Allante had been far enough away to escape damage. As she eased down into the driver's seat, she stole a look at the black rubble, outlined with the bright yellow of the Sheriff Department's official crime scene tape. Her stomach turned, sick and queasy, as she realized she was viewing what could have been the scene of her death.

She deliberately looked away and started the car, just wanting to be home and to forget the tension of the last few hours.

She checked her answering machine as soon as she walked into the house. Alan had returned her earlier call, leaving a message that said he had to go out of town for an indeterminate time and giving her the names and numbers of two people she could call if she urgently had to get in touch with him.

The first was Vera Ward and the second was Barney Coffman. She made a note of both names and numbers and decided to wait to pass on her news until Alan returned.

She headed for the one reclining lounge chair she had and put her feet up thankfully. She felt real relief that Dave Reyes was going to make it. After seeing the anguish of the two wives of Arthur Knudsen, Claire wasn't feeling too charitable toward the man.

As a psychologist she was trained to administer to those who needed her help, but her profession did not make her blind or indifferent to the harm someone like Arthur Knudsen could do.

Claire snuggled into the satiny beige fabric of the easy chair and deliberately closed her eyes. It was after seven-thirty and she was hungry, but she just wanted to relax a bit before she started to think of preparing food.

When she was comfortable, her mind wandered and she thought about Richard Quade. Had he arrived for their appointment only to find the building gone? Had it frightened him? The questions kept bouncing through her mind. There was nothing to do but get up and call him. She dragged herself out of the recliner and walked over to the phone. Sally Quade answered. Claire could hear a child crying in the background.

"Sally, it's Dr. Claire Boland. Is Richard there?"

"Yes, but...I thought Rich said he didn't want to see you anymore."

Claire was surprised. She thought Richard would have explained his change of heart to his wife. Obviously he hadn't. "He called me from work today and we scheduled an appointment for this afternoon."

"He did? I . . . see."

Claire thought Sally didn't sound like she really saw at all. "He didn't show?" Sally asked.

Claire didn't want to explain about the explosion and alarm Sally, so she selected her next words carefully. "I had to leave the office before Richard arrived. I wonder if you would tell him—"

"He's in the shower now. He said he's going out afterward. I'll tell him you called if he stops to talk with me."

"Sally, what's wrong?"

"I can't . . . I can't talk now," she said and hung up.

Claire was disturbed as she replaced the receiver on the telephone base. What was wrong with Sally Quade?

Her thoughts were interrupted by the doorbell. Her heart did a little skip when she found Wyatt on the threshold. He was holding several square white cardboard boxes of Chinese take-out food.

"Lemon chicken or sweet and sour pork?" he asked.

She smiled. "Lemon chicken. Put them on the dining-room table and I'll get the water on for tea."

Less than thirty minutes later the cardboard containers were empty. "That was great, Wyatt."

He smiled in response and removed a tape recorder from a pocket of his suit coat. He placed it on the table. "I need to get your official statement concerning your activities today up to and including Knudsen's visit. Ready?"

She nodded and he began the tape. She gave her statement concerning her Wednesday activities and the attempted suicide. Wyatt found his mind drifting to the curve of her cheek and the glow of her hair. He asked no questions until she was finished.

"You left out the name of the person you had lunch with. Who was it?" he asked as he leaned over to pick up his cup of tea.

"It was Alan. I didn't think it mattered."

Wyatt tried to ignore the swab of jealousy coating his throat. He swallowed some tea as though trying to dissolve it. "Alan Gillette was pretty vague about his business when I asked him last night. What does he do?"

"He works for the Naval Intelligence Service."

"At Puget Sound?"

"No. He's with their district office at the Mare Island Naval Shipyard in Vallejo, California."

"Then what is he doing here?" Wyatt asked.

Claire didn't understand or appreciate the growing irritation in Wyatt's voice or all the questions about Alan. What was bugging him? She found her own tone becoming curt. "You'd best ask him that."

"What's his number?" Wyatt asked.

"You can reach him through the NIS office at the Puget Sound Naval Shipyard."

Wyatt reached over to turn off the tape machine. He kept watching it for a minute. "Is he your lover?"

He looked up as soon as he asked his last question to catch the expression on Claire's face. It was absolute surprise. "Of course not. Alan's my brother. Didn't he tell you that when he answered the door last night?"

Wyatt felt an immense relief and lifting of his spirits. He carefully controlled the smile that tried to curl his lips. Of course! That was why Alan looked familiar. His deep-blue eyes were very much like his sister's. Wyatt should have caught the resemblance before. It also explained why Alan had been so friendly and showed no signs of jealousy.

Wyatt coughed, trying to hide his overwhelming relief that Alan wasn't a rival after all. "Why have you been so vague about him?"

Claire shifted in her chair. "His business is confidential."

Wyatt sat back in his chair as he studied her closed expression. Naval Intelligence Service confidential business? That might bear looking into. But for now he wouldn't push the issue.

"Anything else you would like to add to your statement?"

Claire shook her head. "Would you answer me something?"

Wyatt was feeling particularly magnanimous since hearing about Alan's status. "Anything I can," he said, smiling.

"Were the two women who showed up at the hospital both really married to Knudsen?"

Wyatt marked the finished tape with the case number.

"Yes, but until today, they didn't know about each other. The plump one is Dori-Frances. Her name and number were in Knudsen's wallet, so the hospital administrator called her when he was brought in. Knudsen spent his last couple of nights at their place in Poulsbo."

"She hid him?" Claire asked.

"She didn't know he was wanted. She's twenty-two with barely a second-grade education. Knudsen married her six years ago in Arkansas. The Korean girl is Suzzie. She's barely nineteen. She was a mail-order bride Knudsen sent for about a year ago. He kept her in a run-down trailer in Bremerton."

Claire slumped in her chair. The tragedy of the two women was making her very sad. Wyatt got up and moved over to sit in a chair closer to her.

She looked up as she heard the uncompromising tone in his voice. "Neither woman knew about the other. Knudsen intentionally kept his 'wives' ignorant and broke. We found a key on him for a safe deposit box under a fictitious name in a local bank. There was eighty-five-thousand dollars in it. Knudsen had the money to take care of his wives and children, but he didn't. Frankly, I couldn't care less about his fears of being locked up."

Claire nodded in understanding. "Where did he get eighty-five-thousand dollars working in a grocery store?"

"Good question," Wyatt said, exhaling some anger. "We're interested in finding an answer to that one, too."

"The authorities will help the wives, won't they?"

Wyatt nodded. "I've called four different local welfare organizations."

She looked over at him and rested a hand on his arm. "I'm glad you're the kind of person who cares, Wyatt."

Her slight touch was like a struck match inside him. Its flame flared up and before he realized what he was doing, he had leaned over to gently kiss the hollow of her cheek. The surprise in her eyes immediately caused him to retreat. He stood and purposefully moved toward the door.

He took his time, hoping she would follow. Just about the moment he was turning the knob, he heard her behind him. "Wyatt?"

He turned to see her cheeks slightly flushed and knew his kiss had been the cause. "Yes?"

"I just wanted to say good night."

She looked beautiful and glowing in the dim light. Grasping at the remaining threads of his control, he looked away from the softness in her eyes and fiddled unnecessarily with the tape machine. "The typist will have your statement ready to sign tomorrow. Will I see you at Roger Thayer's funeral?"

"Yes." Her voice was slightly breathless.

He looked back into those eyes and found himself leaning down to kiss the pinkness surfacing on her slightly parted lips. As he moved closer, he saw the awareness of the impending kiss enter her eyes and deepen their blue in both a curious and cautious anticipation. He barely brushed her mouth with his, giving her just an enticing taste of the possibilities before he reached for the knob and opened the door behind him. He smiled to himself as he felt her eyes following him down the sidewalk to his car.

ALAN GILLETTE STRODE through the main Navy corridor of the elite E-wing of the Pentagon in Washington, D. C., past the plush nautical paneling and the scores of refurbished ship-captain's doors, replete with brass numbers and eagle door knocks. As he entered the one leading to the inner sanctum of the Chief of Naval Operations, Admiral Charles Frost, Alan heard the Navy bells chime the hour, just as though they were on a ship.

A medium-sized man stood at the window with his back to the room, staring out at the Potomac River in the distance. Alan waited for a moment, but when the man had still not turned to acknowledge his presence, he called out tentatively. "Admiral?"

The silver hood of the straight, compact man turned in Alan's direction. Alan could tell from the surprise in his eyes that he had indeed been miles away as he stared out his window. But the crispness in his voice assured he was back from his mental journey and ready for business.

"Good, Gillette. You've come directly from the airport, I see. Step over here. I have something to show you."

Alan advanced toward the admiral's enormous desk and reached across it to take an eight-by-ten-inch brown envelope from his hands. He drew out several photographs.

The first was of chalk marks on a gold carpet depicting the outline of a body. Alan could tell the chalk outline seemed strange and distorted for some reason. When he focused on the next picture, he understood why. The image was of the scattered remains of a man's body. Alan put the pictures back into the brown envelope, willing his stomach to settle.

Admiral Frost started to speak. "He was found this morning in his Georgetown house. The medical examiner says he was killed sometime last weekend."

"Who was he, sir?"

"His name was Frank Hotspoint. He was a federal court judge and a commander in the Naval Reserves. A good man, Gillette. A fine officer, a personal friend. He served with distinction on several nuclear vessels. I want you to find his murderer."

Alan's stomach churned at what he must say. He stood as straight and tall as he was capable. "Admiral, respectfully, sir, I ask you to reconsider and assign someone else to Commander Hotspoint's murder."

The Admiral's eyes squinted. "What are you saying, Gillette?"

"Sir, you've gotten my reports. You know I'm already involved in investigating an unexplained explosion at the Puget Sound Naval Shipyard that killed two men."

Admiral Frost's face turned neutral as his hard dark eyes bored through Alan's from across his desk. "Perhaps I should have mentioned that Commander Hotspoint was not just murdered, Gillette. He was blown up by a very sophisticated explosive device. Does that help to clarify matters any?"

Alan swallowed as the meaning and delivery of the Admiral's words sunk in. He mentally kicked himself for not realizing that possibility when he saw the photos of the body. The mode of the man's death had been the reason for the admiral calling him to the Capital. The death was too similar to those he was investigating at the Shipyard not to be considered related.

"Yes, Admiral, the situation is clear now. I'm going to need the use of the computers to compare the Naval Service records of the assassin's victims. Since it is now unlikely these are random attacks, cross-referencing might be the key. Where can I go to get a terminal access?"

"They're expecting you in Computer Central, Gillette. Get me results and get them quick. We must prove to the President that we can protect against an assassin, otherwise he may reconsider putting PALs on our nuclear weapons. If we lose his confidence, we've lost the battle."

RICHARD QUADE WAITED behind the well clipped hedge of Commander Paul Carroll's Seattle residence, not trusting the night's darkness to keep him hidden. He had successfully passed undetected through the security gate to this exclusive community.

Finding the commander's home had proved difficult because of the similarities of the house clusters, but it too had been accomplished. Now he only waited for an elderly man walking an old golden retriever to move on. It shouldn't be too much longer.

Man and dog were in no hurry, but finally they turned the corner at the end of the block. Slowly, quietly, Quade set down the remote-control, foot-high miniature tank on the pavement and cautiously looked around. No one was in sight.

Quade positioned the remote-control panel on his bent knee and pushed forward on the lever. The high wailing sound of the small tank's motor seemed loud to his overly sensitive ears. He looked anxiously around the deserted sidewalk.

Carefully he maneuvered the small remote-controlled tank across the pitched driveway and up the cement walkway to the door. As it came to a stop in front of the door, he was confident he could control its maneuvering from his vantage position behind the hedge.

His eyes searched for movement. No one was in sight. Carefully, quietly, he passed through the hedge and walked to the front porch beside the toy tank. He punched the doorbell, leaped off the porch and ran back to the hedge. His heart pumped loudly in his chest as he grasped the remote-control panel in readiness.

A man in shirt sleeves opened the door and looked around for who had rung the doorbell. Richard Quade did not hesitate but pressed the forward lever hard. The miniaturized tank charged up the aluminum channel separating the door bottom from the threshold and plopped in front of the man's feet. Quade watched as a look of incredulity crossed Commander Carroll's face. He leaned down to pick up the toy tank. That was the moment Richard Quade hit the detonation button.

Chapter Eight

Claire squinted in the already bright morning light as she slowly walked away from the earthy smell of the newly filled grave. She searched inside her shoulder bag for her sunglasses as Wyatt fell into step next to her.

She wasn't sure she was up to discussing Roger Thayer. It would be a long time before she could forget the sight of what he'd looked like on the Safeway floor. Wyatt seemed to sense her mood, for all he did was smile at her as they walked quietly toward their cars.

She was immediately drawn to the welcoming look in his eyes, the broad expanse of his arms and chest so casually contained in his blue suit jacket. A warm hint of Old Spice reached her nose.

Her thoughts wandered to the remembered feel of his arms about her when she had felt so distressed the afternoon before at the hospital and to the whisper of a kiss they had shared later. Those memories had awakened her more than once during that night as they skipped in and out of her dreams.

Now his deep voice dissolved her recollections.

"Going to be another hot one. This weather remind you of home?"

She put on her sunglasses, a little surprised at his chosen topic. "Washington State is home now."

"You don't mind all the rain?"

"Actually I think it's great. It helps to maintain the beautiful green landscape and healthy fresh air. My grandmother was a native. I remember her letters to me while I was growing up always talked about the cleansing rain. That description was one of the reasons I decided to move here when . . ."

Her voice trailed off and the cloaked expression on her face told him whatever she was remembering was not a subject she felt easy about discussing. His interest was aroused.

"When what?" he prompted.

"When I decided to move," she said, but he was sure that was not what she had been about to say. He decided to probe further.

"Why did you decide to move?"

Something about the way Wyatt asked the question told her it wasn't just prompted by idle curiosity. For that reason she decided to answer him without further evasion.

"I had just lost my husband. I needed a place to grieve."

His voice became gentle. "Do you still grieve?"

She looked at him, hearing the seriousness in his question, but he looked away, as though her answer was something he might regret hearing. Suddenly she understood he really wanted to know and she really wanted to tell him. "No, I don't grieve anymore."

"Will you be going back to San Francisco then?"

She continued to watch his profile. "No. I told you. Washington is my home now. As a matter of fact, I love it here."

He still did not meet her eyes. "But you were brought up in a big city. Don't you miss the parties and nightlife?"

She shook her head. "They've never been my style."

As they approached her red Allante in the parking lot, he looked at her car purposely and frowned.

"This isn't exactly the type of car I picture as being owned by a conservative psychologist."

Claire cocked her head to one side as she studied his face. "Are you trying to psychoanalyze me, Sergeant Lockhart?"

Her question and mockingly formal address brought a small smile to his lips and a direct look from his green-blue eyes. "If I was, I would make every effort to see you enjoyed an extended stay on my couch, Dr. Boland."

She read the very warm, personal message in his response. It quickened her pulse in excitement as she once again remembered their kiss of the night before. Then, before her eyes, his playful expression changed abruptly as his head lifted to look behind her. As Claire turned, his hand raised to point to a dark-haired woman walking across the lawn.

"That's Doris, Thayer's sister. I tried to get some information out of her about Roger yesterday when she came to my office, but all she was in the mood for was to yell and scream about why we hadn't found her brother's murderer yet. When I tried talking with her a few minutes ago, she told me she wouldn't waste her time with anyone in law enforcement. Would you consider trying your luck?"

Claire nodded. "Of course. She looks like she's heading for the cemetery's office. I'll wait till she comes out and see what I can do. Will you be in your office later today?"

Wyatt's voice was low and smooth and vibrated warm and enticing just above her left ear. "I'll make it a point to be."

Claire turned and looked up into Wyatt's half smile, finding his face only a foot away from hers. She could feel the heat from his body and smell his after-shave mixing with his own natural scent. Her heart began pounding against her chest as his closeness invaded all her senses.

Her eyes quickly focused on the keys in her hand as she tried to collect her thoughts. "I'll be there as soon as I can."

His hand closed over hers for a moment. "I'll wait."

Her heart was still pounding as he turned and walked away.

Claire realized then he was continuing to show his interest, but also giving her the room to back away if she chose. She felt excited at the possibilities. Of course she would back away if things got too intense. Wouldn't she?

DORIS THAYER was a short plump woman with dark hair in a mannish cut. She had a big mouth with a prominent separation between her two front teeth. Claire asked her if she wouldn't mind talking about her brother. They decided to drive to a restaurant to have breakfast.

Roger Thayer's sister had a kind voice and manner about her. Before she began to talk about her brother, she turned to thank the waitress who'd brought her three scrambled eggs and a tall gin fizz. For the time being she ignored the eggs.

"Roger was a nice person, Dr. Boland. Oh, I know you probably don't believe me. You probably think that because I was his sister, I was blind to his faults. But I wasn't. I knew Roger very well."

"What was the difference in your ages?" Claire said between bites of her blueberry waffle.

"Seven years. My parents had me seven years before they brought Roger home," Doris said.

"Brought Roger home? Roger was adopted?"

The woman's short dark hair bobbed up and down. "We both were. Our dad couldn't have kids naturally, but he sure wanted them. Our parents hounded the agency year after year with requests, but they only got us two. Just as well."

"Why do you say that?"

"Well, Dad died when I was sixteen and Roger was nine. Things fell apart after that. Mom hated being alone. She married again just a year later."

The natural kindness in Doris's voice seemed to submerge beneath an ocean of cold hate. "The guy was a real creep. I remember the day they got back from their honeymoon. He took his belt off and hit me and Roger with it. Told us it was just so we'd know who was boss."

Claire couldn't mask her revulsion. "Didn't your mother know?"

"Oh, she found out soon enough, but by then it was too late. She was pregnant, you see, and she kind of went crazy."

Claire frowned. "I don't understand."

Doris played with the eggs on her plate. "She had wanted her own child so much that she got all wrapped up in the pregnancy. Forgot about Roger and me. We tried to talk to her, but she just kept telling us to try to get along, that everything would turn out all right. Of course, it didn't."

Claire had an uneasy feeling she knew what was to follow. She couldn't help asking the question, however. "What happened?"

Doris's large dark eyes turned fiercely sad. "I was eighteen by then. I left home. Roger was only eleven. I remember his begging me to take him out of the house when I left. I had no money, no job. I didn't know how I was going to feed myself much less an eleven-year-old kid. I had to leave him with that creep!"

Tears had started to stream down Doris's face. Claire waited for a minute while she composed herself. Doris stared down at her untouched eggs, her hands becoming square fists on either side of her plate.

Finally she looked up. The tears had stopped, but her voice lacked its earlier volume. "It was about a year later. Mom had taken her new baby to the doctor for a checkup. Roger and the creep were alone in the house when he came after Roger and started to beat him with his belt strap. Roger picked a long sharp knife out of the kitchen drawer and stabbed him with it. Sixteen times."

Doris reached for the gin fizz and swallowed as much as she could. Claire put down her fork. She had lost her appetite.

"He killed his stepfather?"

"In self-defense! They found Roger's blood on the metal buckle of that creep's belt! Roger shouldn't have been prosecuted. They should have given him a medal!"

"Didn't he explain what had happened?" Claire asked. "Didn't they understand he was protecting himself?"

Doris's bent head nodded. "Trouble was he kept saying he wasn't sorry his stepfather was dead, and sixteen stab wounds didn't sound too good to the District Attorney. Then the judge listened to Mama's testimony that her husband was a good man who just wanted to be sure that boy was properly disciplined. It was all garbage, of course, but Mama really believed it, even to this day. That's why she wouldn't come to Roger's funeral.''

"Roger was put in jail?''

"A boy's labor camp until he was eighteen and then prison until he was twenty-one. That was because he kept running away from the labor camp so when he was supposed to get out, they had added three years in an adult facility.''

"And he had been eleven when he was arrested?'' Claire said.

Doris nodded. "Nine years they locked him up. I went to see him every week. I wanted him to keep in touch with someone on the outside, to let him know there was a reality beyond those cages.''

"What happened when he got out?''

Doris downed the rest of her drink. She signaled to the waitress for another. "He came to stay with me. I taught him to drive and he got his license. Except for his heavy smoking habit, we were real compatible. One of the girls I waitress with thought he was cute and wanted to go out with him. I'll never forget how excited Roger was. Later, she told me he had been real shy with her. I didn't tell her it had been his first date.''

Doris stopped to thank the waitress for the second drink that had been placed next to her still untouched eggs. She looked back at Claire.

"I wouldn't have minded going on taking care of him, but his pride wouldn't let me. He had learned auto mechanics while in the joint, had a real flare for it. He tried for job after job, but no one would hire a twenty-one-year-old who had been in jail most of his life. Then one day, one of his buddies showed up.

"An ex-con. A kid not much older than Roger, but a lot harder. He had gotten out several months after Roger, and he had a job lined up. He wanted Roger's help to rob a liquor store.''

"Did you know?''

"Not at first. Roger asked if this buddy of his could stay a few days. I was happy he seemed to have a friend. Then I got a call at work two days later telling me Roger had been arrested. The guy he was with had a gun when they robbed the liquor store. He shot and seriously wounded the proprietor. A policeman exchanged fire and killed Roger's buddy. Roger was unarmed. He surrendered."

"How many years did he get?"

"Twenty. But he never served them. Five years into his sentence, he and several other prisoners were being taken to a special medical facility. They were volunteers in some medical research on high blood pressure medicine. Their volunteering was supposed to take time off their sentences. It took a lot of time off of Roger's sentence. He escaped."

"How?"

"It was a fluke. The guard watching them in the back of the truck had a heart attack and passed out. Roger and the other prisoners jumped out the back. Of the six prisoners who escaped, five were recaptured within two days. Roger was the sixth."

"The authorities never knew where he went?" Claire asked.

"No. They hounded me for months thinking he would come back to my place. But he was too smart to do that. They would have picked him up immediately. I knew he went in the other direction, north into another state."

"How did you know?"

"He sent me a postcard a month after his escape. It was postmarked from Montana."

"The police weren't watching your mail?"

"Oh, I'm sure they were, but the message on the card meant nothing to them. You see, Roger and I both knew we were adopted ever since we were little. We used to imagine who our real parents were. I loved horses so much, I would tell Roger that my real parents owned a horse ranch in a place called Hungryhorse, Montana. I had seen the name on a map once. And I made up names for my parents, too. My mother's name was Marie and my father's name was Preston."

"So the postcard you got was from Hungryhorse, Montana?"

Doris nodded. "It said 'Feeling right at home. Sorry you can't be with us. Love, Marie and Preston.' Those were names and a place only Roger would know. It was his way of telling me he was okay."

"Did you ever hear from him again?"

"Not until the Sheriff called and told me Roger had been killed here. You said earlier you thought you knew Roger. Had you really met him?"

Claire hedged. She was now certain that in her shock she had only imagined Roger Thayer's grease-stained shirt, blackened thumb and scar to have also existed on her patient, Richard Quade. But she didn't want to admit to being sent by Wyatt, so she tried to think up a plausible excuse for her questions.

"I'm not sure, Doris. I thought he looked like someone I cared about. Did he ever mention a man by the name of Arthur Knudsen?" Claire supplied Doris with a physical description.

Doris shook her head. "No. No one like that ever came around. Of course, he never had a chance to make real friends."

Doris's eyes began to fill again. "All this time I've had the hope that Roger had found a home somewhere with people who loved him. That he'd discovered a bit of happiness in a world turned against him. I suppose that sounds foolish?"

Claire placed her hand on the woman's arm. "Not at all, Doris. And who knows? Maybe he did."

RICHARD QUADE LISTENED to the local radio news, angrily throwing his wrench down on the shop floor. His bomb had missed the damn psychologist! He was sure he had timed it to go off at four-fifteen precisely. She must have been late for their appointment.

At least the police didn't seem to be making the connection to an attempt on her life. All the radio reports still indicated the Sheriff's office was calling the disaster a building "collapse." Quade knew they were trying to hide the fact of a bomb explosion. But if they thought about an intended victim, they must be thinking of Dr. David Reyes, the medical doctor across the hall, or even his dead receptionist. The psychologist hadn't been hurt.

It could still work out fine. She was walking around, accessible. He'd get her yet.

He leaned over to remove the remote-control device he had used on Tuesday afternoon from inside the engine of the incapacitated bus. The Shipyard police had never thought to look there. It had proved a perfect hiding place.

Once the detonator was in his hands again, he quickly stuffed it into his vest pocket and closed the hood on the engine. Then he walked back to his regular work station.

"Hey, Rich, what's your fascination for that broken-down bus? You falling in love with it, or something?"

Richard tensed when he recognized Kevin, another mechanic at the Yard, and then forcibly slapped a quick smile on his face. "Just trying to scrounge up a part for this baby here," he said, as he patted the nose of the bus he was working on.

Kevin pulled out a cigarette and shoved the rest of the pack toward Richard. "So spend the Yard's money on some new stuff. What the hell do you care?"

Richard turned his head away from the offered cigarette and put up his hand. "Hey man, I told you I've quit. If you're going to smoke, don't do it around me."

"Oh, come off it, Rich. Any wimp can breathe oxygen. It takes a real man to suck in the ole carbon monoxide stick. Come on, have one. Let's cough out our guts together."

"Back off, Kevin. I mean it. I've quit."

Kevin drew back the cigarette. "And boozing, too? You haven't been to the old watering hole in days. Hell, I know you're always hot to get home to your old lady, but that's no reason to cut off one drink with your buddies. What's wrong?"

Richard stared down at his grease-blackened nails. "I've got things on my mind."

Kevin's hands came up in surrender. "Okay, okay. But if it's like last year, you know you can talk to me, buddy. I mean, I was there for you then, remember? It was ole Kevin here who helped you to remember where everything was.''

"Yeah, Kevin. Thanks, but this is different. Something I've got to do on my own.''

Richard put his head back under the hood of the bus so that he could escape from the prying look of the other mechanic. Kevin spoke up again. ''The Sheriff's Department left word they'd like to talk with you, buddy. After work today.''

Richard's pulse quickened at Kevin's words. His head jagged upward. ''They were here?''

''Naw. Called in and left word with the Shop Supervisor. Asked if you'd stop by a Port Orchard address. Sup gave it to me to give to you. Here.''

Richard took the offered slip of paper, trying to calm his initial panic. If the Sheriff's Department knew anything, they wouldn't be calling and asking him to drop by. They must just be fishing around to see if they could get lucky in finding out about the doctor's office explosion. It would be okay. This was one fish too smart to swallow any of their bait.

Kevin finally gave up his buddy act and returned to his own work station. The man was proving a continuing pest, but a temporary one. That psychologist was a pest, too, but he'd take care of her. Only not right away. He'd have to let a day or so go by to remove any suspicion that she was the intended target. Then he'd bring her a little present.

She'd get a real blast out of it.

CLAIRE WALKED into Sergeant Lockhart's office just before two. She felt a pleasant warming throughout her body as he stood up and smiled. She took the offered chair next to his desk.

''I would have been here earlier, but I began to realize there was some business I had to attend to right away.''

''What business?'' he asked.

''Well first, I had to send out notes to all my patients and call the few with appointments for today and tomorrow to advise them of the recent trouble. It was amazing, but the ones I talked to seemed to know about the trouble. One man even told me he had spoken with one of your deputies.''

Wyatt's grunt was noncommittal. Claire went on.

"After that I had to see about trying to get another office in some vacant space in Silverdale.''

"Were you successful?''

"I've started the process, but until a lease is signed, some furniture delivered and a phone installed, I'll be seeing patients out of my home.''

"Isn't that a bit risky?'' he asked.

"How do you mean?''

"Well, considering the emotionally disturbed people who come to see you, I wouldn't have thought it prudent to let them know where you live.''

Claire's smile faded. "Wyatt, what are you saying?''

"I'm saying that until we find this creep who blows up people, you've got to be more careful.'' He leaned forward in his chair, his voice becoming softer. "Claire, we don't know who we're dealing with here. It might be anyone.''

She nodded, pleased with his concern for her if not his suspicions of her patients. "Who do you think it might be?''

He leaned back in his chair again. "Frankly, I'm still voting for Knudsen. He was at the market the night of Thayer's murder and he was at your office on the afternoon it was blown.''

"Wyatt, that doesn't make a whole lot of sense. What could he have gained by blowing up my office?''

Wyatt got up suddenly and began to pace around the room. His long stride covered the width of the room in just three steps. "The reason might all be related to Thayer's murder. Something we haven't uncovered yet. Were you successful in getting Doris Thayer to talk with you?''

Claire nodded and filled him in on her conversation. Wyatt came to sit on the edge of his desk as he listened to her. He digested the information for a few minutes after she was finished.

"Do you think Doris Thayer was lying about her brother knowing Knudsen?''

Claire shook her head. "No.''

Wyatt slid off the end of his desk, rubbing the back of his neck with his right hand and looking frustrated. "Knudsen's such a slime, Claire. You understand? I want him to be the one."

Claire nodded, thinking she did understand. "My every instinct tells me he's not, however..." She paused purposely.

He stopped his pacing to look at her. "Yes?"

Claire said her words carefully. "If I were you I'd check with the police departments in some other states to see if they've heard of Arthur Knudsen."

Wyatt stared at her for a moment. Claire watched a look of possibility raise his thick blond eyebrows. "You think Knudsen is wanted elsewhere?"

"Let's just say that men don't generally start being bigamists when they hit fifty. It's often a life-long pattern they never break."

"Any ideas where I should start looking?"

"Maybe his application at Safeway could give you a lead if he hasn't lied about previous employment. I'd also definitely check Arkansas since Dori-Frances is from there."

Wyatt circled his desk and sat heavily in his chair. He straightened his tie as though it had gotten out of place. Claire heard the frustration grabbing at his voice.

"Even if there are bigamy charges filed against him, we probably won't be able to put Knudsen away. The psychiatrist at Harrison will have him for a while because of the suicide attempt. Afterward, well, the judges treat bigamy cases like jokes. And it's hard to get the women to testify. When I mentioned the possibility of going to court to Dori-Frances and Suzzie this morning, they both froze up on me. They're afraid of what they don't understand. He selected his victims well."

Claire now felt herself on firm ground. Her voice carried the conviction she felt. "But he may not have always selected his victims so well. He may have crossed the wrong woman in his younger years."

Claire liked the expression on Wyatt's face when he looked over at her then. It had some hope in it.

"All right. I'm certainly interested in pinning whatever I can on him. But if Knudsen isn't our man, then who is? Thayer didn't have any known associates with explosive experience. And until his death Monday night, we had no evidence of his being in these parts. Knudsen was the only thing tying these two explosion deaths together."

"You don't think Dr. Reyes was the target?" Claire asked.

Wyatt looked at her and frowned. "We thoroughly interviewed Marj Reyes and the Reyes's friends. His patients think Dr. Dave can do no wrong. I can't believe the second bomb was meant for him."

"What about his receptionist? She was the one killed."

Wyatt was obviously not comfortable sitting for long. He got up and stretched, smoothing his suit pants over his long well-shaped legs. Claire tried to keep her mind on his next words.

"Reyes's receptionist was a gruff old gal, but she was harmless. Lived a quiet life, devoid of humans and full of pets. We found ten cats and four dogs in her small house."

A sudden uncomfortable thought occurred to Claire. Why hadn't it presented itself before? She forced herself to ask the question. "You're talking to my patients, aren't you?"

Wyatt was still standing, looking away from her.

"It's getting close in here. Let's go for a walk."

He didn't wait for her response, but headed for the door. If she wanted an answer to her question, she had no choice but to follow. Wyatt told the front desk personnel he'd be gone for a few minutes. They headed down a side street next to the station.

No breeze stirred off the sparkling waters of Sinclair Inlet. Small triangular sails swam through its calm. Several white marshmallow clouds sizzled above them under the hot summer sun. They walked for several minutes along the sidewalk without saying anything. Finally Claire couldn't stand it any longer.

"You are talking with my patients, aren't you?"

Wyatt nodded, still looking straight ahead.

"How did you find out who they were? You didn't present me with a court order or a search warrant."

"We presented one to the telephone company. You've got measured service. The number of every call you make is recorded. You call your patients once or twice a week in addition to seeing them in your office."

Claire tried to control the feeling of helpless anger licking through her. "How did you know?"

"Marj Reyes thinks a lot of your professional expertise. She had no problem about admitting to being one of your patients. She went on at length about how you had treated her with real care and concern, the personal touch of the weekly calls."

Claire felt the burning along her skin. What she thought she could keep confidential he seemed to have gotten so easily, and all without telling her and without her cooperation. The frustration sucked the moisture from her mouth.

"I told you that even identifying someone as a patient of mine was a breach of their right to privacy. You had no right."

Wyatt stopped and turned to her, reaching out his hands to circle her arms. "For God's sake, Claire, I was doing my job."

Begrudgingly she knew he was probably within his rights, but she wasn't ready to let him off the hook. "Why didn't you come to me first? I could have prepared them."

"But that's just the point. I didn't want your patients 'prepared.' Claire, you could be the missing link."

"Missing link? What missing link?"

His hands squeezed the flesh of her arms even more tightly. "The missing link between the bombings. Hasn't it occurred to you that one of your patients might have been trying to kill you in that Safeway store, and when he missed the first time, tried to get you again at your office?"

Claire shook her head. "Wyatt, that's absurd. No one knew I was going to the store that night, not even me. Unless you think I'm treating a clairvoyant, what you're implying makes absolutely no sense."

Wyatt's voice became testy. "Look, these are murders by explosion I'm investigating, and the logical assumption is that a psycho—"

"Stop it, right there." Claire tore her arms out of Wyatt's restraining hands. The anger burned through every pore in her skin. She hardly noticed his look of surprise.

"Psychotics are not candidates for psychoanalysis, Sergeant Lockhart. My patients are sane people who are trying to resolve doubt. Sometimes they just need someone to listen to their problems because the people in their lives can't or won't give them the time. But even if it's more than that, even if they are experiencing torment of some kind, they come to me because they recognize right and wrong and are trying to do the right thing."

"I—" Wyatt began to say.

"I'm not finished. When my patients get antisocial urges, which by the way are statistically less violent than an avid fan during football season, they dial my number. Do you understand me? My patients talk about it because they have a conscience. And now if you'll excuse me, I'd like to get back to them."

Wyatt watched Claire's retreating form in some amazement and amusement. Earlier, he had been drawn to the humanness of her frailties and doubts. Now he was finding himself equally drawn to the displayed strength of her convictions.

He watched her get into the red Allante a block away and drive off. She had proved an eloquent advocate for her profession. He respected that kind of passion and commitment in someone. They were rare. Attractive. Even seductive.

His ex-wife, Jennifer, had left him and taken her new job back east purely for the money and prestige it promised. Claire, on the other hand, was proving to him she was a psychologist because she really cared about people. It was a nice difference.

Now the only question became, was she deluding herself? Did her desire to help her patients blind her to their possible murderous intent?

Chapter Nine

Claire closed her house door on her last patient of the day. She checked her watch and was surprised to find it was already six. She put the tape and the tape recorder away.

She was reminded again that all of her old tapes had gone up in the office explosion. It was a real pity. Sometimes referring back to them had proved important in maintaining continuity with a patient who had missed several sessions. Well, nothing she could do about it now but start a new file.

All in all her patients hadn't responded too badly to being questioned by the Sheriff's office. She admitted begrudgingly that Wyatt had handled the matter very well.

Detectives told her patients their assistance was needed in identifying anyone who they might have seen loitering around the office premises when they came for their appointments.

Each had been told that they were on a list of patients of both Drs. Reyes and Boland, so they had not been singled out as one of her patients. It seemed to help them feel their anonymity hadn't been compromised.

So her anger over the invasion of her patients' privacy seemed to have been unfounded. And now with just her conscience for company, she found herself coolly evaluating Wyatt's suggestion. Did one of her patients follow her to the Safeway store to kill her and then try again at her office?

No. And not just because she didn't want to believe it could be true. Even if one of her patients was an Oscar-award-winning actor, the scenario just didn't make sense. Whoever had exploded that bomb in Roger Thayer's face had planted it beforehand and had been on the scene to detonate it when the intended victim picked it up. And as she had told Wyatt, she had only driven to the grocery on the spur of the moment and she had been on the other side of the store when the bomb exploded. She could not have been the intended victim.

So why was her office bombed?

She turned on the radio and the news blared away. The continuing battle over the weapons control PAL system was still being hotly debated in Congress. But it was soon followed by a report that claimed all her attention:

> "An unexplained explosion earlier this week rocked the Puget Sound Naval Shipyard in Bremerton. The liaison officer for the Shipyard said that fire crackers left over from the Fourth of July apparently were behind the prank that they ascribe to local teenagers sneaking into the base over some wire fence.
>
> In other news..."

Claire turned off the radio. She knew the Shipyard was obviously keeping the facts from the media with this false story about fire crackers. The explosion on Tuesday was hardly a prank, certainly not with two men killed.

She decided she had to try to reach Alan again to see when he might be returning. She strongly felt he must be told about the explosions in Silverdale. She got up and went over to her shoulder bag, reaching for the numbers he had given her to call. The first on her list was Vera Ward. She dialed the number and recognized the woman's voice immediately as the person who answered in Alan's absence the day before.

"Has Alan returned to the Shipyard?" Claire asked after identifying herself.

"He's expected sometime after eight, Dr. Boland. Is there a message you'd like to leave?"

Claire searched her mind for the right words. She realized she had no idea what they were. "Would you ask him to call me? I have some information for him I think is very important."

"Of course, Dr. Boland, but if you leave the information with me, I can tell him immediately upon his arrival."

Claire hesitated. All she had to pass on was a strong suspicion—not evidence. She decided it would be best to share it with Alan alone. "No. The message is all."

Claire hung up the phone feeling restless and uneasy. She really wished she could have gotten hold of Alan. She needed to share her suspicions with him soon. They were beginning to weigh down her spirit.

Also bothering her was the fact that she had still not heard from Richard Quade, despite the several messages she had left at the Shipyard for him earlier in the day. He was the only one of her patients she had been unable to reach. She decided she would try again on his home number and quickly looked it up in the telephone directory. Sally Quade answered on the first ring.

"It's Claire Boland, Sally. Is Richard there?"

"No. He's late getting home. I don't know what's keeping him. He might have stopped off for a drink with his friends. He may have decided to have more than one."

"So you don't know when he might be home?" Claire asked.

"No. He didn't get in until after midnight last night. But I wish you'd come over anyway. I really need to talk to someone, I mean, to you, Doctor. If you have the time?"

Claire remembered the pain in Sally's voice from the night before. The pain and the entreaty in her voice now decided Claire's next action. "Yes, Sally, I have the time. I'll be there in ten minutes."

"WHAT DO YOU MEAN Knudsen escaped?" Wyatt said as he stood up suddenly, slamming his knee against the desk drawer. "How could he possibly escape?"

Tom Watson looked frustrated. "The deputy on duty left the hallway to visit the restroom. When he got back, Knudsen had vanished from his room."

Wyatt rubbed his banged knee, thinking that was the least of his pains at the moment.

"Put out an A.P.B. Comb that hospital area. He doesn't have transportation, so that should be his first objective. Check what bus lines are running. Call the cab companies."

"All that is being done, Wyatt."

"Have you staked out the two wives' addresses?" Wyatt asked.

"Yes."

Wyatt tried to kick the chair out of his way, missed and managed to bump his knee again. He was getting more frustrated by the minute. "Well, what haven't you done?"

"I don't know," Tom said.

"What did you come in here for, inspiration?" Wyatt asked.

"I thought you'd want to know," Tom said.

Wyatt shook his head irritably. "Well I don't want to know. You should have just let me go home ignorant and happy."

Wyatt captured the elusive chair in his two hands and sat down angrily in it. He scooted it up to the desk and hit his knee again. Finally the absolute absurdity of his continuous knee battering struck him as funny. He began to laugh. "Damn it. I'm getting as clumsy as an adolescent."

Tom's previously tense mouth relaxed into a polite chuckle. "You're just punchy. We've all been working a lot of hours."

Wyatt exhaled heavily. "No reason to make this another long night. If they find Knudsen, they'll call us." He looked over at Tom's tired face. "Why don't you go home for a change?"

Tom shook his head. "If you can stick it out, so can I."

"This isn't a contest, Tom. I'm going to need you bright eyed and bushy tailed tomorrow. Go home."

"I'm not leaving you here," Tom said.

Wyatt looked at the fatigue lines in the normally smooth, pudgy face. "Look, I'm staying just long enough to call the Chief and fill him in. Then, I'm out of here."

"You're sure?" Tom said.

Wyatt nodded. "Get going."

As soon as Tom left, Wyatt placed his call to the Chief of Detectives to let him know of Knudsen's escape. Then he went and got himself another cup of coffee. This time he was able to sit in his chair without hitting his knee. He chalked it up as a major coordination victory and tried to concentrate on putting himself in Arthur Knudsen's place. Where would the man go?

After fifteen minutes all Wyatt had succeeded in doing was drinking his coffee. He couldn't second-guess Knudsen. It would take someone who knew him better. Then he thought of Claire.

He reached into his pocket for his notebook and found her number. The telephone rang three times and then an answering machine came on. Her recorded voice, like the echo from a deep wishing well, told him she wasn't there. He didn't leave a message.

Their last parting hadn't been a particularly pleasant one. He had purposely put a little time between them to give her a chance to cool down and think it over. He'd been doing some thinking, too.

He didn't feel he was wrong about suspecting her patients, but on the other hand, he had felt pretty down all day because of her obvious disappointment in him. It had been harder for him to take than he would have imagined. He had enjoyed her earlier warmth and regard. He wanted it back.

And now, not being able to reach her gave him a hollow feeling. His stomach growled. He told himself he was just hungry. He got up quickly, knocking his knee once again on the desk edge.

He shook his head. "I'm degenerating into an adolescent all right, physically and emotionally. I'll probably be getting zits next!"

SALLY WAS PUTTING cookies and milk on the table for her twin girls when Claire arrived. Claire accepted the offer to join in.

"These are my daughters, Tami and Toni. No use in pointing out which is which because everyone soon loses track."

Claire looked at the two identical faces and saw the large bruise on the forehead of one.

"Well, at least as long as that bruise is there I expect you'll be able to tell them apart," Claire said.

Sally's face clouded over considerably. She instructed the girls to take their milk and cookies to their room. Claire felt the woman's anxiety like sparks of storm static in the air. When the girls were safely behind their door, Sally turned to her.

"I'm so glad you're here."

"What's wrong?"

Sally reached behind the cookie jar for a pack of cigarettes. She lit one before answering. It seemed to steady her nerves.

"Richard hit Tami. He caused that bruise on her forehead. All she was doing was sitting on the garage floor playing with some toys she had found and Richard grabbed her and hit her. Then he yelled at me to keep the girls out of his workshop. It's getting worse every day. I'm afraid for us all."

Claire rested her hand on the woman's arm. "Tell me everything that's happened."

Sally nodded and dragged again on her cigarette before she responded. She leaned back and Claire withdrew her hand.

"It all started about a year ago. You remember my telling you about Richard's sailing trip, how he was hit on the head with the mainsail?"

"Yes, I remember."

"Well, he came home to me and the girls afterward, but it was kind of screwy. He seemed so changed."

"In what way?" Claire asked.

"Well, at first he looked so different I hardly recognized him. Rich always wore a full curly beard. When he came in the door, I was surprised to see he had shaved it off. He grew it back right away so at least that strangeness was temporary."

"But something else wasn't?" Claire prompted.

Sally nodded. "He knew us and yet he didn't know us. I mean he knew who we were, but he had forgotten so much of our lives together. Couldn't remember birthdays. I had to keep reminding him where things came from."

"I don't understand," Claire said.

"Where things came from," Sally said more loudly, as though Claire was a little deaf. "The fact that he had given certain things to the girls as presents for Christmas and such."

"Oh, I see," Claire said. "Did Richard ask to be called by a different name?"

Sally looked confused. "A different name?"

"Yes. You've called him both Rich and Richard when you've referred to him. Did he like those names? Did he favor one over the other? Did he suggest you call him something other than Rich or Richard?"

Sally shook her head. "No. I've always called him Rich or Richard. He's never told me if he liked one better."

Claire nodded. "Okay, Sally. Did Richard consult a doctor?"

"A doctor?"

"Because of his head injury?" Claire said.

Sally looked uncomfortable. "Well, I wanted him to, at first. I mean he was having the same problem at work. He knew his job and all, but he had forgotten so many details. I explained to his boss about his being hit on the head. His boss told me to convince Richard to go to a doctor."

"But you didn't convince him?"

"No. Richard didn't want to go. He said it was just a little amnesia from being knocked out. Said he'd get over it."

"Did he?" Claire said.

"Not really. I mean I don't think he really ever remembered things. But within just a week or two, he had re-learned things. I know his boss thought he was doing fine, and he seemed all right at home. Actually better."

"Better?"

Sally looked down at her hands guiltily. She dragged on her cigarette before answering.

"You're a doctor so I guess I can tell you. Richard was always kind of aggressive in bed. You know, trying to live up to a macho image, I guess. But after that hit on the head a year ago, well, he became so much more sensitive, so much better."

"He was better *after* the accident?" Claire asked.

Sally nodded. "At first, he was almost shy with me, and then, so gentle. It was such a turn-on. As the weeks went by, he seemed so much more interested in our times together. Told me sweet things like he really looked forward to coming home every day to see me. He never said that stuff before. I . . . well, Doctor, I wasn't so sure I wanted the old Richard back, if you know what I mean."

Claire nodded. "Were there other personality changes you noticed? Other than his lovemaking?"

Sally dragged on her cigarette again and nodded. "Lots of little things."

"Can you give me some examples?" Claire said.

"Well, he was better with the girls, for one, much more tolerant when they got tired and cranky. He got interested in our going on family outings together and would even get up after dinner and help me with the dishes."

Sally paused but Claire could see she was holding something back. She gave the nervous woman a moment then leaned forward. "What else, Sally?"

Sally's pale eyes darted upward. "He stopped trying to get me to quit smoking. He even started to smoke himself. I know it's a dangerous habit, and I worry about the health problems of secondary smoke around the twins, but you'll never know how happy I was when he started a year ago. Does that sound crazy?"

"No, of course not. That took a lot of pressure off you."

Sally's eyes lit up. "Exactly. I'm glad you understand."

"Why do you think Richard changed after being hit on the head?"

Sally shrugged. "I don't know. I told him he had changed, but that I wasn't complaining. He smiled at me and said he guessed getting hurt had awakened him to what he had in me and the girls. He said he had been taking us for granted and that he'd never do it again. He was so... wonderful."

"But he isn't wonderful anymore, is he, Sally?"

Sally shook as though she had caught a sudden chill. "No, he's not. He's like before the accident, only worse."

"He's worse?"

Sally's shaking hand brought the cigarette back to her colorless lips. She let the smoke escape her lungs with a sigh.

"He's worse now because I know what he could be like, was like just a few days ago."

"A few days? Did Richard seem all right to you Sunday?"

"Yes. And, Monday, too, only he's been sort of nervous for a few weeks. That's why I put off telling him about the baby."

"The baby? You're pregnant?"

"Yes. I took an EPT, you know, home pregnancy test, and it came out positive. I have an appointment with the doctor next week to confirm it, but I can't tell Richard now."

"Why not?"

"If he was still like he was this past year, he would have been so pleased. He even asked me to go off the pill six months ago. But since he's like before, I know he doesn't want any more kids. If only he hadn't changed again...."

Claire tried to refocus Sally's thoughts to the subject she needed to discuss. "You said he'd been nervous recently."

"Yes, even a little scared. And when he came home from work Monday, he said something about not wanting to talk with anyone on the phone for a while. Wanted me to screen his calls."

"Did a call come for him Monday night?"

"No. I remember I got a call from some man wanting to talk with Richard, but when he wouldn't give his name, I hung up. Then I just unplugged all the phones."

"You said Richard seemed okay Sunday and Monday. When precisely did he change back to how he was before?"

"Late Monday night when he...talked to me and I knew."

Claire could see the unhappiness in Sally's face at the memory. She was holding her cigarette as though someone might try to take it away from her. "Was it something about his not smoking anymore?" Claire asked.

Sally looked down at the cigarette in her hands.

"I guess you heard what he said when he came home the other night? Yeah, he doesn't smoke now. Just quit like that."

Sally tried to snap her fingers, but no noise resulted. Her voice was a dejected sigh as though the snap had gone out of her life entirely. "It was a big shock. He never even mentioned he was thinking of quitting. Then, Monday, without warning, he wakes me up in the middle of the night and tells me he's going to sleep out in the den until I stop smelling like a dirty ashtray."

Tears began to sting Sally's eyes. Claire rested her hand again on the woman's arm. "You're not sleeping together anymore?"

Sally's head jerked up and down. "No. After a year of making love nearly every night, not seeming to be able to get enough, all of a sudden my husband can't stand to touch me!"

Sally was biting her lip, trying to hold back the tears. Claire came over to put her arm around the woman's shoulders. "It's all right, Sally. Crying is good for us all. Just relax and let it come."

The thin blond woman collapsed her head into her bent arms on the tabletop. Claire leaned over to remove the smoking cigarette from her fingers and put it out in the ashtray so that the woman wouldn't inadvertently burn herself. She let Sally cry out her unhappiness while she held onto her shaking shoulders.

After a couple of minutes, Sally's pale head rose and Claire handed her a tissue from a container on the table. She wiped away the remaining tears. "It's my fault, isn't it, Doctor?"

Claire pulled up a chair closer to Sally and sat down in it so they were at eye level.

"Absolutely not, Sally. It's premature for me to be telling you this, but I want you to be completely free of guilt feelings. You see, I think I know the source of your husband's strange behavior and it has nothing to do with anything you've done."

"What is it then? Please tell me."

"Do you know what the term multiple personality means?"

Sally frowned. "Is that anything like a schizoid or schizo?"

"No. The media frequently misuse the terms. A schizoid personality describes someone who is reserved, socially withdrawn and seclusive. Schizophrenia is a serious disorder of perception generally involving delusions and hallucinations. Neither have anything to do with multiple personality disorders."

"What is it then?"

"What I'm talking about, Sally, is where more than one 'identity' exists within the same human body. Do you remember the story of Dr. Jekyll and Mr. Hyde?"

"Yes. The man that had a good and bad side."

"It's more than just a 'side' of the same individual. It's called multiple personality because each identity has a disparate self-concept, set of beliefs, memories, typical behaviors."

Sally frowned. "That sounds so weird. Are you saying the changes in Richard are from another personality inside him?"

"Yes, Sally. I think the second personality, let's call him Rich, first emerged after your husband hit his head last year on a fishing trip. But the first personality, we'll label him Richard, decided to come back, and Rich suddenly realized he was in danger. He came to see me because Richard Quade was threatening him.''

''He was threatening himself?'' Sally asked.

''Rich's consciousness was being threatened by the other personality inhabiting his body. I think he lost his consciousness Monday night to Richard, that other personality.''

Sally's eyes enlarged with new awareness. ''The night everything changed! The night he stopped sleeping with me and quit smoking! My God, can it be true?''

''It seems to be the probable explanation with the current facts. I need a lot more time with your husband to be sure. You see, I'm disturbed by a very large inconsistency to this theory.''

''What?'' Sally asked.

''Well, people with multiple personalities insist on very distinct and separate names for their distinct and separate personalities. From everything you've told me, your husband does not. And I'm also bothered by the fact that 'Richard' threw me out of his house and yet called me the next day and apologized, saying he wanted to see me again, admitting to needing my help. Those are inconsistent acts for the 'Richard' personality.''

''What does it mean?'' Sally asked.

Claire put a hand on her shoulder. ''I don't know. But I'll find out. Don't you worry. For the time being, mention none of our conversation to your husband. Just act naturally and relate to him as best as you can. We'll sort it out.''

As she patted Sally's shoulder, Claire couldn't help but hope she was right. Despite her assurances to his wife, she felt uneasy about her diagnosis of Richard Quade's personality changes. It was as though she was missing something very important. Or maybe she was no longer capable of interpreting the information she had correctly. She felt sick at the thought, but she knew she had to consider it.

Claire's ruminations were rudely interrupted by the loud and almost sarcastic voice that suddenly boomed to her right. She felt Sally's shoulders jump uncontrollably beneath her hands.

"Well if it isn't Dr. Boland. How thoughtful of you to drop in," Richard Quade said.

Claire looked over at him from where she stood above Sally. He was leaning against the door to the kitchen, stroking his beard as he had Tuesday night when she had come by. This was not Dr. Jekyll, the gentle Rich Sally loved so much. This was Mr. Hyde, the harsh Richard Sally was learning to fear. Claire forced herself to smile as she gave Sally's shoulders a reassuring squeeze before removing her hands.

"Good evening, Richard. I was just keeping Sally company while she was fixing dinner," Claire said.

Richard moved into the room purposely. "I didn't know you two were such good friends. Or is it that my wife is finally getting professional help on quitting this filthy habit of hers?"

Richard picked up the table's ashtray and threw it into the trash. The force of his swing broke the ceramic piece with a loud crash. Sally winced. Claire felt the barely leashed violence in the man. She understood Sally's fear. Tomorrow she would call to discuss how Sally could protect herself and her children. Now she felt it would be best if she left.

"Good night, Sally. Richard."

Just as Claire reached the door, Richard called after her. "Dr. Boland, wait a minute."

By the time Richard had caught up with her, Claire could see his expression had changed. The anger was gone. There was an anxiousness or eagerness about him, she couldn't decide which. She studied his face, trying to see to the man within, but he was shielded. That, in itself, was interesting.

"We missed our appointment yesterday. I'd like to reschedule. I would have called before this, but things have been busy at the Yard. Are you available soon?"

Claire knew this different Richard Quade didn't need her help to rid himself of fear or threats. But she sensed he was after something. Did he want to discuss the personality he had so recently supplanted? Maybe if she could talk with him just once more, she might be able to clear up her doubts concerning his diagnosis. It was worth a try.

"Tomorrow. I could fit you in late in the afternoon. Say four-thirty?" she said.

"That would be fine. Where's your new office?"

"I'm practicing out of my home for the next week or so. My address is 655 Cedar Lane in Silverdale. Do you think you can find it?" Claire opened the door and stepped outside.

"Don't worry, I'll find it," Richard Quade said, holding the door open and smiling.

Claire shivered as she walked toward her car. She decided it must be because she was hungry. After all, it was still quite warm out despite the thick cloud cover that had rolled in late that afternoon. As she started the car, she looked in the rearview mirror. Nothing was there. She tried to shake her uneasiness as she pulled away from the curb.

By the time she arrived home, she was still feeling shaky. She left the car in the driveway and walked to the front door. She was thinking about what she had to eat in the refrigerator while she fiddled with extracting the house key, when the deep voice suddenly boomed from behind her. She spun around and jumped in sudden fright, her heart leaping into her throat.

"I'm sorry. I didn't mean to scare you," Wyatt said, his hands full with a large pizza carton.

Claire's back collapsed against the front door while she tried to control her nerves.

"Where did you come from?" she said in a voice not quite her own. "I didn't hear or see you."

Wyatt's look and tone emphasized his sincerity. "I really am sorry. I called out from the car when you pulled up. I thought you heard me."

Wyatt turned and pointed in the direction of the front where Claire noticed an old white Chevy Blazer was parked. She knew it hadn't been there a minute ago.

"When I pulled up just now?" she asked.

"Yes. I guess your mind was somewhere else. I saw you driving down Silverdale Way and followed you home. I was picking up a pizza." He lifted the large carton he held in his hands for emphasis. "It's extra large and has everything but pineapple and anchovies on it. There's enough for two."

Claire smiled. Now that her initial fright was past, she felt very happy to see Wyatt. She opened the door and gestured him inside. "Sounds great."

"While we're sharing the pizza, would you mind if we talk a little about Knudsen?" he asked as he stepped through the doorway.

Claire fought a small twinge of disappointment. Had he only come to see her as a consultant? "Okay. But I need to check my answering machine before I do anything else. The kitchen's back there." She closed the door behind him.

Wyatt walked past and Claire ran her messages back. She picked up the phone and dialed Alan's number. After the eighth ring, she gave it up. His call had come in about ten minutes before. He must have gone to whatever hotel he was staying at. He had only left his office number on the answering machine.

"What would you like to drink? I have low-fat milk, cola and orange juice," she said as she entered the kitchen.

"You don't have anything alcoholic?" Wyatt asked. He had spread the pizza on the table and its aroma was filling the room.

"Yes, but I didn't think you'd want to drink while on duty."

He looked over at her and smiled. "I'm always on duty, but the hours I don't get paid for I consider my own."

"In that case I have vodka, brandy and white or red wine."

"Red wine definitely to go with the pizza."

When they talked again, only a fourth of the pizza remained, and half the bottle of red wine. Claire leaned back and stretched. "That hit the spot. I'm glad you showed up tonight."

Claire could feel Wyatt watching her as he nursed his second glass of wine. "Does that mean you've forgiven me for this afternoon?"

His smile was small but Claire still felt special under its light. "I overreacted, Wyatt. Your people approached my patients with tact and diplomacy. I'm sorry I became angry."

He smiled in relief. "It's okay. You get angry about the right things. I'm a firm believer that there are no negative emotions, only negative reasons for becoming emotional."

Claire thought about his statement. "That identifies reason as the impetus for all emotion. What an interesting concept. You're certainly surprising, Wyatt."

His smile enlarged. "I'm glad you think so."

Wyatt could see the deepening color in her cheeks and knew she was neither unaware nor immune to his interest. The knowledge was exciting. With difficulty, he refocused his mind on business.

"There's something I need to tell you. We got the report in this afternoon. Arthur Knudsen is wanted for murder in California under the name of Arthur Knute."

Claire swallowed, her initial glow over Wyatt's interest fading into a sudden chill. For a moment, she couldn't speak. When she finally found her voice, it sounded like a squeak.

"Knudsen's a murderer?"

Chapter Ten

Wyatt leaned forward in his chair, seeing the shock on Claire's face. "You were right. It all stems from his repeating bigamy pattern. We've located at least four previous wives in that state. Apparently his fourth wife, a Judy Norris Knute, proved his nemesis. His mistake was leaving her and cleaning out her substantial bank account to the tune of one-hundred-thousand dollars. The eighty-five-thousand we found in his safe deposit box is probably what's left."

"Why did you say she was his nemesis?"

"She put a private investigator on his trail. The investigator found him and the existence of the other three wives. Then, Judy's brother went after Knudsen."

Claire drank some more of her red wine as Wyatt went on to describe the scene with Knudsen and his brother-in-law.

"Judy's brother threatened to have Knudsen locked up for stealing Judy's money. Knudsen went crazy and shot the brother in front of two witnesses. When the police arrived, Knudsen displayed amnesia for what had happened. He was committed to a mental facility for observation and evaluation."

"What did the mental evaluation reveal?" Claire asked.

"It was incomplete. Knudsen went into a frenzy when they took him to the facility, kept accusing them of trying to bury him alive. The medical personnel decided he was reliving some earlier traumatic experience and sedated him heavily. When they let the medication wear off so they could conduct the medical evaluation, he bashed in an attendant's head and escaped. That was twelve years ago."

Claire still felt numbed by the news. "I thought there might be something, but this . . ."

"There's more," he said. "Knudsen escaped from the hospital late this afternoon. Where do you think he'll go?"

"As far away as he can get. His attempt at suicide tells me he now feels trapped here."

Wyatt frowned. "If we catch up with him, confront him, what do you think he'll do?"

Claire shrugged. "I think he'll fight like a cornered animal and maybe even try to kill himself again if he thinks he'll be captured. From that information the California mental institution sent you and from what I've seen of him, I believe Arthur Knudsen thinks being locked up is worse than death."

Wyatt nodded his understanding. "We've tried to limit his avenues of escape. His wives are being watched. We've alerted the bank to contact us if he tries to get into the safe deposit box. Do you think it possible he might come here for help?"

Wyatt watched her face as she digested the thought.

"I told him I think he's innocent of Roger Thayer's murder, but he also knows I'm a psychologist and that puts a mark against me. I don't know, Wyatt. He can't think I'd help him. On the other hand, he's not rational and that makes him unpredictable."

While Wyatt paused to consider her words, Claire rose to clean off the table. She automatically wrapped up the rest of the pizza and set it in front of him. He watched her while he sipped the last of his wine.

"Is this a signal to me that now you've eaten my pizza you want me to leave?" he asked.

She was so immersed in her own thoughts that his question took her by surprise. As she looked over at him, she noticed the small smile at the corners of his mouth and struggled to keep one off her lips as she cocked her head to one side.

"Are you fishing for an invitation to stay?"

His eyes searched her face for a minute as his smile slowly broadened. "Am I likely to catch one?"

Claire's heartbeat began to quicken at the intimate teasing of his words. She glanced away, trying to avoid looking too closely into the depths of his disturbing green-blue eyes.

"Are you always this friendly to the people you meet on assignment?" she heard herself ask. The question surprised her as did the realization that she really wanted an answer.

Wyatt waited to answer her until his prolonged silence brought her eyes back to his face. Then he leaned across the table and took hold of her hand. There was no tease in his voice this time as his eyes searched hers. "No, Claire. As a matter of fact, I make it a point to keep a discreet distance. But I'm finding it impossible to do so with you."

His eyes were pulling her toward him as was the warmth seeping through his hand and spreading through her body. She felt breathless and expectant as he leaned closer and closer across the small table.

His lips rubbed against hers slowly, gently at first and then faster, more insistent as she sighed in pleasure. He tasted warm and full-bodied like the wine he had drunk. She parted her moist lips in invitation, wanting more of him and the delicious dizziness whirlpooling her thoughts into thin air.

Suddenly the doorbell rang like a thunderous gong, making both of them jump apart. Wyatt was on his feet and had his gun drawn before Claire had a chance to blink. "Are you expecting anyone?"

His words had been spoken urgently. Their implication drove a shiver up Claire's spine. She whispered back. "No."

He took her arm and led her from the kitchen to the darkened entry hall. She felt his breath caress her ear. "Ask who it is."

He still held onto her arm, a firm grip. She saw the evening light shining through the window gleam off the barrel of his drawn gun. Her voice sounded harsh in her ears as she called out. She heard a muffled answer.

"Do you recognize the voice?" Wyatt whispered.

"No."

"Ask again. Louder this time."

Claire called out more loudly asking her visitor to speak up.

"Claire, it's okay. It's Alan."

Claire had the door open in a second and Alan came rushing in, immediately putting his arms around her.

"Every time I telephoned I kept getting that damn answering machine. I'm sorry to just drop by like this, but Vera said you sounded anxious about something so I—"

Claire felt Alan's involuntary start and then his immediate relaxation as he recognized the man next to her holding a gun.

"Hello, Wyatt. Didn't expect to find the Sheriff's Department here. Is everything okay?"

Claire looked over to see Wyatt putting his gun away.

"Under control. I'll be on my way," he said to Claire. "Be sure to keep all your doors and windows locked. I'll have a unit patrol by here during the night. You have my number in case Knudsen should try to contact you?"

"Yes. Thank you, Wyatt."

Wyatt nodded to Alan, then left. Claire closed the door behind him and turned to her brother.

"What's all this about, Claire? Why does Wyatt treat you as though you might need protection?"

Claire took his arm and led him into the kitchen. "It's only precautionary, Alan. A mentally disturbed individual involved in his case escaped from the hospital this afternoon. Wyatt just wanted to be sure I knew in the unlikely event the man came here."

"You're sure that event is unlikely?"

"Relax, Alan. You heard Wyatt say there would be a unit around. I'll be fine. Now how about some leftover pizza Wyatt brought by. I could heat it up in the microwave?"

Alan's face wore a satisfied smirk. "So he's gone from cold fresh fruit to hot pizza? That's a good sign. Things must be warming up all around the cave."

Claire smiled but said nothing as she led the way to the kitchen. Alan shrugged. "Okay, your love life's off bounds. Pop the pizza into the microwave and tell me why you've been calling."

Claire put aside her thoughts of Wyatt and set the microwave timer. "I've got a feeling that this murder I'm involved in and the ones that have taken place at the Shipyard might be connected."

Alan frowned. "How?"

"Explosions, Alan. The man I discovered had his face blown off, and a receptionist was killed when my offices were bombed yesterday. Could it be the same person setting these explosions?"

Alan's frown had dug a deep canal in his forehead. "Claire, forget the pizza. Sit down this second and tell me everything you know about this dead man you found. Everything."

CLAIRE PACED impatiently in the hospital's waiting room early Friday. The deputy on duty had passed her, but the duty nurse had advised her that Dave Reyes's condition was still listed as serious and unless and until the doctor's morning examination proved he was up to seeing visitors, only family members would be allowed in. Waiting for the doctor to show and perform such an examination was trying Claire's patience.

She checked her watch for the umpteenth time only to assure herself that less than a minute had passed since the last check. Determinedly she put the timepiece out of sight beneath the sleeve of her blouse, reminding herself that time was as unlikely to cooperate as a watched pot. She must put her mind elsewhere.

Thoughts of Wyatt instantly surfaced and she found herself smiling. She became so engrossed reliving the warm message in his words and kiss of the night before that it was several moments before she realized someone was tugging at her suit jacket. She gazed down into the dark eyes of a small boy, about seven.

"Why are you looking at that blank wall?"

Claire smiled at the youngster's question. "I was really seeing things in my own mind."

The boy frowned at her words so she tried again.

"In my mind I was somewhere else. Don't you ever do that?"

He said nothing, but another voice spoke up instantly from her left. "He knows what you mean."

Claire looked over at this new young voice and blinked, not quite believeing her eyes. The face was a duplicate of the one on her right. "You're twins?"

The dark-haired boy on her right stayed motionless, but the one on her left was nodding. "Except I'm not anything like him. We just look alike," the one with the nodding head said.

"Jimmy, Jerry. Come here and sit still for a change." Claire watched as the two youngsters by her side retreated to their mother's seated position in one of the waiting-room chairs. She followed.

"I hope they weren't bothering you?" the woman asked.

Claire shook her head. "No. Not at all. Are they really very different in personality?"

She shook her head tolerantly and smiled as she wrapped an arm around each, hugging them to her like identical bookends. "In a way. Jimmy, the one on the right, is the one who likes to ask all the questions, and Jerry, on my left, pops up with all the answers."

"Do you ever get a complete conversation out of one of them?"

"Only when I separate them. Still, even when by himself, Jimmy will insist Jerry's still in the room and is the one answering my questions. And Jerry insists he's Jimmy when he asks questions."

Claire found the process fascinating. "You don't sound like their behavior disturbs you."

"Oh no," their mother said. "Each feels the other's absence so acutely he tries to pretend his twin is still there with him by playing his part. My sister and I were twins, too. We did some pretty crazy things ourselves when we were kids.

Being a twin is a special relationship. The bond is very strong.''

Claire found the woman's words stirring the creative juices of her thoughts. "You say you were a twin, too? The tendency to have twins is hereditary, right?''

"Oh yes. Out of six generations in my family, four have produced twins and two of those generations have had multiple sets.''

Claire's mind raced. She was reexamining the heredity component of twins and remembering the identical faces of Richard Quade's twin daughters. These were new waters for speculation and she found herself diving right in. Was Richard Quade also a twin?

Everything she had ever read in the psychological literature said this woman was right—the bond between twins was very strong, sometimes even neurotically so. Could it be what she was thinking?

Each feels the other's absence so acutely he tries to pretend his twin is still there with him by playing his part.

The words played through her mind, dark and ominous, yet compelling, too, like a tortured Mozart work.

"Dr. Claire Boland?''

Claire jumped at the sudden calling of her name, so deep had her thoughts taken her. She looked up to see the face of Dave's doctor.

"Yes. How is Dave? May I see him?''

"He's improving, but I'm not going to allow him to see anyone but his wife for the present. I'm sure you understand he's still very weak. Give him a couple of more days. As they say, time heals all wounds.''

"Not necessarily the emotional ones, Doctor," Claire said, as she turned and walked away in obvious distraction.

"I HAVE THAT INFORMATION you wanted on the Gillette guy," Tom said as he walked into Wyatt's office.

"I'm listening," Wyatt said as he leaned back in his chair.

"He's a big shot with Naval Intelligence Service. Flew into SEATAC from San Francisco on Tuesday. Stayed a day. Flew back to D.C. on Wednesday and then returned here last night. Something is up for him to have been called in, but nobody's talking."

"The news mentioned exploding fireworks at the Shipyard on Tuesday," Wyatt said. "Perhaps that brought Gillette in."

"That might explain Gillette coming on Tuesday, but what about his coming back last night?" Tom asked.

Wyatt remembered Gillette's presence at Claire's Tuesday night and again last night. "His second visit could be personal."

Tom shook his head. "No, something's up, Wyatt. Newsmen have been sniffing after Shipyard rumors since Tuesday. Isn't it a little coincidental that it was also Tuesday Gillette first arrived?"

"What were the rumors?" Wyatt asked.

"They were all over the board. One said a visiting Pentagon commander had been shot and killed. Another said cars had been set on fire in front of the captain's office. And a third said some kids with firecrackers had set them off causing the personnel to panic."

"I assume none of these rumors was substantiated by the media liaison officer at the Shipyard?"

"He freely admitted to the firecracker incident, but the press was hesitant to report it because something smelled fishy. If it was only kids with firecrackers, why did Shipyard personnel who normally talk openly with reporters all of a sudden clam up? The guys in the newsroom said it was almost as though whatever really happened was under a tight security lid."

"Did they tell you what they thought it was?" Wyatt asked.

"No. But the pressure's building under some big secret. Want to bet me it's going to blow?"

"I'll take that bet," a third voice suddenly said from the door, causing both Wyatt and Tom to start in surprise.

Wyatt stood and approached the light brown-haired man who was casually leaning against the doorjamb.

"Well, Alan, you're quite a surprise. As you no doubt overheard, we were discussing the events surrounding your arrival to the Puget Sound Area."

Wyatt introduced Tom and the men shook hands.

Alan eyed the detective carefully. "Watson. You must be the one calling around and asking questions about me so furiously this morning. Find out everything you needed?"

Tom couldn't seem to find his voice. At a signal from Wyatt, he unceremoniously excused himself. Alan sat down in an offered chair, leaning back comfortably.

"What brings you here?" Wyatt said, still standing.

"Actually Claire suggested I see you. It seems we have some interests in common. Certain events at the Puget Sound Naval Shipyard appear to be coinciding with certain events taking place within the Silverdale community."

Wyatt's interest was more than peaked. "What events?"

Alan leaned forward slightly in his chair. "I know you've been investigating two murders caused by explosion."

Wyatt circled his desk and sat down, trying to hide the sudden disappointment he felt. "Claire told you the method?"

"Yes, she told me, but only because she couldn't tell you."

"You're being mysterious, Alan. What's this all about?"

Alan got up then and paced around the front of Wyatt's desk. Finally he rested his knuckles across Wyatt's desk blotter and leaned over toward him. "What I tell you now must not leave this room. It's a matter of national security. I need your word on this."

Wyatt watched Alan's eyes. They held an expression of concern and worry. "You have it," he said.

Alan straightened and began to pace again.

"We've had our own explosion on the Puget Sound Naval Shipyard this past week that killed two men. Claire knew of this explosion. Her involvement with two murders in this community, both of which also occurred by explosion this week, gave rise in her mind to the possibility of a common killer. Frankly, I agree with her."

Wyatt was alarmed and puzzled by Alan's information. He got up from his chair and came around to the front of the desk.

"Do you know who it is?"

Alan sat back down in one of Wyatt's side chairs. "I think we may be dealing with an assassin and one or more accomplices. And, no, I don't know who they are. Yet."

"What kind of explosive was used?" Wyatt asked.

"Primarily high-powered gelatin. But an unexploded bomb we also found tells us this assassin has a knowledge of various kinds of explosives. He's not an amateur. He sets out precisely enough to take out the area he wants."

Alan's words set off a familiar ringing in Wyatt's brain.

"Precisely enough?"

Alan smiled. "Yes, he could have been the one to take off the face and left hand of Roger Thayer Monday night in Safeway."

Wyatt battled disappointment. "I see she told you everything."

Alan leaned forward in his chair. "She knew it was important to do so. And she knows me, trusts me, as I trust her. You understand why she did it?"

Wyatt nodded, aware that Alan didn't want him to be angry at his sister. That thought at least comforted him.

Alan got up and began to pace about Wyatt's office again. "If we make the assumption Claire did, and I think we should, then the motives for your recent murders might have their origin in our assassin trying to either hide his identity or his reasons for the explosions at the Shipyard."

Wyatt nodded. "Tell me more."

"There are a couple of scenarios that could fit. One might be that our assassin comes to town and kills Roger Thayer because Thayer is the one person who could recognize him and blow the whistle on what he's about to do. We're launching an investigation into Thayer's background searching for that match."

"Okay. I can see that's a possibility. What else?"

Alan's face wore a pensive look. "Maybe Roger Thayer was supposed to be in on the assassination attempts but got cold feet or wanted more money for the job so he was taken out by his cohorts."

Wyatt rubbed his chin. "Either of those might explain the Thayer killing. But what about the bomb that went off killing the receptionist and injuring the doctor?"

Alan looked ready, as though he was expecting the question.

"I think the bomb was meant either for Arthur Knudsen or Claire. They both were in Safeway on the night Thayer was killed. Either one of them might have seen something that could identify who the killer was or the killer thinks they might have seen something and doesn't want to take the chance they might talk."

Wyatt read something in Alan's look. "You really think the assassin's after Claire?"

Alan nodded. "She's the more likely candidate."

Wyatt tried to control the uneasiness that was gathering in his stomach. "Does she know?"

Alan exhaled heavily. "She hasn't said anything to me."

Wyatt paused for a moment and then reached over his desk for a file. He took out some pages and handed them to Alan.

Alan glanced at the top of the investigative report and then back at Wyatt. "Another explosion death?"

Wyatt nodded. "Victim was a lawyer. Worked out of the Naval Legal Service Office in Seattle. Lt. Commander Carroll. Looks like the explosive device was in a toy car of some type."

Alan flipped through the report. "How did you find out about this death?"

"I made inquiries to surrounding law enforcement for similar explosive methods used in homicides. This happened Wednesday night."

"Can I keep this copy of the police report?" Alan asked.

Wyatt nodded. "Do you want to work together?"

Alan shook his head. "I can't. What I've told you this morning you may not use in any way other than to help focus your investigation. The Shipyard explosions have far-reaching effects and a significance beyond the individual murders. I can say no more. But whether it's you or I who catch this assassin, he'll be tried in federal court for crimes against the federal government."

"So you want me to turn him over to you?" Wyatt asked.

"Assuming I don't get him first, and I do believe I will. In all honesty, if Claire hadn't insisted I tell you, I wouldn't have even come here today. And if I hadn't thought she was in danger, I might not have even come then."

Wyatt moved away from his resting spot on the edge of his desk. "It's not my investigation you've been trying to help, is it? You're really telling me all this so I'll protect her, aren't you?"

Alan quickly closed the distance separating them to stand in front of Wyatt, his eyes looking directly into the other man's. "It's the major motivation, yes. Are you going to tell me you'd rather not have the job?"

Wyatt looked for a moment into the knowing eyes and found his first appraisal of Alan's intelligence correct. He smiled and shrugged. "Leave me your number and I'll keep you posted."

Alan smiled as he put out his hand and Wyatt returned his firm shake. "Good luck," Alan said, and then he was gone.

Tom bounded into Wyatt's office. "Can you believe that? Here we are discussing the guy and he walks right in! I was speechless!"

Tom's voice barely penetrated Wyatt's thoughts. He was standing with his hands in his pockets, looking out the window at the retreating form of Alan Gillette.

"We're going to solve these bombing murders, Tom. Go to the FBI. Request their files for all known saboteurs. Put a rush on it. Go wherever you have to go to get a terminal access. I want the information by this afternoon at the latest."

"Wyatt, I don't think—"

"And get a detective or deputy watching Dr. Claire Boland twenty-four hours a day beginning now. This is a protective surveillance, you understand. If anybody suspicious approaches her, put the cuffs on first, ask questions later. Are you with me, Tom?''

The uncompromising tone in Wyatt's voice finally got through to Tom. "Yes . . . sir.''

"HOW WERE THINGS after I left last night, Sally?" Claire asked. She heard Sally's sigh over the telephone line and wished she could see the woman's face.

"He left right after you did, barely looked at what I was preparing for dinner. Just came back into the kitchen and told me he was going out to eat.''

"When did he get home?''

"It was about an hour and a half later. I had gone to bed. It was early but I just didn't want to face his anger and disapproval again. He slept on the couch as usual. This other personality we talked about, Rich. Do you think he might ever come back?''

"It's a good question, Sally, but one I can't answer. I haven't been able to confirm my diagnosis of multiple personality yet. Can I ask you a few more questions?''

"Sure.''

"Sally, there have been cases of people losing a twin and attempting to keep the twin alive by acting out what they perceive to be the lost twin's behavior. Sometimes they use a separate name for their 'lost' twin. Sometimes they don't because they consider the twin just another part of themselves. I'm mentioning this so you'll understand my next question. Is Richard a twin?''

Sally's voice sounded surprised. "No. He's an only child like I am. I've known him since we were both twenty. That's when he came down to this area to work at the Shipyard. Before that he lived up in Port Townsend with his parents. I'm sure he has no twin.''

Claire thought for a minute. "Could Richard be adopted?''

Sally's voice sounded confused. "I never asked him, but that's something he would have told me, wouldn't he? Anyway his folks have never mentioned anything about Richard being adopted.''

"Do you have his parents' number in Port Townsend?"

"Sure." Sally gave Claire the number.

"Does Richard get along with his parents?" Claire asked.

"Pretty well, I guess. We don't see them much."

Claire had heard the slight hesitation in Sally's response. "Is there a problem between them?" Claire asked.

"No. He's just neglectful. They feel it, of course. I still get a lot of calls asking when they are going to get another chance to see their grandchildren. They're real nice people. I hate to put them off but Richard..."

Sally's voice trailed off, but Claire got the idea. "You know he's agreed to see me this afternoon?" she said.

Sally's voice sounded confused. "No. He...didn't tell me."

"I've told you because I believe your knowing what is going on is important for your own piece of mind. But I think you and I should also talk, Sally. You have needs, too. These changes in Richard are as disruptive to you as they have been to him. Frankly you and the girls are my primary concern at the moment."

The phone line was quiet for a moment and then Claire heard the muted sobs in her ear.

"Sally? Why are you crying?"

It was a moment before the woman was able to answer. "You're so nice to me. I've needed to talk with someone so badly and you've...been there."

Claire's mind flashed back to graduate school and the most-asked question of each professor: Why do you want to be a psychologist? Sally Quade had just answered that question far more eloquently than she had ever been able to.

"I'll continue to be here for you, Sally. Together we can work it out. Can you see me Saturday? I practice out of my home for the present. Bring the girls if you like. They can play in my backyard." Claire gave her the address.

"Yes, of course, I'll come see you," Sally said. "You're the only one who really understands."

After they agreed on a time, Claire hung up the phone feeling almost like a fraud. What exactly did she understand?

For a moment that morning, just for a moment as she looked at those twin boys and listened to their mother's explanation about their unusual behavior, she had thought she might have an answer. Richard Quade did have twin daughters and twins did run in families. If he had been a twin and had lost his brother, he might be acting out his brother's personality to deny his loss.

But Sally had just denied Richard was a twin. Did that close the book on this pursuit? Absolutely. Unless...

If he wasn't a twin now, had Richard Quade been one when he was born? Did the other child die before it was named? Had Richard Quade made up a second personality, an antithesis to his own, in an effort to bring back his dead twin? Is that why the other personality didn't have a separate name?

Claire got up to look out her window at the muggy hot day before her. She looked past the cloud-muted rays of the summer sun to the dense row of fir trees all around her, looking cool and content in their robes of green. Interspersed among the green fir trees was the occasional red bark of a fast-growing Madrona tree, shedding its too tight skin as it shot for the sky.

This afternoon I'll know, she thought, *because that's when I'll ask Quade what happened to the man I spoke with on Monday.*

RICHARD QUADE STAYED at his work position when the noon whistle blew. He knew it was the only way to discourage Kevin from trying to get him to go off the Yard for lunch. Fortunately today was the last day he'd have to put up with the pest.

That is, if contact was made. He'd been anxiously waiting all morning, but nothing. They had agreed he would stay close by his work position after the completion of phase four. The final phase might require his help. And if it did, he would be contacted here with instructions. Only here and only today.

He stopped for a moment and got out the sandwiches Sally had prepared for him. She wasn't all that bad when he thought about it. He might have enjoyed her if she hadn't been a smoker. But there was no sex appeal in the stale, rancid smell of tobacco, or the yellowed residue on her fingers and teeth.

Their memory caused him to lose his appetite. He threw the partly eaten sandwich away and tried to lose himself in the business of overhauling the engine. The shadow fell across his line of sight before he heard a sound. He started at the breathy voice that spoke into his ear.

"It's me."

Richard's nerves were instantly taut and ready. He began to turn toward his visitor.

"No, don't turn around. Stay exactly where you are. Your instructions and new I.D. are in this envelope."

At that moment, Richard felt something being slipped into his pants' pockets. "Why do I need a new identification?"

"It's the identification of a man who works in the Mobile Technical Unit 15. I've decided I'll need a diversion tomorrow. The tag you'll find is to be hung from your rearview mirror and means your car is part of a car pool. With it you can pass on to the Shipyard so you can make a quick getaway. The rest of the instructions are included in the envelope."

"If I need to reach you—"

The breathy voice interrupted. "You cannot reach me. You must not try. Shipyard calls are being monitored."

"They found the bugs?"

"Don't worry. I planned for it, and it makes no difference. Tomorrow is our day." The shadow moved away. Richard kept his head down, pretending to concentrate on the engine in front of him while his mind feverishly explored the next day's events. He had waited a long time for this revenge. It tasted so very sweet.

ALAN LOOKED over the Seattle police report, shaking his head. If only he had had this information the day before, he could have fed it into the computer back in D.C. It might have exposed right then the connecting thread in the explosion deaths. Cross-referencing the service records of Commander Corson, Commander Hotspoint and Captain Kent had produced no tie-in.

When Claire had told Alan the night before about the similar explosion deaths in Silverdale, he had run Roger Thayer's name and background against the other three men but received no matches at all. However, this death of Lt. Commander Paul Carroll by the same explosive method might be just the clue he needed. He was glad he listened to Claire and shared some information with Wyatt.

Now it was up to him. He picked up the phone and subjected it to his own personal scrambling device before punching in the number for Computer Central. He wished he could discuss his most recent line of inquiry with Vera but the computer report had connected her to two of the dead men. It could be nothing. Still, until he knew for certain, he would have to keep his investigation to himself.

It was times like this when he most missed Jerry Boland. He'd been able to talk to Jerry. But Jerry was gone and with him went another secret Alan had to keep. And, perhaps of all his secrets, that one hurt the most.

Chapter Eleven

Claire looked at her watch again as she paced the floor of her living room. It was four-fifty. Where was Richard Quade? This was the third time he had made an appointment with her in the last three days and the third time he hadn't shown. Well, that wasn't exactly fair. He had been detained the first time by the Shipyard investigation and the second by the explosion of her office. Those reasons were hardly capricious.

The earlier clouds had evaporated and the temperature was rising perceptibly as the rays of the afternoon sun stabbed through her floor-to-ceiling living-room windows. She turned on the fan in the corner and began to pace in front of it.

After another five minutes had passed and Richard Quade still hadn't appeared, Claire picked up the phone and dialed his home number. Sally Quade answered.

"You don't have to tell me why you're calling, Dr. Boland. I can guess. He didn't show for his appointment, did he?"

"No. He's not there?" Claire asked.

Sally sighed. "No."

"Well, don't worry about it. We have our appointment for tomorrow. We'll discuss your options then, Sally. You've got lots of them, by the way, so don't lose heart. Understand?"

"Yeah, okay. I just wish he had kept his appointment with you."

"So do I, Sally. So do I."

Claire hung up the phone, once again feeling unsettled. Had there been more trouble at the Shipyard? Two of her patients today had mentioned the added security precautions being taken when they entered to go to their jobs. One had even had her lunch searched as Marines carrying M16s stood by.

Claire picked up the phone and called Alan. He was characteristically unavailable. Without hesitating, she dialed Vera Ward's number. She was told Vera was in a meeting and not expected back. On a hunch, Claire asked if Alan Gillette and Barney Coffman were also in that meeting.

"Mr. Gillette is conducting the meeting. But Mr. Coffman is in his office. May I give you that number?"

"No. I have it. Can you tell me if any employees were detained at the Shipyard today?"

"I don't know what you mean," the secretary said. Claire thought she pulled off the innocent act very well. No doubt she had been told not to say anything. Claire tried a gentle probe into the official story that had been released.

"I know some of the Shipyard employees were detained earlier this week because of some firecrackers that were set off. I just wondered if a similar situation might have occurred today."

"I have no such knowledge, Dr. Boland. Perhaps you might wish to try Mr. Coffman. I believe he is working late tonight so you should still find him in his office."

Claire thanked the secretary and placed her next call. The Shipyard police detective who answered the phone waded her through several introductory questions before Barney Coffman finally came on the line.

"I'm Claire Boland, Mr. Coffman. Alan Gillette told me to call you if he was unavailable."

"Yes, Ms. Boland. Alan mentioned you were his sister. What can I do for you?"

"I was wondering if you could tell me if any of the Shipyard employees were detained this evening."

"Detained? For what reason?" Coffman asked.

"I don't know. Perhaps because of a second firecracker incident?"

"Who did you have in mind, Ms. Boland?"

Claire hesitated. She didn't like mentioning Richard Quade's name to the head of the Criminal Investigation Division. Bringing attention to him might cause Richard unnecessary focus and questioning. She tried to retreat.

"No one specifically. I just know some of the men are late getting home. I hoped it was nothing serious," Claire said.

"What men are late?"

The man's voice was direct, probing. Claire knew how to change her own to solicit information from a repressed patient. She recognized the technique in the man questioning her. The only way to get out of this gracefully was to lie. She didn't like doing it, but she was beginning to feel cornered.

"Oh, here they come. Never mind, Mr. Coffman. The pickup is pulling up now. Thank you for your help."

Claire hung up the phone before Barney Coffman could say anything. Lying always made her feel rotten, no matter what the reason. Why couldn't the man just have told her if employees were being kept late? Alan must have explained that she wasn't a security risk. It wasn't as if she was asking for secret information.

Claire began to pace the living room again as she reconsidered the situation. No, she wasn't being fair. If there had been another incident, everything would be considered secret information. Well, that call yielded exactly nothing but irritation. What next?

She felt an increasing need for movement, somewhere, anywhere. She shoved her hand into her bag for the number of Richard Quade's parents. The phone rang several times before a man's voice answered.

"Mr. Quade?" Claire asked.

"I'm Quade. Who is this?"

"Dr. Claire Boland. I've been counseling your son, Richard."

"Richard has a counselor? What for?"

"Richard is going through some emotional concerns. I'd very much like to talk with you about him so that I could understand Richard better and perhaps be more effective in helping him."

Richard's father hesitated. "I don't discuss anything over a phone. If you want to talk to me concerning my son, you'll have to do it in person."

"I could drive up now if that would be convenient for you and Mrs. Quade."

Her sudden offer caused a much longer hesitation. Claire heard some muffled voice sounds in the background. She imagined Mr. Quade's hand over the telephone mouthpiece as he conferred with his wife. Then his voice returned.

"Okay, you can come tonight, if you think it that important. How soon would you be here?"

"About an hour and a half. Hold on for a moment while I get a pencil. I'll need to write down your address and directions."

Claire had the address and directions and was in her car within ten minutes. As she drove north, she gave some thought to the impropriety of talking with a patient's parents without first getting his approval. She assuaged her conscience by reminding herself that Sally Quade was also a patient and that she had given her permission for Claire to talk with Richard's parents when she had passed on their telephone number.

The thought of the telephone number brought to mind that she had forgotten to turn on her answering machine before she left the house. She was already thirty minutes on her way. It would be off for only a few hours. After all, she reasoned, what could possibly happen during that time?

As soon as Richard Quade had lifted the hood on his pickup truck, he saw the reason the wheels wouldn't move and the engine just continued to race. The universal joint had broken and the drive shaft had come loose.

Angry blood rushed into his face and hands. He wanted so much to smash something, anything. He stood with his hands on his hips, kicking the pickup truck with the heavy sole of his boot and cursing. This was one of the worst times for the thing to go belly-up on him.

What could he do? He had no way of fixing the damn thing without a new universal joint, and he had no way of getting a new one while he remained standing and fuming in the right lane of Highway Three. There was no alternative. He'd have to start walking toward the nearest offramp and get to a phone. It was bound to be a few miles. Somewhere he'd have to find a garage that was still open and had the part.

He'd have to call the psychologist, too, and let her know why he was late. He had to appease her until he could take care of her. As long as she thought she could manipulate him, she'd probably remain quiet. But if she thought he was unmanageable, she might go for the cops. Tomorrow would be a big day. If he could get her tonight, he could be assured she wouldn't be around to cause trouble.

Richard looked back at the truck and his eyes met with the toys sitting on the passenger's side. A new frown dug into his face. What would happen if a deputy stopped to examine the abandoned pickup? Would he just write a ticket or would he have the truck towed away? Richard stood looking at the explosives and biting his lip as he thought about the possibilities. He couldn't take the chance. He'd have to hide the toys now.

He looked around for something to put the toys into. On the floor of the truck was a scuffed but otherwise intact double-strength paper shopping bag. He got in the pickup, reached for the bag, snapped it open and carefully gathered the toys, placing each gently into the bag. Then he folded the bag shut and slipped across the seat to the door.

Once he got out of the pickup, he headed for the bushes along the side of the highway. He waited until the oncoming cars had driven by, then he quickly ducked into the greenery and shoved the bag between two sturdy bushes. He looked up again toward the highway. No cars were in view. No one could have seen him. The bag's contents would be safe until he returned for the truck.

He looked at his watch. His stomach tightened as he noticed it was already after five. The psychologist would know he wasn't going to show on time. What would she do? The police didn't know anything yet. Everything about his interview the afternoon before told him that. But he was sure that psychologist knew the score when she came by the house again last night. Would tonight be the night she spilled everything to the cops?

Damn it, she should already be dead. He would have seen to it last night if that guy in the old Chevy Blazer hadn't followed her home and decided to stay. He was the same big blond detective he had seen with her on Monday night at Safeway. The guy was probably staying close to her because he was suspicious of the psychologist. She was the only thing tying the two explosion deaths in Silverdale together. And knowing the Navy like he did, he was sure no one at NIS would discuss what was happening at the Shipyard.

Richard circled the truck, watching the traffic whiz by. He'd get to her in time. After all, it would be pretty awkward for her to come forward now after holding back from the cops. It might also bother her that she hadn't been able to treat him as a patient. Her egotism might delay her just long enough for him.

He put his hands into the tight pockets of his blue jeans as he started walking north to the nearest offramp. He'd like to make hers a slow death. She had cost him a lot of time and inconvenience. He'd think about a nice painful method on his long walk to a telephone.

"WE'RE GLAD you're seeing our son, Dr. Boland," Richard Quade said. "He's seemed quite troubled this last year, so forgetful. I even thought that the boy's purposely avoided us."

Mr. Quade had shown Claire into the sea-green living room of his home overlooking the Strait of Juan de Fuca. She was sitting on the couch. Mrs. Quade sat across from her in a matching chair. Richard Quade Sr. remained standing.

"Avoided you?" Claire repeated, hoping for enlightment.

Mrs. Quade shifted on her foam chair. "Oh, Sally has tried to cover for him, but his dad and I understand. We know he suffered a head injury in that boating accident last year. I suppose a memory loss is natural in that kind of situation?" Ellie Quade's tone was inquiring.

"I'm not a medical doctor, Mrs. Quade, but it's possible part of Richard's problems stem from a physical injury. Have you seen or talked with him this past week?"

"No. It's been several months."

If Claire had entertained any serious thoughts about Richard being adopted, they were dispelled when she saw the Quades. Both parents had his same black curly hair and light brown eyes. And although certainly not identical, Claire was amazed at how close in appearance even Richard Sr. and Ellie Quade were.

She thought that had she seen them for the first time in a crowd, she could have picked them out easily because of their likeness to each other and their son.

Still, with all that evidence literally staring her in the face, she asked the question. "Was Richard adopted?"

"Adopted? Oh, no," Ellie Quade said. "Richard is our natural child, Doctor. Sadly, our only one."

"Did you try to have other children?" Claire asked.

Ellie nodded. "Both our parents were dead. Our family was quite small. We wanted to have lots of children to fill our lives."

"It didn't work out that way?" Claire said.

"Richard was my only successful pregnancy. All the others were gone before they were born, you understand."

"I'm sorry, Mrs. Quade. I hope you don't mind my asking. Was Richard a twin by any chance?"

Ellie Quade looked at her husband, then back at Claire. "Why, no. Whatever made you ask that?"

Ellie Quade's question was a good one. Claire tried to think of an answer that might suffice. "He has twin daughters. I'm aware that twins run in families. I thought perhaps...?"

Ellie's head was shaking back and forth. "No, Richard was a single birth. But I admit to you that we hoped he would be twins. You see, I'm an identical twin and so is Richard's father. We felt sure we had a good chance of having twins. As it turned out . . ."

Ellie's voice faded away and Claire imagined the woman must be thinking about the babies she had been unable to carry to term. But Claire was fascinated at the information about Richard's parents both being twins. It seemed to fit so beautifully with Richard imagining himself as a twin personality.

"Mrs. Quade, I know this question might sound a little odd to you, but could you really have delivered twin boys?"

"What are you saying?"

"If you had twins, could one of the babies have died? Or is it possible the hospital inadvertently gave you only one child? I know it's rare, but such things do occasionally occur."

Ellie Quade smiled at Claire tolerantly. "I had Richard at home, Dr. Boland. He came quite unexpectedly and my husband delivered him. You can believe us. Richard was a single birth."

Now she was sure Richard was not a twin, Claire began to concentrate on the area in which she had the most hope of finding an answer to her patient's strange behavior.

"Did Richard know about the fact of twins running in his family?" Claire asked.

"Well, yes. We told him quite early. I remember his asking us about having brothers and sisters. We were still trying at the time and asked him how he would like to have twin brothers or sisters. He seemed quite intrigued with the idea, as I recall. I remember he always wanted to see his aunt and uncle."

"That would be your sister and Mr. Quade's brother?" Claire said.

Richard Sr. had been quiet through most of the conversation. But at the mention of his brother and sister-in-law, an angry sadness had descended over his face. Claire wanted to know what was behind those conflicting emotions. All

Richard's father did, however, was nod. Claire turned back to the more open face of Ellie Quade.

"How was Richard as a little boy? Did he seem moody to you?"

"No, not really," Ellie said. "He liked getting his own way, of course. But I suspect that's natural for all youngsters. He always wanted to be out playing with his friends."

"Did he have any imaginary friends while he was growing up?"

Ellie shook her head. "He had so many real ones, I don't think imaginary ones would have occurred to him. He wasn't one for fantasy of any sort. Didn't even like fairy tales much. Wanted toy guns and camouflage outfits and such. A typical boy."

"He never pretended he had a brother, a twin perhaps?"

Ellie looked confused at Claire's continuing questions. "No, Doctor. Or at least if he did he never told me."

"Neither you nor your husband are close to your identical twins?" Claire asked.

Ellie Quade sighed and then paused a long moment as she looked up at her husband. When she turned back to Claire her voice sounded spiritless. "They're dead."

A dark sadness dwelt on both their faces. Claire had seen the look before in her patients. It was a pain and regret. It laced both their eyes, but Richard Quade's eyes seemed more deeply scarred.

"What happened?" she asked.

Once again, it was Ellie Quade who spoke. "We were all so close, once. Identical twins live a special kind of life, Doctor. You never feel alone. You see yourself as two halves of a whole. And when the other is gone, you feel kind of lost without her."

Claire thought Ellie did indeed have a lost look in her eyes. She wondered how long it had been there. Before she could give it much thought, Richard Quade's mother continued her story.

"Of course, a sister that close can also be a bit of a nuisance where men are concerned. We had some early fights over liking the same boy and such. Elaine always wanted to prove the boys liked her better. Maybe all sisters go through these petty jealousies when they're young."

Ellie's voice faded away into a bittersweet past. Claire sought to bring her back to the present.

"Did the rivalry end?" she said.

"I suppose it would have. I'll never forget when Elaine and I met Richard and Robert. I became so concerned Elaine might mess things up. You see, I knew right away Richard was the man for me, so sensitive and shy. He was very unlike his brother."

"They weren't identical?" Claire asked.

"Physically, oh yes, but not in the important, intangible things. Robert was outgoing and flashy. I could see even from the beginning that he thought himself a ladies' man. He was always talking loud or showing off. Elaine had always been attracted to that sort so I suppose it was just as well. Otherwise, she might have been drawn to Richard, and, well, I don't know what I would have done then. As it turned out, it wasn't Elaine's attraction to Richard that became the problem."

Ellie had stopped at just the wrong spot. Her eyes studied her hands as they lay folded in her lap. Richard Quade Sr. stood stiff and staight next to the chair in which she sat. Claire felt herself on the edge of the couch.

"What was it?" she asked.

Ellie looked at her husband for approval before continuing. He nodded affirmatively and Ellie looked back at Claire. "Everything was okay, at first. We were married in a double wedding ceremony. Richard and I and Robert and Elaine. We even went to the same resort for our honeymoon. Then, at the end of our second week, Robert—"

Ellie had stopped suddenly, obviously uneasy. She looked away from Claire's face and stared at the sea-green carpet.

"Yes?" Claire prompted.

Ellie's voice resumed, slowly, hesitantly. "I had gone back to our bungalow to lie down in the afternoon. I felt sleepy from too much sun. After a while, I was awakened by Richard kissing me. I realized he had left the others to be with me and we made love. Then, he suggested I shower for dinner. When I came out, he was gone. Then a few minutes later, Richard came back.''

From the uneasiness in Ellie's voice, Claire got the picture. ''Only this time it was the real Richard and you found out you had been with Robert earlier?''

Ellie nodded. ''Yes. I was so angry, so ashamed. My Richard understood, of course. He knew whose fault it had been. We both went over to their bungalow and confronted Robert. He denied everything. Elaine started shouting at me, saying I was a liar, accusing me of trying to steal Robert away from her beause I was dissatisfied with Richard. It was a terrible scene. We all said so many horrible, hurtful things. They were not things that could be easily forgotten.''

''So you parted. When next did you see Elaine and Robert?''

Ellie shook her head. ''We never saw them again. Robert took a job in Nevada right after the honeymoon.''

''You never tried to get in touch? To mend the rift?''

Ellie shrugged. ''It was a case of pride. I had too much to forgive my sister's accusations. And then when I found out I was pregnant with little Richard a couple of months later, well the possibility of Richard being Robert's child . . .''

Ellie got up and put her arm through her husband's.

''Richard and I were in agreement to focus our love on the child and to forget any doubts. We didn't want to remind ourselves of Robert's betrayal. Deciding not to see our twins was our way of forgetting the more unpleasant possibilities.''

From their faces, Claire had no doubt that Richard and Ellie Quade still lived with the ''unpleasant possibilities.''

''Your twins never tried to reach you?'' Claire asked.

''No. I finally sent a Christmas card to the address I had for them last. It was when Richard was around eight and started to ask me more and more about his aunt and uncle who looked exactly like Mommy and Daddy.''

''They didn't respond?'' Claire asked.

Ellie shook her head. ''The card came back with a postal stamp, the kind that says Not at this Address. Actually, we only found out much later that they had both been killed before their first wedding anniversary.''

"Killed?''

"An automobile accident.''

"So, they died less than a year after your honeymoon. How did you find this out?'' Claire asked.

"It was Richard. He was so interested in the idea that his dad and I had identical twins that at the age of twenty he went looking for his aunt and uncle. It was then he learned of their deaths.''

"How did he respond to the news?'' Claire asked.

"He was sad they were gone, seemed to genuinely feel their loss, despite what Robert had done. We had to tell him, you see. We had to explain why we never went to see our only blood relatives.''

"I understand, Mrs. Quade. By the way, was Richard always left-handed?''

"Absolutely. I'm right-handed myself, but Richard's dad is left-handed, too. I knew our son was left-handed as soon as he picked up his first spoon. Reached right across the bowl with his left hand. Never a doubt in his mind which hand he preferred. I knew then he was my Richard's son.''

Richard Quade's father did not look happy. He turned to his wife with a look of a long-standing disagreement between them.

"Robert was left-handed, too, Ellie. It was no proof.''

Claire could see Ellie clung to the only belief possible for her to enjoy her son and their lives in general. But Richard Quade Sr. would never know the truth, and not knowing had obviously eaten away at the man for many years. Robert Quade's one afternoon of stolen passion had affected many lives.

Claire rose and thanked the Quades for their time. Ellie Quade walked her to the door. "Why is Richard avoiding us, Dr. Boland?''

Claire tried to smile reassuringly. "Sometimes, Mrs. Quade, we avoid the people we most love because we don't want to burden them with our concerns.''

"Is that what Richard is doing?''

Claire bit her lip, wanting to give reassurance, but feeling her words striking a wrong note. "It could be, Mrs. Quade. It could be."

"WHAT DO YOU MEAN you don't know where she is?" Wyatt said, quickly flipping the folder closed on the dining-room table.

Detective Tom Watson's voice on the other end of the telephone hesitated before responding. "I had my unit behind some trees across the street all afternoon. I know she was home. I kept watching patients we had interviewed earlier come to her door and leave after an hour or so. I could see her letting them in and then out again."

"When did you lose track of her?" Wyatt said.

"It was sometime after five, I think. I had to leave the unit for a few minutes. I was only gone a short time. When I got back, no cars had driven up. It never occurred to me then that she had driven off."

"When did the possibility occur to you?" Wyatt asked.

"Just a few minutes ago the sun's rays fell below the trees and no lights came on in the house. I rang the doorbell, but there was no answer. Then I checked the garage and found the car gone."

"Okay. Hang on, Tom. I'm going to try her number."

Wyatt switched his phone to his second line and dialed Claire's number. After six rings he switched back to Tom.

"Damn it, I'm afraid something's wrong. She wouldn't have left without putting her answering machine on. She would want to know if any of her patients had tried to reach her while she was gone."

"But if she was just expecting to be gone for a few minutes, maybe just a short trip to the store, she might not have thought it was important." Tom suggested.

"You told me you left the unit sometime after five. It's after nine. She's been gone four hours. That's hardly a short trip."

Tom's sigh was audible. "What do you want me to do?"

Wyatt drummed his fingers on the dining-room table as he tried to consider the options. "Stay put. I'm going to make some calls to see if I can find out where she went."

Richard Quade immediately noticed the man in the green car partially hidden by the thick trees. He was glad he had taken the precaution of parking a couple of blocks away. The surveillance on her house underlined the Sheriff's Department's suspicion of her. He almost laughed. Moving soundlessly through the trees, he approached the back of the house unseen. He knew he would be able to leave the place just as easily.

The single-car garage was attached to the house at the back end. He got out his flashlight and shone it into the back window of the garage. The psychologist's car was gone. He turned off the flashlight and moved toward the backside of the house.

He broke the lock on the bedroom window, pushed it open, removed the screen and slipped quietly inside. Each room he walked through was empty. He didn't think she'd be home.

He had tried her by telephone before he had decided to come by. She hadn't turned on her answering machine, which meant she couldn't have gone far. She'd be back soon. He'd wait.

He reached into his pocket for the small packet of explosives he kept there, but his fingers touched nothing but fabric. Surprise quickly turned into anger. Damn it! It must have fallen out when he leaned over the pickup's seat to get the shopping bag. There was nothing else he could do but find something in the house to use. The kitchen was the most likely source.

He didn't risk turning on the flashlight, although the dining-room's drapes were drawn, making it dark and difficult to find his way.

As soon as he reached the kitchen, however, the twilight sky shone through its undraped windows giving plenty of light to see by. He reached into a drawer and pulled out a short steak knife. He ran his thumb along the edge. A little thrill of anticipation licked through him as its sharpness drew blood. Then he heard the distinctive sound of the garage door opening. She was home. He smiled.

Chapter Twelve

Claire left the radio off on her long drive back to Silverdale from Port Townsend. Her mind churned with the information she had learned from Richard's parents.

So Richard was not a twin. He hadn't dealt in fantasy or imagined friends. All of which meant that the emergence of a second personality called Richard Quade was even more unusual. But it had to be what had happened. The personality now inhabiting Richard Quade's body was not the one inhabiting it Monday in her office.

He came to her because he believed he was being menaced by telephone calls from a man he met a year before, a man who he claimed was dead and yet who he also believed to be himself.

And now he wasn't himself at all. He was this other man. No matter how much she had read about multiple personalities, she found this actual experience with one very disturbing.

Her thoughts masked the passage of time and the automatic motions of her driving. When next she took conscious notice of her surroundings, she was pulling into her driveway. She pressed the garage-door opener and watched the large wooden door shudder to a shaky halt.

The trees moaned abruptly in a sudden evening breeze, their shadows dragging grotesque black shapes over her home in the deepening twilight. Suddenly the house's square shape seemed like a crouching wild animal, its windows like black eyes watching her. She felt a primitive foreboding, an incomprehensible urge to back up, to drive away, to seek an inhabited dwelling of light and company.

She looked toward the garage's interior. The light would stay on for a minute and a half more. She sat in the driveway for several seconds, neither going forward nor backward, suspended in an instinctive immobility, almost as though she was waiting for a sniff of the predator's scent so she could tell its direction.

I'm acting strangely, she thought. *There's no reason for this feeling.*

She drove her car into the garage and pressed the button to close the door. The screeching hinges protested as she got out of the car. She unlocked the connecting door to the house and turned on the light before stepping into the kitchen.

Despite the normality of the scene before her, the jumpy feeling remained. Since she hadn't eaten since noon, she decided it must be hunger. She set her purse down and opened the refrigerator.

She took out some leftover chicken and closed the door. But as soon as she put the chicken on the counter, she turned around suddenly when she felt something, like an angry spider biting at the top of her spine. The kitchen stood before her as always—quiet, bright and...empty. She rubbed the back of her neck, finding no spider lurking there, but aware her hands had begun to quiver.

Low blood sugar, she thought. She turned back to the counter and shoved the chicken into the microwave. But as she set the timer to begin the reheating cycle, no amount of self talk could steady her shaking fingers. She pressed the start button.

The microwave came on in a sudden roar in the quiet kitchen. Its noise was deafening. Then, just as quickly, it went off. Silence. Claire stared at the appliance, baffled. Finally she read the programmed time. She had set it for two seconds instead of two minutes. She exhaled an imprisoned breath and shook her head.

But before she could reach up to reset the timer, she heard the other noise. She whirled around, facing the blackened entry into the dining room, her heart hammering the wall of her chest. Several very long seconds passed, but she heard nothing further. Yet she could have sworn she heard a sound from the dining room. Only one way to find out. She would have to go see.

Without taking her eyes off the blackened entrance into the dining room, she reached into the silverware drawer and felt the comforting cool steel beneath her fingers. She pulled out the steak knife and held it tightly by her side as she closed the silverware drawer silently with her hip.

She walked slowly through the bright kitchen toward the dark dining room, her hand at her side. The light switch was just inside the doorway. She would only have to step through and feel the wall. Her foot was just stepping onto the dining-room carpet when a loud gonging jolted through her already stressed senses.

Her body jumped uncontrollably, blood pumping wildly through her overly taxed arteries. In relief she identified the loud terrifying gonging sound as only her front doorbell. She leaned against the whiteness of the kitchen wall for a moment trying to will her heartbeat back to normal. The doorbell rang again, insistent.

She automatically looked at her watch. It was after ten. She certainly wasn't expecting anyone. Another insistent ring. Whoever was there wasn't going away. She stepped into the darkened dining room, switched on the light and walked toward the entry hall.

For some reason, she felt less on edge. Maybe it was because she doubted a burglar would ring the doorbell and announce his presence. She automatically switched on the porch light. Her voice seemed to be her own when she called out. "Who is it?"

"It's Wyatt, Claire."

Claire immediately opened the door, and looked in welcome surprise at the casual shirt, vest and blue-jeans attire of the man before her. His tanned, well developed arms bulged out from his rolled up sleeves. Curly blond hair climbed out of the V-neck of his unbuttoned shirt.

She had found Wyatt elegantly masculine in his business suits. In these casual clothes, he oozed sensuality. Her pulse quickened as she stepped aside for him to enter.

His eyes quickly surveyed her, as though looking for something. She saw them rivet on her right hand. She looked down and realized she was still holding the steak knife.

"Has there been trouble? Who did you think I was?"

Claire shrugged and closed the door behind him. "You interrupted me as I was about to investigate a noise."

Wyatt followed her back into the kitchen as Claire opened the silverware drawer to replace the knife.

"Noise? What noise?" he asked.

But Claire didn't answer his question. She was standing in front of the silverware drawer staring into its contents with a quizzical frown on her face. Wyatt came to stand next to her to see if he could discover the reason for her preoccupation.

"What is it? What's wrong?" he asked.

"The knives. There are only seven knives."

"You have one in your hand," he said.

"Even with this one in my hand, there are still only seven."

"How many should there be?" Wyatt asked.

"Eight."

Wyatt moved to the sink and opened the dishwasher. He moved quickly to the refrigerator and looked inside for the missing knife from the freezer section to the crisper. By the time he had closed the door, he had drawn his gun from a side holster beneath his vest.

"Where did you hear that noise?"

Claire blinked, the full import of his question and her own intangible fears of the last few minutes forming into the very real and tangible shape of a possible intruder.

She pushed the words out of her closing throat. "The dining room. I was about to investigate when I heard the doorbell."

They walked back in, Wyatt leading the way. The now bright dining room was empty. He turned to Claire and whispered.

"Stay here and see if anything's missing. I'm going to check the rest of the house."

As soon as he left, she looked around slowly. She was momentarily distracted as lights kept coming on throughout the house. Then, her eyes searched. She could detect nothing specific, yet she had a strong sense that something wasn't quite right. What was it?

She stood back in the doorway of the kitchen and looked directly across at the small table in the corner of the dining room. It was then she saw it. The cocoa-colored china vase that normally sat on that table was missing.

She walked up to the table, looking around its base, and saw that the vase had fallen onto the carpet. She bent down to pick it up, noticing a chip in its neck. She frowned, instantly puzzled. She was straightening up as Wyatt returned.

"You found something?" he asked.

"This vase fell off the table. It has a chip here. I'm sure it was intact earlier today. Still it doesn't seem possible that its falling was the noise I heard."

"Why not?"

"The thick carpet should have cushioned the noise of the fall."

Wyatt squatted down and ran his finger across the edge of the table. "It didn't fall by itself. It was knocked over. Look here."

Claire followed his pointing finger to the table. A noticeable gouge appeared on the edge where the china vase had impacted.

"Knocked over?" she repeated, a black sickness churning at her insides. "So it hit the table here and that's the noise I heard. I didn't imagine the feeling. Someone was here."

Wyatt nodded as he straightened. "The lock's been forced on your bedroom window. Whoever was here might still be around. Come on."

He took her firmly by the hand, as though he was expecting resistance. That thought never crossed her mind. But she did pause to step back into the kitchen to pick up her shoulder bag.

"Don't lock the door when we leave," Wyatt said. "The crime scene investigators are going to need to get in."

Claire nodded as she laced the strap over her shoulder. Wyatt turned off the porch light before he opened the door. He stood in the doorway a moment, like a bloodhound sniffing for the scent.

"Stay directly behind me. Keep pace. If I tell you to drop, hit the ground and keep rolling over. Got it?"

She nodded, finding the warmth of his hand in hers very comforting and steadying. "Where are we going?"

"Just to my car at the curb. Ready?"

She nodded again and he gave her hand a last reassuring squeeze. Then he wrapped both his hands around his gun and started forward.

It was only about twenty-five feet to the car, but it seemed a lot farther to Claire. She felt the tension vibrating in the man before her like a tightened wire. By the time Wyatt finally handed her into the passenger's side of the white Blazer and locked the door, her breath was coming in shallow sighs.

"Stay put," he said. "I'll be back in a minute." She watched him head purposefully toward the trees on the other side of the street.

Claire leaned back against the seat and tried to remain calm. She wasn't successful. Possibilities kept looming their ugly heads. All those strong perceptions of danger she had tried to fight against had been right. Someone had been in her house when she arrived home. Someone had taken a knife out of her kitchen drawer. Someone had been hiding in her darkened dining room, knocking a vase off a table while he watched her. She shivered.

What would have happened if she had gone into that dining room before the doorbell rang? A vision of a dark shadowy figure with a knife in his hand flashed into her mind. The doorbell must have frightened him away. Saved by the bell. How apt.

Claire was beginning to shake in earnest now. She knew dwelling on things that never happened was foolish. Deliberately she brought to mind the advice she would have given any of her patients: Face your reality, not your imagined reality.

She inhaled deeply. *I am perfectly safe.* She looked at her hands. They were still shaking. Damn it. It was just so much easier to give that kind of advice than take it.

She looked around the interior of Wyatt's car, trying to refocus her thoughts. A police radio and separate telephone competed for room between the bucket seats. He'd obviously made his Chevy Blazer an extension of his work.

She looked up in relief to see him returning from his conference with the driver of the marked Sheriff's Department unit. Its lights had flickered on and it was pulling away from its parked position behind the camouflaging trees. Wyatt unlocked the door of the Blazer and got in, giving her a little nod.

"There'll be another unit along in a minute. Then we'll leave."

"Leave?" she said.

"I'd like to keep you away from the house while the burglary folks dust for fingerprints. Could you use a drink?"

Claire didn't hesitate. "A stiff one."

After about a thirty-minute drive, Wyatt and Claire pulled in front of the end house on a private, dirt cul-de-sac in a hilly area of Port Orchard. The distinctive clank-clank of the old Chevy Blazer engine finally died away as Wyatt turned the ignition key.

He looked over at her. "You've been quiet all the way from your place. Is anything wrong?"

Claire shook her head. "No, I just didn't think I could compete with the old heartbeat of America here," she said as she patted the Chevy Blazer's dashboard.

Wyatt smiled. "Not everyone can afford an Allante, you know."

Claire suddenly felt the need to explain. "It was my husband's car. We only needed one in San Francisco. He liked the idea of a red convertible. It wouldn't have been my pick."

Wyatt looked over at her, a tone of satisfaction in his voice although his expression was barely readable in the darkened interior. "Even from the first I didn't think it would be."

She felt warmed by the approval in his words. They got out of the car and walked up to the house. Claire knew this was his home. An eagerness to see the inside quickened her step.

She always got feelings from people's houses. She smiled as she walked into Wyatt's home of hard-oak wall panels, thick plank floors and warm, fuzzy throw rugs and furniture. It bespoke of a strong solid man who nevertheless had his need for tenderness.

She couldn't help admiring the living room's deep brown, overstuffed sectional and sleek black marble-top cocktail tables, highly polished and spotless. But when she looked over at the next room's enormous cherry dining set, she found it cluttered beyond belief. Papers, files, books and sections from newspapers were strewn all over the table and its eight surrounding chairs.

This closer examination of the two rooms proved a puzzling contradiction of attitude and life-style.

"You live here alone?" Claire asked as she took an offered seat on the living-room sectional.

"Yes. Why?"

"Oh, I don't know. There just seems to be a difference in housecleaning tactics between rooms."

Wyatt moved over to a portable black marble bar in the corner of the living room and fixed a couple of drinks. He looked around at the two visible rooms as though seeing them for the first time. His response didn't come until he had handed Claire what looked like a tall orange juice.

"The dining-room table is where I work, and when I work, I get messy, involved."

Claire disliked psychologists who psychoanalyzed everybody they knew. She strove to keep her professional obser-
vations confined to the paying patients. But she was more
than intrigued by this attractive man and her desire to know
more about him had nothing to do with her profession. That
desire prompted her next question.

"And your personal life is neat and orderly?"

He sat across from her, his biceps flexing automatically
as he lowered himself in the chair, the light from the nearby
lamp playing across the golden tan of his exposed arms and
chest. She was finding she couldn't keep her eyes off him.

"I was married once, Claire. It was a very cluttered affair of two unhappy people full of mismatched needs and
expectations. I've been divorced four years now."

"What happened?"

Wyatt took a large gulp of his drink, watching her face for
a long moment before he answered. "She didn't need me."

Claire's forehead puckered in a frown. "I don't understand."

He shrugged. "After being married awhile, she felt very
dissatisfied with the simplicity of our life. She worked in
Seattle for an advertising company. When her company offered her a New York promotion, promising money, travel
and prestige, she jumped at it. She didn't even ask me if I'd
come with her. She just had her attorney send the divorce
papers in the mail."

He related the story very calmly, but Claire could still hear
the disillusionment between the lines. "Would you have
gone with her had she asked?"

Wyatt shook his head. "Even if she had wanted me to, she
didn't need me to. And I need to feel needed, Claire. It's a
basic part of my nature. Perhaps as a psychologist you'd say
that's neurotic."

He was sitting watching her very closely, a tight, tense half
grin on his handsome face as he waited for her response.
Suddenly she knew her answer was very important to him.

She leaned forward, the words coming from her heart.
"I'd say that's very human, Wyatt. It's in no book I've ever
read, no lecture I've ever heard, but personally I've always

thought that when need reinforces desire, there's no stronger support for love.''

The tenseness eased around his mouth as his fingers moved to capture hers, circling the glass in her hand.

She felt the pull of his look, the tingle traveling through her body at the claiming touch of his hands. As he leaned forward to take the drink from her and place it on the coffee table, she inhaled the exciting scent of his Old Spice, heated from contact with his body. Still holding her eyes with his, he moved to sit next to her on the soft fuzzy couch, drawing her back with him to rest against its yielding fabric.

He began to kiss her hair and then the pink of her ears and the beating pulse in her neck, tenderly, unhurriedly. She moaned in pleasure under his caresses, feeling his passion, beating wildly in the sizzling heat of his touch, yet caged with his controlled concern for her arousal. He was reaching not just for her body, but for her, and the message came through loud and clear.

Surprisingly that message gave her pause and she sat up.

Wyatt felt her body stiffen, and although disappointed, he didn't try to stop her as she moved out of his arms. Something was making her unsure. He'd have to wait. Mentally he could accept the fact, but his body was rebelling quite strongly. He got up and went to stand over at the portable bar and took some more ice cubes out of the small refrigerator, letting them melt in the heat from his palms.

Claire tried to steady her conflicting emotions. Wyatt was handsome, intelligent and caring. Since she had met him the Monday before, exciting thoughts of the big, powerful detective sergeant had continually claimed her attention. Even now as she watched the broad expanse of his back as he stood at the portable bar, her hands ached to touch him and to once again feel him touch her.

He turned as though he had felt her desire pulling him back and she gulped at the heat radiating out of his green-blue eyes. "You understand this is not just physical attraction for me, don't you?''

Claire sighed. "Wyatt, I think that's the problem."

He walked back to the chair opposite her and sat down. He folded his hands together, trying to control his desire to reach out to touch her. He took a deep, steadying breath. "Can you be a little more specific?"

"Wyatt, it's been two years since I've let a man touch me."

He nodded. "Since your husband's death. I can understand how grief can subjugate desire. Knowing the person you are, I'm not surprised."

His hands reached out to circle hers again, his voice so deep she felt it vibrating through her. "But you told me earlier your grief was gone, Claire. And I know you're attracted to me. I feel it even when I look at you. And when I touch you . . ."

Claire quickly pulled her hands away, afraid another minute of listening to the deep sensuality of his voice would deafen even the screams of fear echoing in her ears.

"Your touch reaches inside me, Wyatt, in more ways than just physical. I feel as though I'm losing control with you. I feel as though if I did . . ."

He sat next to her on the couch and pulled her to him. "You might learn to care too much? Claire, I want your feelings to grow for me. I'll cherish them. As long as you trust your feelings and mine, there's nothing to stop us."

She did not relax in his arms. If anything he felt her stiffen even more. "I've trusted before, Wyatt. Both my feelings and those of the person I loved. I lost them both."

He heard the sadness in her voice and something else he couldn't place. "But he died, Claire. You're too level-headed to mistrust your feelings or those of someone you loved just because death ended them. After all, he couldn't help that."

"Oh but he could," her sad voice said.

The message in her words sent a jolt through Wyatt. He leaned back away from her for a moment to see her face more clearly. "Are you saying your husband committed suicide?"

She didn't have to answer. The look on her face told him that and so much more. "I don't believe it," he said.

Her smile was a painful affair. "My very protest at the time. I thought Jerry loved me and we were happy together. He was outgoing, confident, even a bit flamboyant at times. Nothing about his personality bespoke of a depression or pain that would lead him to suicide. At least, that's what I thought. God, how could I have been so wrong!"

He saw the pain on her face. And the doubt. Two years and still it was festering just below the surface, an unhealed wound for which time had not proved a salve. She put her head in her hands, trying to stop the unbidden tears stinging her eyes.

Wyatt suddenly felt incredibly helpless as he watched her pain. He wanted so badly to be able to take it away, but he felt powerless to do so. All he could offer was comfort. He cradled her in his arms and gently stroked the silk of her hair.

When she stopped crying, she moved out of his arms. He wondered with a sudden pang how he could fight this new rival. Vanquishing self-doubt was a very personal affair, and until her self-doubt was gone, he could see she would not be open to a serious relationship. What could he do?

Claire reached for her drink on the coffee table, finding it had a good shot of vodka in the cool fresh orange juice. She summoned all her resolve to put aside her personal failings and resume her professional demeanor. "This is good. Thank you. I've been meaning to ask, why did you come by my house tonight?"

Wyatt reached for his drink, disappointed with her deliberate avoidance of their previous subject. His growing feelings for her wouldn't let him swim away and her shield of doubt prevented him from swimming toward her. All he could do was tread water and hope for an opening. Strange. Her all-too-human doubt had been one of the things that had drawn him to her. Now he was finding it might be the thing that kept them apart.

"Where did you go tonight?"

Claire knew she couldn't tell Wyatt where she had been if she hoped to keep her patient's case confidential. "Just for a drive."

"You were gone for several hours," Wyatt said.

"Yes, I was. What did you want to talk with me about?"

Wyatt finished the rest of his drink and got up to get another. He picked up Claire's glass and it was only then she realized she had finished hers, too.

"Just make the next one orange juice, please," she said.

Wyatt nodded. "I had a talk with your brother this morning. I appreciate your asking him to come see me."

Claire shifted to a more comfortable position on the fuzzy couch. She took the second drink from Wyatt's hand. "I thought it might be a good idea if you and Alan could work together."

Wyatt sat across from her. "He's opened my mind to some new possibilities, but we're not working together."

Claire felt confused. "But if the murderer is the same as the one at the Shipyard..."

"Then I'll have to find him on my own. NIS doesn't collaborate with local law enforcement on areas involving national security."

Claire looked up at his words. He was staring over at her, looking frustrated. She knew he cared for her and wanted their relationship to grow. A part of her ached to say yes. But that other part, the part that doubted, kept her silent.

She felt suddenly weary. She looked down at the drink in her hand. "Then your meeting wasn't of any real use."

Wyatt set his new drink on the coffee table. "Oh, I don't know. Without it, I probably wouldn't have realized the danger you're in, and I doubt whether I would have gotten to your place in time."

She looked up. "You think the murderer came after me tonight?"

"What do you think?"

Claire tried to collect her thoughts. "It can't have been Thayer's murderer. Explosions connect his crimes. The person in my home tonight took a knife out of my silverware drawer. Maybe it was just a burglar who heard me coming home."

Wyatt shook his head. "When burglars panic, they head out the nearest exit, not grab a weapon and hang around. Besides, I don't believe in coincidences. I think someone tried to murder you by that office explosion Wednesday. And since whoever it was missed, he's come back a second time tonight."

Claire took a sip of her new drink as she watched Wyatt finishing his. Thoughts of a murderer stalking her were making her limbs feel numb. She inhaled, trying to keep her voice natural, and not exactly succeeding. "Why is he after me?"

Wyatt shrugged. "You saw something that night in Safeway when Roger Thayer was murdered. It's the only explanation."

Claire leaned farther back into the soft cushions, feeling frustrated. "What did I see?"

Wyatt leaned forward, holding his drink in his hands. "In my office Tuesday, you told me you weren't alone with the dead body of Roger Thayer. Who else was there?"

"I'm . . . not sure," she said. But as she closed her eyes, the blurred movement of a face that seemed to be Richard Quade's flashed across her shut lids. Her eyes popped open and she sat up straight. She felt Wyatt's eyes watching her.

"You've remembered, haven't you?" he asked.

"Not exactly. I keep seeing the blurred face of Richard Quade, but it might just be because I thought he was the dead man."

"You didn't see him in the store that night?"

Claire unconsciously reached for the drink on the coffee table. "No. I don't think so."

"Which is it? Are you sure you didn't see him or are you not sure at all?"

Claire placed the cool glass on her forehead as though she might be able to rest her fevered thoughts against it. "Wyatt, I don't know for sure. God, I don't know anything for sure."

Wyatt watched her, knowing that she wasn't only talking about what she had seen Monday night in Safeway.

The telephone rang from the next room. He got up to answer it.

Claire overheard Wyatt's side of the telephone conversation as a series of affirmative and negative grunts. When he came back into the room, he was frowning.

"Is everything okay?" she asked.

"They didn't find any explosives at your place."

His voice said there was more. "And?"

"Have you cut your hand on your back bedroom window lately?"

"No, why?"

"The crime scene people found a smudge of fresh blood on the sill. They're running a sample to the Seattle lab where they'll DNA code it. When we catch the right suspect, we can match the blood samples and prove he was in your house tonight."

"So it's evidence that's only good to nail a suspect?"

"Yes." Wyatt was staring into his glass.

"What is it?" Claire asked.

"I'm curious why he took one of your knives. Is there some information he wanted to coax out of you? Or did he not want this murder to look like the others."

Claire was getting more than uncomfortable with this candid discussion of her aborted murder. She put her hands to her temples, glad when Wyatt's next question refocused the discussion.

"Psychologically, how would you solve this crime?"

Claire sat back, allowing the question to take her full attention. "Well I think I'd first ask myself why Roger Thayer was killed the way he was killed."

"How do you mean?"

"Psychologically, murderers aren't just ending someone's life. They're ending it in a particular way. Often, the method is as important as the act itself. We know this person is proficient in the use of explosives. Correct?"

Wyatt nodded.

Claire plunged on. "Okay, so this person who knows explosives kills Roger Thayer by blowing up his face. Why?"

Wyatt leaned forward in his seat. "You mean why damage the face and leave the rest of the body intact?"

"Yes."

"Okay, let's say that was intentional. What would be the motive?"

Claire leaned forward. "The reason I'd want to blow someone's face off is because I wouldn't want it recognized."

Wyatt's initial interest seemed to dissipate as he leaned back in his seat. "That doesn't make sense. His right hand was intact. Fingerprints remained for identification."

Claire leaned back and sipped some more of her drink. "I said recognized, not identified. If this murderer did everything for a specific purpose, then he killed his victim in a way which prevented people from recognizing his face and yet enabled him to be easily identified. Why?"

Wyatt stood up and paced his living room, seeming to digest Claire's words. "Yes. Why would that be important? Had the man lived in our community under another name? Had he assumed another identity, one which the murderer didn't want discovered?"

Claire nodded enthusiastically. "His sister told me Roger had escaped from prison almost a year before while he was being transported for medical research relating to high blood pressure. He might have been hiding out under another name all this time."

Wyatt stopped pacing. "Claire, you may have something here. If he had established himself under another identity, there must be people in the community who are missing him since last Monday night. Perhaps I might find a lead in the missing person's file. Just a minute. I think I brought home a routine printout of it yesterday. I'll compare it with his description."

Wyatt strode over to his dining-room table piled high with his work. He reached in a hand. Miraculously it came out holding Thayer's expired driver's license. He read from the description. "Roger Thayer was twenty-eight, five-ten, one-hundred-eighty pounds, curly black hair, light brown eyes."

Claire got up and came to stand next to Wyatt as the similarity of the description poked at her memory. She looked at the driver's license picture of Roger Thayer. There was something about the eyes. She placed her finger over the bottom half of the face on the license, simulating the camouflage quality of a full beard. She gulped in shocked recognition.

"Wyatt, look! My God, that's Richard Quade!"

"What?"

"It's him! Don't you see? Put a beard on this picture of Roger Thayer and he's a dead ringer for Richard Quade!"

Wyatt studied the picture carefully. "There is a similarity, isn't there? Too bad Richard Quade isn't a missing person. Then we'd know what identity Roger Thayer had assumed this last year."

Claire grabbed Wyatt's arms, sucking in a shocked breath as the import of his words registered. The bits and fragments of all the previous evidence revolved in her head like a giant kaleidoscope.

A year ago, Roger Thayer, a smoking man who was shy and gentle with women and suffering from high blood pressure, escapes from custody. At almost the exact time, Richard Quade, a non-smoker who was aggressive with his wife suddenly changes into a smoker who is shy and gentle with his wife and suffering from high blood pressure.

Could it be what she was thinking? Of course. How could it be anything else?

Wyatt turned toward her. "Claire? What is it?"

Her voice rose in excitement. "Wyatt, remember how I described to you the clothes my patient wore? Remember how I told you about the marks on his hand being the same as the dead man's in Safeway? Remember my telling you that's how I knew it was Richard Quade?"

Wyatt shrugged. "We have a positive identification of the dead man as Roger Thayer, not Richard Quade. You were mistaken."

"Was I, Wyatt? Seeing Roger Thayer's picture has helped me to see there's a way for those distinctive marks on the patient I saw in my office Monday afternoon to have been the same as those on the dead man I discovered in Safeway Monday night."

"Claire, what are you getting at?"

"What if it was Roger Thayer who I saw Monday afternoon?"

Wyatt was trying to clarify in his mind what Claire had proposed. "You mean you think Roger Thayer was wearing a beard and pretending to be Richard Quade when he met with you Monday?"

Claire took a deep breath. "Not just with me, Wyatt, and not just Monday. What if Roger Thayer has been pretending to be Richard Quade with everybody for the past year?"

Chapter Thirteen

Wyatt looked at Claire in disbelief. "Do you know what you're saying?"

"Yes, of course I know. Roger Thayer's clothing, the scars on his right hand. He was the man I had seen in my office Monday, just as I originally thought. Only when he came to see me, he called himself Richard Quade!"

Wyatt was shaking his head. "How can that be possible? Richard Quade is alive and well. There couldn't have been two of them."

Claire began to pace. "Couldn't there? No wonder I've been having such difficulty figuring out what was going on. I was treating the case totally like a psychologist and that's what has made it so confusing. When I saw two different personalities, I tried to explain it away as a rare case of multiple personality when the real reason was obvious—I saw two different personalities because I saw two different men!"

Wyatt was shaking his head next to her with his hands on his narrow hips. "I'm not following you."

Claire ignored his faint protest. She wondered at the simplicity of the explanation. Everything fit. A dragging uncertainty lifted from her shoulders as she turned toward Wyatt.

Wyatt heard the new confidence in her tone and saw it shine through the deep blue of her eyes.

"A year ago Richard Quade went on a sailing cruise up the Hood Canal. He met a man, Roger Thayer, a fugitive on the run who just happened to resemble him closely enough to be a twin."

"His twin?"

"Well, not biologically. Quade doesn't have a biological twin. But you've seen the picture. The similarity is uncanny."

Wyatt shrugged. "How can someone look exactly like someone else and not be a twin?"

Claire shook her head. "I don't know. Such a thing would be extremely rare, I agree. But even if there were some minor differences between the two men, the full beard Richard wore would help to cover them."

"How do you know they met last year?" Wyatt asked.

"Roger Thayer told me. At least now I understand that's what he was trying to tell me. You see, last year I think he met Richard Quade by chance and that's when Roger Thayer took over the other man's identity."

Wyatt wasn't convinced. "Assuming all this were somehow true, why would Richard Quade agree to such a switch?"

Claire felt eager to explain. "From what Roger Thayer said to me in my office Monday, a switch wasn't involved. Let me give you the scenario of what I think happened."

She began to pace again. "Two men meet who look identical. They are curious about each other. They spend time together and maybe try to find a possible family link. Then one night Thayer and Quade get drunk while sailing along the Hood Canal. Quade suffers a sharp blow from a sudden repositioning of the mainsail. Thayer, thinking Quade's dead, and being himself on the run from the police, decides to slip his look-alike's body overboard."

"Or kills him and pushes him overboard," Wyatt said.

Claire shook her head. "No, you're forgetting I talked with Roger Thayer. Considering everything he told me and how he told me, I'm sure he didn't kill Quade."

"Okay, I'll concede that point for the moment," Wyatt said. "So Thayer, thinking Quade dead and being on the run from the police, decides to assume the identity of his look-alike?''

Claire smiled at him. ''Exactly!''

Wyatt was still shaking his head. ''Quade had a wife, kids, friends—all people who would be able to detect an impostor.''

Claire continued to pace, as though she was marching the pieces into place. ''That's why he told them he'd been hit on the head.''

''He'd been hit on the head, too?'' Wyatt asked.

''Not really. He only claimed to have had an accident that caused him to lose his memory so that people wouldn't think it odd when he couldn't remember things. Quade had probably shared with him a lot about his life when they talked about their backgrounds. Later, when confronted with a missing piece of Quade's life, all Thayer had to do was claim a convenient amnesia.''

''But how could he keep his job? Bosses aren't particularly keen on having to retrain an amnesiac.''

''That's where his prison training came in handy. His sister, Doris, told me Roger had taken auto mechanics. Quade was also a mechanic. Learning the specifics of Quade's job was probably easy.''

Wyatt was still shaking his head. ''I might be inclined to consider this theory except for one thing.''

''Which is?''

''Richard Quade isn't dead. Since he didn't have a fatal accident about a year ago, where has he been while Roger Thayer has been impersonating him?''

Claire plopped back down on the couch.

''Damn good question. I admit it doesn't fit, but there's got to be an explanation. Maybe he was seriously injured a year ago in the accident Thayer thought took his life. Maybe he was in a hospital recuperating. Maybe he even had real amnesia for a while. You could check that kind of thing, couldn't you?''

''Probably. But what you want me to believe is that after almost a year, Richard Quade comes back, finds Roger

Thayer impersonating him, kills Thayer, and takes over his life again as though nothing ever happened?''

Claire looked at him. ''Thayer told me he was getting threatening calls from Richard Quade. Why couldn't it have happened that way?''

''He told you he was getting threatening calls from Richard Quade while he was pretending to be Richard Quade? Claire, that was evidence. How could you have held it back?''

Claire felt so sure and relieved with the rational explanation of her perceptions that she didn't feel at all upset at Wyatt's redress. She walked over to him and put a hand on his arm, then lifted her head to look in his eyes.

''Wyatt, I've only just realized my real patient is dead and that the information is evidence. Prior to that awareness, everything that was said between Richard Quade, I mean Roger Thayer, and me was under the doctor-patient privilege. Please understand, I could not tell you before now.''

He covered her hand with his, feeling the beat in her pulse quicken as he stepped closer. Her blue eyes held a new sparkle and confidence and he found himself excited by the flush in her cheeks. He brought her hand to his lips, planting a hot kiss in her palm and hearing the sharp intake of her startled breath.

He read the fear in her eyes, so he released her hand. But he couldn't release the huskiness from his voice. ''Okay, Doc.''

Claire's palm felt singed where his kiss still burned. She rubbed it with her other palm, but then both seemed to start burning. She turned away from Wyatt, trying to control her voice and her emotions. ''Now that you know, what do you plan to do?''

Wyatt's voice sounded strained. ''What is it I know?''

''Richard Quade killed Roger Thayer.''

Wyatt shook his head. ''Before I accept that as fact, I need the answers to a few questions.''

''What questions?'' Claire asked.

''Well, for one, why did Richard Quade kill him? Why not just expose him as an impostor? That would have been the logical thing to do and you have contended the murderer was logical.''

Claire's next words sounded as though she was trying to convince herself as well as Wyatt. "He might have killed him out of anger and revenge. Perhaps he had been conscious but unable to communicate when Thayer dumped him overboard. Perhaps he even thought Roger meant to harm him. Pain and suffering often seek scapegoats.''

Wyatt considered her offered explanation. "If Richard did kill Thayer, then he is probably also the man who blew up your office, killed two men at the Shipyard and another in Seattle. Why?''

Claire shook her head and sighed. "I don't know about the Shipyard business or that person in Seattle. But he might have feared me because I was someone who could connect Thayer with him. I remember when I met the real Richard Quade after Thayer's death, he didn't know Roger had come to see me about his threatening calls. Perhaps he was afraid of what Roger had told me.''

"What did Quade threaten on these calls?''

"He tried to scare Roger by pretending to be a voice from the grave. At first he seemed to be trying to get Roger to commit suicide. When that didn't work, Quade said he was going to kill him.''

"So Richard Quade, a mechanic with no previous tendencies toward violence nor any experience with explosives, gets so angry at a man who impersonates him that not only does he kill the man, but he also decides to go after two men at the Shipyard, a Navy lawyer in Seattle and a psychologist in Silverdale? Do you know how flimsy your story sounds?'' Wyatt said.

Claire decided he sounded more frustrated at not being able to believe in her theory rather than arbitrarily not wanting to believe. She reached down for the rest of her orange juice, drank it and replaced the glass on the coffee table.

"There's a rational explanation for the rest somewhere,'' she said. "It isn't because I'm wrong about Thayer and Quade. Wyatt, for the first time in a long while, I know I'm right.''

He looked over at her, hearing the relief in her voice. Before he realized what he was doing, he had closed the distance between them. ''It's been rough, hasn't it?''

Claire looked into his searching eyes and sighed. ''Since the body was identified as Thayer and not Quade, all the old doubts about Jerry have come back. I saw no hint of his torment, Wyatt. For two years I've been struggling under that failure. I thought my perceptions were again distorted.''

She was standing tantalizingly close to him, the light dancing through her red-gold hair, hot and exciting. He was impaled by her beauty, her honesty as she revealed her feelings so openly. He had backed away before because he knew she had wanted him to. Now he reached for her, because he was no longer able to battle against it.

Claire felt his passion flowing through his arms as he crushed her to him. Her muscles went numb as his desire took control of her willing body. She started to speak, but he snatched the very breath from her soul as his mouth devoured hers into a sizzling silence.

She tingled from the heady taste and feel of his lips as her whole body seemed to flow into the kiss, melt in its heat, be consumed by its promise. She clung to Wyatt, totally engulfed with no thought of what had gone before or what was to come. The intense feeling of the moment carried her into a joyful, sublime and sweet insanity. When their lips finally parted, she looked up to see a green-blue fire alight in his incredible eyes.

He pressed her head to his chest, his hands gently rubbing her neck. She could hear the wild beat of his heart.

He didn't speak for a moment, just held her firmly, fighting for control. Then his slightly thick voice came from somewhere above her ear as he eased her out of his arms. ''Preview of the coming attractions should you decide to buy a ticket for the entire show. I'll take you home now.''

Claire swallowed as the warmth of his arms withdrew from around her. She tried to catch his eye, but he had turned to get the keys to the Chevy where they lay on the coffee table. Then he turned toward the door.

He wanted her, of that she was sure. But he was waiting for her to offer more than just the physical part of herself. She wanted to, but could she? Figuring out the relationship between Richard Quade and Roger Thayer had cleared some doubt from her mind, but it wasn't enough. The enigma of Jerry's suicide still remained. Claire stooped to pick up her shoulder bag and followed sadly in Wyatt's retreating wake.

RICHARD QUADE DIDN'T like the idea of giving up on getting the psychologist, but it didn't look like he had any choice. He had gotten away all right tonight, but it had been close.

He doubted whether she'd be going to the cops now with whatever Roger Thayer had told her in his confession session. She'd let too much time pass. Her credibility would be at stake. Besides, it looked like they were watching her pretty closely. No doubt she was suspect number one on their list. He turned his attention to the business at hand.

He had gone into his garage quietly to get ready for the part he was to play the next day. Sally and the twins had gone to bed hours before so he should be left undisturbed. He reached into the front seat of the pickup to get the explosives ready, only to stop and stare. They were gone.

A moment of confusion passed in which his brain searched for possible explanations. The twins had taken them? They had somehow fallen out of the truck? Conjecture turned to certainty as memory inched back. He had taken them out when he had gone to get a new universal joint. When the garage mechanic had driven him back and together they had fixed the truck, he had completely forgotten the explosives he had hidden in the bushes on the side of Highway Three. Damn it, he had left them there.

Richard looked at his watch. It was already almost midnight, but he didn't have any choice. He had to go back to get the explosives. He didn't have enough to do the job tomorrow. Not properly, anyway. He had been so preoccupied with getting his truck fixed and getting to the Boland woman that he had made a mistake.

Damn it, she had ruined his concentration for the last time. If he didn't succeed at anything else tomorrow, he was going to get that psychologist.

CLAIRE'S HAND GROPED for the ringing telephone as her eyelids refused to unlock and help with the search. Once her fingers finally made contact with the elusive receiver, she yawned her hello.

"Hi, it's Alan. Can we get together for a quick breakfast?"

Her left eye worked itself open. The clock on her nightstand flashed nine o'clock, alternating with the date. The red pulsating light felt as though it was stabbing her.

"Breakfast?"

"Come on, sleepyhead. I'll razzle-dazzle you with an award-winning breakfast of my famous pancakes."

Claire yawned again as she forced herself to sit up and coax the other eye open. "And exactly who was it who gave out this award?"

Alan's tone held good-humored shock. "Claire, I'm surprised at you! A gentleman never tells such things."

Claire smiled in spite of her half-awake state. "Humph. I think, my footloose fancy-free brother, that you should have been married long ago."

"And disappoint a large segment of the female population? Never. I'll see you in five."

"Better make it ten. I had a late night."

"Oh? Perhaps it's big brother who should be bringing up the subject of marriage to little sister?"

"No, it's big brother who should get off the phone so little sister can wash the sleep out of her eyes."

Alan laughed as he hung up. Claire's smile at their lighthearted exchange turned into a sigh as she reluctantly threw the covers aside and padded into the bathroom. Despite how late it was, she had only really gotten a couple of hours' sleep. Most of the night she had tossed and turned, reliving Wyatt's mind-melting kiss and embrace.

He hadn't said anything to her when he drove her back to her home in Silverdale. When she had said good-night at her door, he had curtly informed her a deputy would be on watch and then just left.

She knew it was only her doubts keeping them apart. That knowledge gave no comfort.

When she opened the door about ten minutes later for Alan, her hair and teeth were brushed, her face was washed but she had just covered her pajamas with a light blue robe.

"Do you know some deputy just asked me to identify myself outside?" Alan asked.

"Sorry, Alan," Claire said as she closed the door. "I had an intruder last night. Wyatt has taken precautions."

"An intruder? Are you okay?"

His arms reached for her shoulders. Claire wished he wasn't looking at her so intently. "I'm fine."

His expression told her he wasn't convinced. "You don't look too fine, Claire. What happened?"

Somewhere she found a laugh. "Not enough sleep is what happened. Come into the kitchen. I'll tell you all about it while you make our breakfast."

By the time Claire finished getting the coffee ready and Alan was deftly flopping the last of the pancakes onto his plate, she had told him about coming home and sensing an intruder and Wyatt's timely arrival. She had just gotten to the part where Wyatt had driven her to his place when the doorbell rang. She got up to answer it while Alan continued to enjoy his pancakes.

At the sight of Wyatt on her doorstep, Claire's heart skipped a beat. He was clean-shaven and back in a suit, but she was perversely happy to see that he, too, looked just a little tired around the edges this morning.

"I need to talk with you," he said.

It was then Claire remembered she was dressed only in a robe and wished she hadn't opened the door. It was too late to worry over vanity, however. "Come in. Alan's in the kitchen."

Wyatt stepped inside the door as Claire closed it behind him, but he went no farther.

"I know he's here. The detective outside called me when he arrived. What I have to say is for both your ears. Have you told him yet about last night?"

Despite all her self-control, Claire felt the blood starting to collect beneath her cheeks, until she realized Wyatt couldn't possibly be referring to their kiss and embrace. "Oh, you mean about my theory concerning the impersonation of Quade by Thayer."

Wyatt smiled. "What else?" he said, knowing full well what had been on her mind.

"Why, about the intruder in my home, of course," Claire said, happy she had another subject to substitute in place of the one that she knew was really on both their minds.

Wyatt shrugged. "Yes, well have you told him?"

"Only about the intruder. I didn't have time for the other."

"Then let's do it together," he said as he took her arm and led her in the direction of the kitchen.

When they walked in, Alan and Wyatt nodded at each other. Claire and Wyatt sat down at the table and Claire continued her recanting of the previous evening's discussion. When she was finished, Alan put down his coffee cup and turned to Wyatt. "Do you think Thayer impersonated Quade?" he asked.

In answer Wyatt pulled out two eight-by-ten-sized drawings from his suit pocket and handed them to Claire. Alan moved closer to his sister so he could see them, too.

"I had an artist enlarge the picture from Thayer's driver's license. That's the first one. The next picture is Thayer's driver's license drawing with a black curly beard drawn in."

Claire studied both pictures, nodding.

Wyatt handed her a third. "This is a picture of Richard Quade from the State Licensing Bureau with beard intact. It was taken two years ago before the 'accident.' You were right, Claire. This picture of Quade and the altered pictures of Roger Thayer with a beard look so identical, the two men could have done a Doublemint commercial. Yes, Alan, I think Thayer did take over the identity of Quade last year."

Alan got up from the table and began to pace around the room. "And Quade came back and killed Thayer in such a way that no one ever realized the switch had taken place?"

Claire nodded but Wyatt was shaking his head. "No, I think Thayer impersonated Quade all right, but Quade didn't kill him."

Alan sat back down at the table. Claire studied Wyatt's face. It was very sober and very serious. "What is it?" she asked.

"After I brought you home last night, I got to thinking more about what you said. So I did some calling around to emergency stations along the Hood Canal. I got some answers earlier this morning."

The tightness in Wyatt's shoulders had drawn them into a straight line. His hands tensed around the coffee cup. She looked at him expectantly. "What is it? What did you find out?"

"There was a boating accident about a year ago. A man with a blow to the back of his head was fished out of the water."

"Foul play?" Claire asked.

Wyatt shook his head. "It was considered an accident. The body had no identification on it, so the morgue took a set of prints to run a check. Before the prints could be circulated, however, a man came in and identified the body.

"His story was that his brother was hit by the mainsail. He said he had been frantically trying to locate him. The evidence backed up his story. The authorities were satisfied with the explanation and the dead man was cremated under the name of John Luther, a visiting Canadian."

"Was that the only boating accident on the Hood Canal last year?" Claire asked.

"The only reported one," Wyatt said.

Claire shrugged. "Perhaps the one involving Richard Quade never got reported because he saved himself."

Wyatt looked over at her. "He didn't save himself."

"What is making you so sure?" Claire asked.

"The morgue sent me the set of fingerprints this morning from that drowned man last year and there's no doubt about it. That man they fished out of the Hood Canal was Richard Quade, not a Canadian named John Luther."

Claire sat on the edge of her seat. "Richard Quade died in that boating accident? But how could the man have been identified as John Luther?"

"The authorities believed the man calling himself the brother. And it's crazy but the medical examiner there tells me the fingerprint on the Canadian license matched the corpse. He's not a fingerprint expert, but he says he remembers the loop pattern was just too close for chance. That's rare for two sets of prints to be that close. Very rare."

Claire wasn't listening. Her mind had grabbed hold of what she knew was the real import of Wyatt's discovery. When she could speak again her voice had become a hushed whisper.

"If the real Richard Quade died a year ago and Roger Thayer died last Monday night, then who is the man calling himself Richard Quade today?"

Chapter Fourteen

The man calling himself Richard Quade walked past the sign just above the entry to Building 455, which read vertically: Truck Dispatch, Driver Training, Driver Test and Truck Repairs. He looked quickly around the length of the large warehouse structure. As he had expected, no one was in the work area on a Saturday. He reached down to pick up Quade's hard hat and sauntered over to his work station, an old-fashioned wooden work bench with metal legs.

He took out the solutions he had painstakingly mixed, heated and cooled the night before. He had driven far south into Tacoma and broken into a warehouse to steal the sulfuric acid, the nitric acid and the toluene. Since he had lost the explosives shaped like toys on Highway Three, he had had to improvise this new batch of TNT.

Everything was going smoothly, except the guard at the gate had really checked over his vehicle. Fortunately he hadn't hidden the homemade TNT in the truck but in his vest. When he watched the guard record his license plate number, he knew it would be too chancy to use the pickup as his escape vehicle. Now he walked into the supervisor's office to make a call.

"Sally? It's Richard. I'll be home in the early afternoon, and I'm going to need the station wagon then. I've got some errands to run, and I don't want to use the pickup."

"But Richard, I have an appointment with Dr. Boland. I don't know when I'll be getting back."

The muscles tensed in Quade's jaw. "What are you doing going to that psychologist?"

"I . . . just need someone to talk to. Whatever I tell her is confidential, don't you see? No one will know."

"She'll know," Quade said.

He didn't like the sound of it. He'd be taking a lot more chances at the Shipyard today as it was. He had to carry around identifiable TNT instead of what had masqueraded as children's toys because it had been just too dark the night before to find the explosives he had left on the side of Highway Three.

He had to get away when the explosions started, before they knew what hit them, before they could trace anything to him. Then the thought came to him. Maybe he could use Sally's meeting with that psychologist. "What time is your appointment?"

"One-thirty."

"Sally, honey, why don't you let me have that appointment? I could pick up the station wagon first and then go see the shrink."

He waited through a long pause on the other end of the line. "Really, Rich? You mean it?"

Quade's stomach turned at the eagerness in her voice. He tried to keep the contempt out of his voice.

"Of course, honey. We both know I'm the real problem. I've had such rotten luck making my previous appointments, what with the truck breaking down last night and all. What do you say?"

"Of course, Rich. I'm so glad you're going."

"I've got to hang up now, Sally. Don't call the shrink. Let me just walk in and give her a good surprise. Okay?"

"Yes, Rich. I'll see you this afternoon?"

"Right." He hung up the phone and smiled. Everything was going to work out well. By the time they figured out what happened, it would be too late. Finally he would know his revenge.

VERA WARD STOOD in front of Alan's desk at her customary attention. "The President won't be coming next week,

Vera. Not unless we can ensure his safety. A lot's riding on our success. If we don't get these people today, we'll both be looking for new jobs."

"Understood, sir. All of my people are in position. Have you contacted the Criminal Investigation Division?"

Alan watched the masked face in front of him. Absolutely nothing showed, not excitement, not anxiety, not displeasure, not enjoyment. She was like a machine.

"Yes. Barney Coffman has been told. No doubt—"

Alan was interrupted by the telephone. He waved Vera out of his office when he picked it up.

"It's me, Gillette. Can you talk?"

"Yes, Admiral Frost. The lines are secure."

"Has the trap been set?" Admiral Frost asked.

"We should have our pair of assassins today."

"Their identities came as an unpleasant surprise."

Alan exhaled, consciously keeping his voice low although he was sure he couldn't be overhead. "Yes, sir."

"Just get them both, Gillette. The President will visit next Wednesday only if we can successfully conclude this business today."

"We will, sir. Everything will be over today."

AFTER THEIR breakfast conversation, Claire had gotten dressed and Wyatt had driven her to the Port Orchard Detective's unit to record her statement concerning the break-in to her home the night before and her new evidence concerning the information passed to her by both Thayer and the man currently calling himself Richard Quade. Her experience guided her through the interview smoothly.

Watching her long hair rustle loosely around her shoulders, Wyatt remembered how he had been struck by her overwhelming femininity when he first saw her that previous Monday night. But today, even in her summer dress of white lace, he recognized the straightness of her shoulders, the lift of her chin, the steady light in her eyes, the confidence in her tone.

Her initial beauty was now honed by his knowledge of her intelligence and passion for her work, and it was all he could do not to take her in his arms and feel her trembling against him once more, responding to his touch. It was her unrestrained response that had made last night's kiss so devastating. She had melted into him. The hardest thing he had ever done was to step back and release her.

But he had done it. He wasn't going to go through another relationship with a woman whose lack of commitment could lead him to more heartbreak. Those were the thoughts running through his mind as she spoke into the tape recorder giving her statement. Those thoughts and also how the light played along the silky peach nylons that clung to her slim legs.

Her voice interrupted his eyes' journey. "Wyatt, would you like me to wait for these to be typed?"

Wyatt got up to head for the typist. "If you have time. You can sit here in my office."

When he returned a moment later, Tom Watson was in his wake. "I've got it!"

Wyatt sat down in his chair. "Got what?"

"The sealed records on the adoption papers of Roger Thayer. The original paper ones were stolen about five years ago, but these are faxed copies from the microfilmed documents. You're still interested in them, aren't you?"

Wyatt leaned forward. "Of course. Good work, Tom. Let's see."

Tom scooted the file across Wyatt's desk, seeming to notice Claire for the first time. Her presence caused him to retreat from Wyatt's office with a small knowing smile.

Wyatt started to read through the papers but soon became aware of a light, sweet scent reaching his nostrils. Suddenly he felt Claire's nearness invade all his senses and found his concentration gone as he looked up to see a long red-gold curl resting on his suit coat as she stood reading over his shoulder. "Want a chair?"

Claire wasn't listening. "Wyatt, look at this!"

Wyatt was distracted from Claire's nearness, by the urgency in her voice. His eyes traveled to her pointing finger.

"'Roger is the orphaned child of Robert and Elaine Quade.' *Quade*. Yes, I see. Roger started out with the same last name as Richard. Somehow, they must have been related."

Claire had stepped back, as though she felt herself on the brink of a precipice. The faces of Ellie Quade and Richard Quade Sr. flashed before her eyes duplicated a hundred times as though they had been caught in the trick mirrors of a fun house. "And I know how!"

Wyatt turned to her. "You know how?"

Claire felt the excitement raising her voice. "They're first cousins, Wyatt. Richard Quade's parents each were identical twins. And their twins married each other. But a violent disagreement separated the married identical twins soon after the double weddings. Richard was born about nine months later. Roger Thayer, his cousin, must have been born around the same time."

Wyatt was obviously having trouble absorbing everything Claire was saying. "How can first cousins look exactly alike? This sounds pretty farfetched."

"For average cousins, it would be bizarre. But Richard Quade and his first cousin would not be the norm. Consider that genetically they both come from identical parents. That makes them literally genetic brothers. And I've seen Richard's parents. Even they look alike. The possibility that the sons born around the same time to each set of parents looking alike is not farfetched at all. And even if there were some minor differences, the full beard Richard wore would help to cover them. A close resemblance is not only possible, it's probable."

As Wyatt had been listening to Claire's explanation and nodding his head in understanding, his eyes had also been scanning the rest of the information on the adoption papers. What he now read collapsed the air in his lungs. "It can't be!"

Claire grabbed his shoulder. "Wyatt? What's wrong?"

"Listen to this. 'Roger was a month old at adoption time. He and his brother—'"

"Brother?" Claire's voice echoed as her eyes flew to the pages in front of them and she finished reading.

"...were found homes immediately after the automobile accident killing both their parents. Roger was placed with the Thayer family of Carson City, Nevada. Robert was placed with the Seaton family of Vallejo, California."

Claire clutched the edge of Wyatt's desk as she felt her legs go stiff. Her voice sounded so far away it was even faint to her own ears. "Dear God, Roger Thayer had a twin brother. Wyatt, are you thinking what I am?"

Wyatt spoke their thoughts aloud. "There were three of them. Three look-alikes. Twins and a first cousin. Then Richard died and there were two. Then Roger died and there was one. Robert Seaton. He must be the man impersonating Richard Quade. The twin brother of Roger Thayer must be behind all these explosions."

Claire nodded, feeling herself gulping as though it was so hard to swallow all the news. "It seems to be the answer, but what's the reason? How did Robert Seaton learn of his relatives? Why did he kill his own twin brother? Why is he impersonating his cousin?"

"They're good questions, Claire, and I'm going to find the answers for them, starting with a background check and an A.P.B. on this Robert Seaton, alias Richard Quade."

Claire nodded. "May I use your phone? I need to call Alan."

Wyatt smiled as he handed her the receiver.

Claire felt a lift of her spirits at his smile and the warmth in his look. She punched in the telephone number for her brother. Once again a secretary told her he was unavailable.

"Can I speak to Vera Ward?"

"I'm sorry, Dr. Boland. Special Agent Ward is also unavailable."

Claire thanked the secretary and dialed Barney Coffman's number. He answered his own phone this time.

"It's Claire Boland. I've got a very important message for Alan Gillette. Can you get it to him?"

"What is the message, Miss Boland?" Coffman asked.

"I know who the assassin at the Shipyard is. He's a man posing as Richard Quade, a mechanic, but his real name is Robert Seaton. I believe he's Roger Thayer's twin and Richard Quade's first cousin. You don't have to know who these people are. Just please take down the information and give it to Alan as soon as possible."

"I see. And how did you find out this information?"

"That doesn't matter, Mr. Coffman. Please, don't waste time in questioning me now. Get to Alan and tell him."

"Of course, Miss Boland, I will tell Alan. You were right to call, but you must keep this information quiet. Don't tell anyone else or you could be in danger. You understand?"

Claire was reassured that Alan's friend was taking the matter seriously. "Yes, I understand."

She hung up feeling relieved. Alan would soon know. If Richard Quade's impostor was on the Shipyard, Alan would find him and know how to deal with him. He wouldn't be planting more bombs to blow up more people. She turned back to Wyatt.

"He'll be told."

Wyatt was watching her. "We could be wrong."

Claire shook her head. "You know we're not. Since you found out that the real Richard Quade was killed in that boating accident, haven't you tried to pick up the impostor?"

Wyatt shrugged. "We've been watching the Quade house since about eight-thirty this morning. His wife and daughters are at home, but Quade, I mean this guy calling himself Quade, isn't. Do you think Sally Quade has been in on this deception?"

Claire's head shook emphatically.

"Absolutely not. She has an appointment with me today because the changes in her husband this last week have been driving her wild. Frankly, although the death of Richard Quade is going to be anything but easy to take, I think it might be preferable to her continued living arrangement with the one calling himself her husband. Can you protect her if he comes home?"

"Don't worry. This guy will never get inside. She's safe as long as she stays home. When is your appointment with Sally Quade?"

Claire looked at her watch. "At one-thirty. About three hours from now. You haven't approached her?"

"We couldn't chance telling her because we didn't know if she was involved."

"I understand," Claire said. She shook her head in disbelief. "It's incredible to think about what Sally Quade has been through! The woman has lived with three different men in the last year and has thought each one to be her husband. No wonder she's been feeling so confused!"

"She really didn't know they were different men?" Wyatt asked.

"Physically, she thought they were the same man. She noticed the emotional differences, of course. You know, I think of the three, Roger Thayer was the best husband to her."

"The Nevada murderer?"

Claire nodded. "I believe what his sister told me about the extenuating circumstances surrounding his stepfather's death. The boy was provoked."

"Why are you so sure?" Wyatt asked.

"His behavior since. He was the gentlest and the nicest to Sally and the kids, much better than even her real husband. God, I've got to tell her everything this afternoon. You realize that?"

Wyatt nodded. "I'm confident you'll be able to put it to her in just the right way. You're a talented psychologist."

Claire glanced up at Wyatt's encouraging words. The look in his eyes was gentle and supportive. She sighed, feeling suddenly torn and uncertain.

Wyatt got to his feet. "Come on. I'll take you home."

BARNEY COFFMAN SAT staring at the names he had written on the piece of paper near the phone: Richard Quade, mechanic, Robert Seaton, assassin. Finally, he put the paper in his pocket. Yes, it was time Alan learned about Robert Seaton.

Coffman checked his watch. He'd have to start for his position soon. He took a key out of his pocket and walked over to the file cabinet. He unlocked it and reached into the bottom drawer for the briefcase. He drew it out and checked the identification tag near the key latch. It read: Barney Coffman, Criminal Investigation Division. DO NOT OPEN.

Before he left he reached down for the picture beneath the briefcase for one last look. His wife and son smiled back at him. They had been his life and now they were both gone. Soon he would be gone, too. He was sure now the most difficult thing in life was not fighting for its continuance, but finding meaning for it all. He clutched the picture a moment more before replacing it in the file.

WYATT PULLED IN front of Claire's house and waved to Tom Watson in the green Sheriff's unit at the curb.

"I'm going to talk to my detective over there for a few minutes," he said to Claire. "Then, I'll be heading back to the office to see what might have turned up on Robert Seaton's background. I'll call you later if I learn anything. Promise me you'll stay put?"

Claire nodded and let herself out the passenger's side of his white Chevy Blazer. She headed toward the front door of her house, her head down and distracted as she dug for the keys inside her purse. She was still searching as she stopped at the front door.

A faint rustle of leaves in the nearby hedge sent an instinctive quiver of warning beneath the skin along her arms. It was the only one she got. In that fraction of a second her nerves pulled tight and her head jerked up in the direction of the sound. But it was too late! The dark shadow lurched at her from behind the hedge.

Her mouth opened to scream, but a large, cruel hand had already squeezed it shut, while another grabbed at her body, jerking her backward into the hedge on the side of the house.

A blazing fear struck her stiff and immobile as she felt the strong arms dragging her behind the thick bushes. Her heart kicked against her chest wall as the foul breath of her attacker raked across her face. A frantic voice rasped in her ear.

"Don't scream. I'll kill you only if you make me."

Her initial immobility eased as she turned her head to see the side of Arthur Knudsen's fleshy face. Then her muscles tightened involuntarily as she saw the knife in his hand. He was her burglar of the night before! A cold fear leaked into her muscles.

"Remember, if you scream..."

Claire nodded since the large hand over her mouth precluded her answering in any other way. Arthur Knudsen looked at her for a moment and then removed his hand from over her mouth. He slipped his arm quickly around her body, however.

She found herself having a hard time catching her breath, then realized the hard grip Knudsen had on her middle must be crushing her diaphragm. She panted up at him. "Please. I can't breathe."

He let her go but kept a restraining hand on her arm and watched her warily. "Why are the cops here?"

Her breath was shallow. It didn't seem to carry much volume.

"They're after the man who killed Roger Thayer."

"Thayer?"

"The dead man I found in Safeway Monday night."

Knudsen paused. Claire could see he was carefully watching Wyatt and his detective as they conversed at the side of the curb.

"If they're after a murderer, why are they hanging around you?"

"I saw him," Claire said and realized at the same time that she really had. The blurred face she thought was Richard Quade was the murderer, Robert Seaton. She had seen the face while she was falling over the dead body of Roger Thayer. Seaton must have been stooping over the body to steal Quade's I.D. when she came around the corner and tripped over Thayer's leg.

Unreasoning panic laced Knudsen's words. "You're lying. They're looking for me."

Claire tried to regain her voice and imbue it with calmness. "Why would they be looking for you here, Arthur?"

His breathing was heavy. Claire could smell the unwashed sweat on his body. He didn't look like he had shaved for days. He turned to nervously watch the street through a crack in the hedge while he considered her last words.

Claire stood waiting, realizing Wyatt must not have seen or heard her abduction. Soon he would drive away. And if he looked back at her house and she was no longer in sight, he would just assume she had gone inside. She was on her own.

"You better be telling the truth," Arthur Knudsen said. "Where's your car?"

"In the garage. The keys are in my bag."

Knudsen kept looking through the hedge. He gave no sign he had even heard her. "Only one of them is leaving."

Claire heard the frustration in his voice. "If you saw the detective watching the house, why did you chance coming here?"

He looked fully at her then and Claire saw the wildness deep in his eyes. As she heard the anger in his voice, she realized she had become both the focus of his hope and his hate.

"They won't let me near my women or my money. There was no place else to go. *You* dragged me into this. Now *you're* going to get me out, or I'll kill you. Now how do we get to your car without being seen?"

He raised the knife to her throat. He was putting the burden of his escape on her. If she succeeded in getting him away, he might let her live. If she didn't, he would kill her because in his mind, she would deserve it. She read it all so clearly in his desperate face and words.

Her mind groped frantically, trying to think. She felt the knife scraping at the soft hollow in her neck, as though it was reminding her of what would happen if she failed. A frantic thought fought its way through her fear.

"There's a high utility-room window at the edge of the hedge. I've gotten into the house that way once before when I locked myself out."

"What good will getting into the house do? The car is in the garage," Knudsen said.

The knife blade sank perceptibly deeper into her throat. Claire was afraid to swallow. "There's an inside connecting door from the house into the garage. Once in the house, you can get into the garage without being seen by someone outside."

Claire wasn't positive, but Knudsen's grip on the knife seemed to slacken. "Where is this window?"

She raised her hand to point farther down the hedge. "About twenty feet. The hedge will hide our movement the entire way."

His acceptance of her escape method was evident by the push he suddenly gave her shoulder. Claire stumbled forward, trying to regain her balance so she could pick her way through the dense, sharp branches. She felt a million scratches against her stockings and wished fervently she had worn slacks.

It was slow going. The stiff tough limbs beat at her arms and legs and a couple even scraped across her face. Strands of her hair were painfully pulled by stiff twigs she had difficulty avoiding.

When she paused briefly to move aside a branch, she felt her shoulder roughly shoved and the hot stinking breath of Knudsen on her neck. She pushed forward, less concerned with scrapes and cuts now than she was with antagonizing the crazed man behind her.

Finally they reached the small window. It was about five feet off the ground. Claire looked around for the small wooden crate she used to stand on. It had fallen over on its side. She pulled it upright and dragged it beneath the window. She was about to step onto it and begin to work on the latch when she felt Knudsen's hand digging into the flesh of her arm and jerking her away.

"I'll do it."

He stood on the wooden crate dividing his attention between the latch and Claire, standing just inches from the knife in his right hand. His left hand was slow in loosening the latch. It took a few minutes before he was able to work it free. He pushed up on the window frame and it shuffled up noisily on weather-rusted hinges.

Claire stood stock-still, listening for what she hoped would soon be the approaching footsteps of a curious detective on watch across the street. From the look on Knudsen's face, she knew he was listening, too. With each passing second Claire's hope sank. The only sound was the buzzing of some yellow jackets along the outside of the hedge.

Knudsen stepped off the crate and grabbed her arm pushing her forward, positioning the knife at her back. "You go first."

Trying to control her muscles from going numb in fear, she stepped hesitantly onto the crate and reached up toward the sill. She had let herself in this way before, but it wasn't easy. Her elbows didn't reach the sill and raising her body nearly five feet with the strength of her arms alone was difficult.

Her shoulder bag kept getting in the way so she finally pitched it through the parted window. Less burdened, she tried again. When her progress proved slow, she felt several painful pokes of the knife in her back.

It angered her, temporarily pushing aside her fear. She was doing her best. She hadn't asked for her pear-shaped body and she suddenly resented the lack of understanding of her physical limitations that the man beneath her was exhibiting so painfully. An uncharacteristic heat began to pulsate in her body.

The anger fed her strength. Her hands, arms and legs were badly scraped and cut, but she was up and through the window before she realized it. She quickly swung off the ledge and landed on top of the washing machine.

She looked back out the opened window, the anger beating hot against her cheeks. Knudsen had both hands on the sill as he braced himself to lift his body through. In a couple of seconds, he'd be up and in. It was now or never. She didn't hesitate but grabbed the top of the open frame, pressing her total body weight against it and shoving with all her might. The window came crashing down on his hands, still grasping the sill below.

He screamed in pain. She kept the pressure coming, knowing that if she let up before help came, Arthur Knudsen would come through that window and kill her.

It seemed like forever before the detective threw open the door to the utility room. Tom Watson's gun was drawn and he looked worried until he saw Claire literally sitting on the window, keeping it securely pressed against the pinned hands of her now verbally abusive captive.

Tom smiled as he turned the business end of his weapon in the direction of the ceiling. "Detective Watson, Dr. Boland. Perhaps you remember me?"

Claire returned his smile. "Yes, of course, Detective Watson. You'll forgive me for not getting up? I'm trying to...stay on top of things at the moment."

"HOW IS SHE?" Wyatt said as Tom filled him in on the events immediately following his departure from Claire's house.

"Great. She's a gutsy gal. Had Knudsen in tow by the time I broke through the living-room window. All the screaming I heard turned out to be coming from him."

Wyatt seemed only partially relieved. "How did he get in?"

Tom shrugged. "He grabbed her when you brought her home, before she could get into the house. We were so busy talking, I didn't notice. I mean, who would have thought he'd take her almost right under our noses?

"Anyway, he held a knife on her and tried to sneak into the house by climbing through the utility window after you'd gone. That's when she proved to be a bit too much of a 'pane' for him."

Tom laughed at his own pun. Wyatt still wasn't finding anything funny in the situation. "Where's the knife?"

"One of the deputies spotted it outside the window where Knudsen must have dropped it. He left it there for the crime scene investigators. They'll be finished in a few minutes."

Wyatt's tone was still agitated. "Where is she now?"

"In the kitchen. She got the deputies a couple of cold drinks and I took her up on the offer of a cup of tea. She's in there brewing it now. You know, Wyatt, I like her. She has a way of looking straight at you that makes you feel like she's really seeing you, not just looking through you like most people do." Tom smiled at him knowingly. "Of course you've noticed that no doubt?"

"No doubt," Wyatt said as he left his detective and went back to the kitchen to see Claire. The teapot was puffing away on the electric stove. She was standing by the sink washing her bare forearms, which he could see were covered with tiny cuts. The running water must have drowned out the boiling water sounds.

He stood within the doorjamb for a moment and watched her wince as the water stung the open wounds. He must have made an involuntary sound, because she turned partially toward him. It was then he saw the dried blood from the sharp gash across her cheek.

"You're hurt." At some level he realized the voice was his. Without thinking, he moved over to the paper towels and pulled one off the roll. He rinsed it under the flowing water, spilling into the sink, and gently patted the dried blood off her cheek.

Wayward strands of red-gold hair fell around her shoulders. He removed a clinging hedge leaf from one gleaming lock as he continued to dab at the crusted blood. Her face was upturned to his, her deep blue eyes soft and searching.

"Wyatt?" It was Tom's voice. Wyatt tore his eyes away from Claire's and tried to focus on the face of his detective who had just entered the room. He put the used towel on the counter.

"What is it?"

Tom looked apologetic. "We're ready to take Knudsen down to the station, unless you want to give me enough time for that cup of tea?"

Wyatt walked over to the stove and turned off the heating unit under the teapot. "Teatime can wait. Process Knudsen. We'll be along shortly. Keep a unit across the street, and get someone back here to board up that picture window until it can be repaired."

Tom nodded as he left. As Wyatt turned back to her, Claire turned off the water. She patted her arms dry with a dish towel in the suddenly quiet kitchen. "Do I have time to change?"

At first Wyatt didn't understand. Then he looked down at her dress. Its delicate white lace was torn and soiled and her stockings were ripped and bloody. He remembered sitting in his office less than forty-five minutes before, admiring her smooth legs in those peach stockings. A helpless anger gripped at his insides, crying out for action. He closed the distance separating them and scooped her up in his arms.

He was aware on some level that she hadn't resisted his picking her up, but what he was most aware of was the incredible feel of her soft and safe in his arms and the continuous string of cursing in his ears. In some surprise he realized it was his cursing.

He made directly for the bathroom. Gently, he set her down on the rim of the bathtub and reached over to turn on the faucets, letting them run until they reached the right temperature. He knelt down beside her and began to pull away the strips of torn stockings from her scraped legs, gently loosening the dried blood with the warm, flowing water. Gradually he could hear his cursing subside as he bathed her legs with his bare hands, carefully, lovingly. She hadn't said a word.

When he reached for a soft white towel to pat the moisture clinging to her freshly washed skin, he looked up to see tears in her eyes. His heart squeezed inside his chest as his hands dropped the towel and cupped instead around her shoulders. "Oh Claire, did I hurt you?"

She reached out a hand to touch his face as much more than tears glistened in her eyes. Her voice swept inside him. "No, and I know you never would. Oh, Wyatt, please hold me."

His arms were instantly around her as he leaned over to kiss a tear escaping onto her cheek. His lips traveled over her closed eyes and her forehead and her nose and the indentations beneath her cheeks, tenderly, lovingly. By the time he reached her parted lips, they were moist and trembling and seared longingly into his.

He pulled her closer, reveling in her uninhibited response, her arms about his neck, her fingers running through his hair, her hands pulling him closer as he carried her into the bedroom.

Claire was conscious of every caress of their lovemaking, every deep, breathless kiss. She found such awareness a new experience. Even with Jerry there had been that moment in their joining when her body's desire had become mindless. But not with Wyatt. He was her conscious focus every passionate, pleasure-filled second because she was his. For the first time, she felt she had truly made love to a man and had been made love to without even a thought for the physical act it involved.

The experience was so exhilarating, she found she couldn't find the words to express it afterward as she lay happy and fulfilled in his arms. She opened her mouth to tell him, but the words wouldn't form, so she just curled complacently against him.

He held her closely, as though somehow she might slip away. "I love you, Claire. You realize that, don't you?"

She smiled as she brushed her fingers through the blond curls hugging his chest "Yes. You've just shown me in a most unforgettable way."

"I want to show you in all ways, every day for the rest of our lives."

Claire shifted in his arms as worrisome memories tugged at her. "I've told you about the doubts Jerry's suicide have brought me. Those doubts are not easily erased, Wyatt. I'm not sure I can believe in a love that will endure."

He was quiet for a moment before he drew away and got up to dress. Claire looked over at the disappointment on his face as he buttoned his shirt, feeling a new sadness grip her heart.

"Wyatt, do you understand?"

He finished tucking his shirt into his pants before responding. "I understand you're not giving us a chance because Jerry's suicide has made you think the love in your marriage wasn't real. Now you're afraid to believe in your feelings or mine. But I need your belief and commitment, Claire. I need a woman who needs me."

He leaned down on the bed and bent over to kiss her lips, the passion in his touch making them full with desire. "This is real. These feelings that bind us together. Whatever caused Jerry's death is past. Let it go. Otherwise, I'm the one who'll have to go."

Claire saw the waiting expression in his eyes as she battled with her internal doubts. She wanted so much to give him the reassurance of her love. But she felt confused and uncertain. The pain and disappointment in his expression told her he was accurately reading her hesitation. She was almost happy when the sound of the telephone exploded into the uneasy quiet, allowing her to refocus her thoughts. She answered the phone and then handed the receiver to Wyatt.

Wyatt heard Tom's agitated voice on the other end of the line. "Wyatt, can you come down here right away?"

"What's up?"

"We've got trouble. A guy just walked into the station with a sackful of explosives."

Chapter Fifteen

Wyatt sat down in the white wicker chair next to Claire's bed as he put on his shoes and listened to Tom's voice.

"Okay. Keep him there. I'm on my way. Have you arranged for the repair on the front window here?"

"We've got a carpenter coming in a few hours. A unit will remain in front until he gets there. Are you going to bring Dr. Boland in for her statement?"

Wyatt's eyes traveled over to the mass of red-gold curls staining her pillow. Her head was averted and he sensed she needed time to herself.

"It can wait. I'm more interested in talking with this guy with the explosives first. I'll send a car around for her later. Give me twenty minutes to get there."

Wyatt hung up the phone and turned to Claire.

"I have to go back to the office. I'll phone you later."

She nodded and raised her head. He moved toward the bedroom door, turning back at the last moment to look at her. Her eyes watched him, large and luminous and filled with uncertainty. He didn't know what more he could offer to help extinguish her doubts. He turned and left with a heavy heart.

ROBERT SEATON DROVE slowly past the contingent of Marines as they circled the ships. The *Nimitz* sat on the keel blocks in Dry Dock Four, waiting for its refueling preparations. Its two pressurized water-cooled nuclear reactors had been shut off long before coming into port. Still, all that was needed was a detonation to rupture the reactor vessel and hull of the ship to disperse the radioactive fuel into the environment.

But that wasn't his job. His base contact would be taking care of that part. He turned the pickup toward Dock One where the *USS Wichita* lay. His Navy duty told him she was an AOR, an Auxiliary Oiler Replenishment vessel. The *Wichita* had pulled into port for repairs two days before when she encountered problems with her navigational radar. His forged identification had a name that was on her Access List.

It should be easy for him to get on board, wire a clock to the TNT then make it to the gate before she blew. The explosion would divert attention to the AOR. It would be precisely the diversion needed for his contact to get on board the *Nimitz* and set the bomb. Today was the day they would make history.

CLAIRE FELT restless as she paced through her house waiting to hear from Wyatt. She had put on shorts and a tank top to avoid irritating the many cuts on her arms and legs that were stinging like mad. But her real discomfort was the slow passage of time since Wyatt left.

She looked out the window at the overcast sky, but her mind was on the pleasant memories of lying within Wyatt's arms. As the minutes ticked by and she relived their time together, she knew she loved him. She hadn't wanted it to happen, but she couldn't help it.

Expanding clouds challenged one another as they crowded the sky. She could feel the moisture in the air and wondered if a summer rainstorm was on its way. Everything smelled so alive. Her love for Wyatt was awakening all her senses. She longed to be outside in the midst of nature, feeling a part of its miracles.

She looked at the clock ticking away on the mantle above the flagstone fireplace. Sally Quade wasn't due for another twenty minutes. Why not take a walk? No sooner was the thought in her head then she was turning the answering machine on and heading for the back door, keys in hand.

BARNEY COFFMAN HURRIED unnoticed through the chaos that had ensued after the explosion on board the docked *Wichita*. Bodies scurried around Dry Dock One like frightened ants. But not him.

He headed directly for Dry Dock Four, where the multipurpose aircraft carrier *Nimitz* sat. Two Marine guards raised the business end of their M16's as he approached the Navy guard to sign-in on the log sheet. He had his identification card ready.

"I'm Chief of CID, investigating a threat made against the nuclear reactors on board."

The Navy guard checked the identification picture over carefully and then handed it back to him. "Everything's in order, sir."

One of the Marines spoke up. "Sir, do you know what that explosion was just now?"

Coffman waved the Marines aside as he boarded the Nimitz. "Don't let it concern you. Just maintain your post here and let no one pass."

"Do you need any help, sir?"

Coffman gestured at the briefcase he carried. "I have everything I need." He turned and made his way aboard the ship.

The immensity of the ship immediately dwarfed Coffman. When fully manned the *Nimitz* had one-hundred and fifty-five officers, two-thousand nine-hundred and eighty-one enlisted men and two-thousand eight-hundred assigned to the air wing. Fortunately he had studied its interior design thoroughly during the past week, preparing himself for his mission. Now he knew exactly what deck and passageways he would take to reach the reactor compartment.

The few sailors he passed paid him no attention. It wasn't until he was at the entrance to the reactor section that he was challenged at all. The guard on duty stepped into his path.

"Sorry, sir. No unauthorized personnel past this point."

Coffman flashed his red badge. "I'm the Chief of CID."

The sailor maintained his position. "I'm sorry, sir, but I can't let you pass."

Coffman felt the sweat on his spine. "Look, sailor, a threat of sabotage has been made against the reactors. I must check it out immediately. Now step aside."

"I'm sorry, sir, but nobody goes past this point without a dosimeter. In the event of any radioactive leakage, it's the only way we can be sure you haven't received a critical dose."

Coffman's tension eased as he reached into his pocket and pulled out the radioactive-measuring device that he had forgotten to wear. He clipped it on his pocket. "You're quite right, sailor."

The guard checked the dosimeter, then he stepped aside and Coffman entered the reactor area.

He worked feverishly, not bothering to take time to even check his watch. Seaton had supplied him with an extremely powerful shape charge—one that would explode inward toward the reactor and outward to rupture the hull. He was just about to press the final button when the voice behind him made him jump.

"It's all over, Barney."

Strong arms grabbed Coffman's shoulders and wrists and dragged him to his feet. The two Marines who had admitted him aboard the *Nimitz* were on either side of him.

"Alan, what is this? I was just trying to deactivate this bomb. Vera Ward called me ten minutes ago about the sabotage."

Vera walked into the room as though on cue. Her face wore its characteristic marble countenance. "I made no such call."

Coffman turned to Alan as perspiration began to bead on his skin. "She's lying. She planted this bomb and sent me to disarm it so as to implicate me in her sabotage."

Alan shook his head. "The Marine guards were wired. So was the sailor guard to the reactor compartment. Over there is the camera we planted in here so we could watch you take the bomb out of your briefcase and prepare it for detonation. We've got you cold."

Barney looked from Vera to Alan. "It's not what you think."

Alan watched him as though he was a painful sight. "Vera found the map to the nuclear reactor of the *Nimitz* locked in your desk along with the biographies of seven men—the men who sat on your son's court martial five years ago, including the trial judge, Commander Frank Hotspoint, the prosecuting attorney, Lt. Commander Paul Carroll, and senior board member, Commander Antonio Corson."

Barney's look was defiant. "What does that prove?"

Alan continued. "We also have the airline verification for your round-trip ticket to D.C. last week when you killed Commander Hotspoint. The other two men were killed here and you planted the bomb in the Captain's corridor to throw suspicion off the real targets. No doubt you were counting on getting the final four men today when they came on board the *Nimitz* at noon for an officer's briefing. You knew they'd be here because you tapped the phones."

Barney's face lost its mask and became harsh and unbending. "They deserved to die!"

Alan shook his head. "No, Barney. They were doing their duty."

"Duty? What do you know about it? My boy was only trying to show the necessity for PALs. He wanted to show how command of a nuclear ship could be taken over! Vera, you must understand."

Vera shook her head. "I'd never understand incitement to violence. Your son tried to get other sailors to physically overthrow their officers in an attempt to undermine military command. His actions were mutinous."

Barney's voice quivered in anger. "Mutinous? Never. The charges of mutiny were trumped-up by a vindictive command."

Alan stepped forward. "The record shows your son, Larry Coffman, conspired with a fellow seaman, Robert Seaton, to incite the entire crew of the *Nimitz* into seizing the ship. Forty sailors testified to those facts. How can you say command was vindictive?"

"My boy was doing what he felt was right. That court martial sentenced him to Ft. Leavenworth for four years!"

Alan shook his head. "According to military law, that court martial was lenient."

"Lenient? He died in that hole. They murdered him!"

"No, Barney. He was killed when a steam generator exploded. It was an accident. The Navy was not responsible."

Barney's face got red. "They were responsible! He never would have been there if the Navy hadn't jailed him. You didn't have to see his body blown apart. You didn't have to tell his mother how her son had died. God, it killed my wife!"

Alan took a deep breath. "I know you and your wife suffered, Barney. But how could you have thought these deaths would bring you peace? You were about to release radioactive waste, for God's sake!"

"It was to bring attention to my boy's murder, to the danger of operating without PALs! Even if this explosion killed hundreds, it might have saved millions! The President would have been forced to withdraw support. The Navy would have been forced to accept protection devices!"

"Barney, this bomb has nothing to do with nuclear weapon deployment. You were trying to deliberately expose employees of this Shipyard to deadly radioactivity."

Barney's watery eyes looked crazed with pain. "What's the use of talking to you? Only Robert Seaton understands. Only he knows how much my boy suffered."

Alan shook his head sadly. "How did you get mixed up with Robert Seaton?"

"He was my son's good friend. They took on command together aboard the *Nimitz*. He was there on that day the steam boilers blew and killed my Larry. His prison term was over a month later. He began to plan for the retribution. He explained to me how he would impersonate a close blood relative. He had been an explosive expert before getting duty on the *Nimitz*. He knew his stuff."

"He came to you? It was his idea?" Alan asked.

"Yes, six months ago when my wife died. He had it all worked out. Told me about the opening at CID. From my position there I could coordinate all the details. He was really angry about Larry's death, the way they were both treated at the court martial. He was a real friend to my boy."

"A real friend, Barney? I very much doubt it. You don't know his complete background. He was kicked off Trident subs because of an unexplained explosion that killed an officer. Many on board believed Robert Seaton deliberately set the explosion because the officer had disciplined him. He's a vindictive man, Barney. But command personnel couldn't prove he was at the back of the explosion so they got rid of him. That's when he went to the *Nimitz* and started inciting trouble there with your son."

Barney's lips folded in tightly. "You're making that up."

Alan shook his head. "Barney, Seaton used your sorrow for your son to serve his own revenge. He waited until you were most vulnerable, right after your wife died. Can't you see that?"

Tears waded into Barney's eyes. "I watched my wife die of heartbreak after Larry's death. They made the innocent suffer, too!"

Alan shook his head. "What about the captain's driver who was killed with Commander Corson? What about the innocent people you were about to kill today on board this vessel and the hundreds, maybe thousands you were ready to expose to an overdose of radiation? No, don't talk to me about innocence, Barney. It's not a word I think you understand. Take him away, men."

Alan turned to Vera. "Still no sign of Seaton?"

"No, sir. There's no doubt that he was responsible for the explosion on the *Wichita*, however none of the gate guards passed him through on Richard Quade's I.D. I don't know how he got in."

"Well it's a good thing we knew the *Nimitz* was their real target or they might have succeeded in diverting our attention. When the computer linked up the deaths of Corson, Hotspoint and Carroll to Robert Seaton and Larry Coffman's court martial, I knew then our inside man had to be

Coffman. But until you found the *Nimitz* map and those files in Coffman's office, we had no proof. Good job.''

Vera's face almost smiled. ''Thank you, sir.''

Alan shrugged. ''The gates were closed right after the *Wichita* explosion. Do you think Seaton is trapped inside the Shipyard?''

''If he is, sir, it's just a matter of time before we find him.''

Alan's frown returned. ''And if he isn't?''

ROBERT SEATON CONGRATULATED himself on exiting the main gate of the Shipyard not more than two seconds before the explosion on the *Wichita*. Immediately the gate was barred behind him. He had timed it perfectly. He drove directly to Richard Quade's house. He didn't want Sally to see him so he parked his pickup on the next street in back of some large fir trees. It would be a while before someone noticed it. By then, he'd be long gone.

He walked confidently up the street in the direction of where the house stood on the next block. The station wagon was always parked in the front. He had his own set of keys for the wagon with him. He'd just get in and drive away.

But as he turned the corner, he stopped dead in his tracks and then quickly moved to the cover of the trees on the side of the street. Just a few feet in front of him, in the same fir trees he walked alongside, three Sheriff's Department patrol cars were parked. His house was staked out. How did they know?

The psychologist. She must have talked after all. Damn it!

He had been lucky. If he had driven up in the pickup as he had originally planned, they would have grabbed him. Angrily his fists dug deep into the pockets of his vest. He felt the wooden handle and brought out the steak knife. It gave him an idea.

He'd go back to the pickup and drive to the psychologist's house. He'd take care of her and then escape in her car. The only tricky part would be getting in if the cops were still watching the house. But he'd think of a way.

"When did this guy with the explosives come into the station, Tom?" Wyatt said as he leaned forward in his office chair.

"Soon as I got back from processing Knudsen."

"This is incredible. Have you called John Sanders?"

"Yep. He's on his way," Tom said.

"Well, what do we have on this Timothy Shutz?"

"Nothing. He owns a local paint store. Looks legit."

"So how did he know the toys were made out of explosives?"

"When he served in Vietnam, he worked a lot with plastic explosives. The bottom of the toy plane hadn't been painted. When he saw what the kids were playing with, he nearly had a coronary. He confiscated the 'toys' and came in. He's sitting in the waiting room now eating his fingernails for lunch."

"Could this be the same type of explosive that took out the doctor's office?" Wyatt asked.

"Plastic explosive is plastic explosive, isn't it?"

"I don't know. John Sanders has got to tell us, I suppose. He better get his behind in here quick. God, it's got to be. How many lunatics do we have running around setting off explosives? Where did Shutz say the kids found these 'toys'?"

"In the bushes off Highway Three. The kids were playing there this morning when they saw a paper bag in the bushes and decided to investigate. The toys were in it."

Wyatt got up and began to pace. "Why? Why would he stash them there? It doesn't make any sense."

"Maybe somebody was after him?"

Wyatt shook his head. "Who? Until Claire put some pieces together last night, and we got that adoption report, we didn't know who we were looking for. Now, at least we have a physical description and the name he's using. Damn, Tom. We've got to think this through. There's got to be a logical answer."

Tom sat down in the chair opposite Wyatt's desk swinging a plastic bag in his hand.

Wyatt was watching the motion. "What have you got there?"

Tom looked at the bag as though he had just realized he had it. "This? Oh, it's the knife the crime scene guys picked up outside Dr. Boland's utility window. I thought I'd give our fingerprint expert a chance at it before sending it to Seattle."

Wyatt reached over for the bag. He looked at the curved hunting knife closely. "This isn't a steak knife," he said.

Tom looked confused. "I never said it was."

Wyatt was frowning. "Are you sure this is the knife Knudsen used on Claire?"

Tom nodded. "What's wrong, Wyatt?"

"Since Knudsen attacked her today with a knife, we've all been assuming he was the one in her place last night. But this isn't the right knife. What if her intruder wasn't Knudsen?"

Tom shrugged. "Who else could it be?"

"What if it was the guy who blew up her office?"

"But he'd use explosives, wouldn't he?" Tom asked.

"Unless he somehow lost them on Highway Three." Wyatt leaped to his feet. "I shouldn't have left her alone, Tom. He's out there and he's after her. Get on the phone and alert the deputy watching the house. Then call and warn her. I'm on my way."

Tom didn't have a chance to answer. Wyatt was already out the door.

ROBERT SEATON WATCHED the lone deputy on duty, sitting in his marked green car across the street from Claire's house. His car phone rang and the deputy picked it up. It was while he was talking on it that Robert Seaton quietly picked up the large rock and circled around to the back of the car. At the moment the deputy hung up the phone, Seaton struck him hard. He fell over the steering wheel with a barely audible grunt.

Seaton made his way to the back of the house, looking into the garage window. The car was there. He could hear the telephone ringing inside the house. After two rings it stopped. She must have answered it. He forced the window lock at the bedroom again with a feeling of déjà vu, but he knew this time he would get her. This time she would not escape.

Slowly, quietly he searched each room, but she was nowhere. Then he saw that her answering machine had been turned on.

He looked at his watch. It was one-twenty. She'd have to be arriving home soon. Her appointment with Sally was for one-thirty.

But Sally and the house were being watched. Had Sally been told about him? Probably not. They'd have a hard time believing the woman hadn't known someone else was posing as her husband. Unless the psychologist knew and told them?

He reached for the phone. Sally answered on the second ring.

"It's Richard. I'll be at the psychologists's house in a few minutes. I just thought I'd call to tell you I won't need the station wagon after all."

"Oh, okay. I'll take the girls shopping then. Is there anything special you want for dinner?"

Her voice was the same. No anxiety. No fear. Seaton knew the police hadn't talked with her. Sally Quade was no actress.

"No, why don't you and the girls just stay home and relax. I'll bring home dinner tonight."

"Really, Rich? That would be so...nice."

He hung up, not feeling he had the stomach to reply to such slush. Seaton looked around and saw Claire's shoulder bag sitting on the bureau dresser in her room. He reached for it and dumped its contents on her bed. She couldn't have gone far, but wherever she had gone, she had taken her keys with her.

He began to pace in agitation. He wouldn't be able to kill the psychologist right away. He'd have to find out first what she told them. He felt again for the knife in his pocket and smiled.

CLAIRE WANDERED contentedly through the forest of fir and spruce around her home. She leaned against a tree, two-hundred years thick, and closed her eyes, trying to experience the woods with all her senses. The faint odor of a wild honeysuckle carried on the breeze. The leaves were beginning to rustle, heralding in a weather change, and she could feel the damp air cloaking her skin.

Somewhere a slender bark of a swaying tree moaned happily as it rubbed up against its neighbor. She looked up just in time to see a chipmunk drop a nut from its overfull cheeks as it leaped from branch to branch. She smiled, feeling in tune with her surroundings and basking in the warmth of her love for Wyatt.

He had told her he loved her. He had made it clear he wanted her for a lifetime. Her heart swelled in memory.

A big black shadow suddenly swooped down into the clearing, yelling out its raucous call. Claire felt herself tense as the crow came to rest on the soft, mossy earth in front of her feet. Its rapid descent and unearthly cry seemed so out of place in the peace and harmony surrounding her.

Just like your doubts, a small voice inside her said. And suddenly she knew it was true. She had been allowing her self-doubt to fly into all the most treasured parts of her life bringing shadows to extinguish the light of joy. Why?

Because she'd never know why Jerry killed himself. Did she really want to live with that pain forever? *It's your choice,* the voice inside her said, increasing in volume.

And suddenly she realized it really was her choice. She had come to a crossroads. She could continue worrying over the reason for Jerry's death, or she could finally put it aside and offer the love in her heart to Wyatt and accept his in return to build a new life together. And now that she saw her choice clearly, her future also seemed clear.

With a wave of her hand, she shooed the black bird away.

With its exit, the kiss of a cool breeze suddenly swept through the clearing and raindrops began to pelt the top of her head in a fervent baptism. Feeling brand new and reborn, Claire's heart smiled as she turned back to the house.

STANDING AT THE kitchen window, Seaton watched her exit the woods. So that's where she had been. The rain shower must be bringing her back to the house. He could see she was holding something in her right hand. Yes. It was the keys. He'd have his fun questioning her and then he'd escape in her car. He willed her to walk faster as his thumb played with the sharp blade of the knife.

CLAIRE KNEW if Sally wasn't due, she might have gone on walking in the summer shower. She felt so alive and cleansed. Love. What a wonderful, happy, rejuvenating emotion! How lucky she was to have it in her heart again. Suddenly she couldn't wait to phone Wyatt and tell him her doubts were gone. She quickened her pace.

The raindrops fattened as she headed in the direction of the back door. Her head raised to a sudden blinding flash of lighting, striking like a sword through the house. Claire stood transfixed, her feet anchored to the ground as a deadly chill grabbed at her spine. Illuminated only in that split second of the lighting strike was the dark silhouette of a man standing at the kitchen window. She couldn't move. As the thunder crashed all around her, Claire's heartbeat thudded back like an echo chamber.

She knew instinctively it was Robert Seaton and he had come for her. He was just waiting for her to come inside so he could kill her. She stood under the now pouring rain immobile with fear.

She wanted to run, but reason prevented it. If she were to turn tail now, he would know she had seen him and he would come after her. No, she had to be smart about delaying coming inside.

Then she remembered the deputy left on watch at the front of the house. All she needed to do was circle around to the front and gain his attention. What ruse could she use?

"Here, kitty, kitty," she yelled out loudly over the increasing sounds of wind and rain as she bent down and slowly moved in the direction of the house's corner. "Come on, girl. Let me pick you up so we can both go inside and get warm and dry. Come on."

She kept her eyes purposely on the corner of the house as she headed toward the nonexistent cat, continuing to call out. Then she deliberately changed the tone of her call. "Oh, bad cat! Don't run away. Come back here! I'm getting soaked in this rain. Now come on. You've got just one more chance."

As she called out her last admonishment to the phantom cat she circled the side of the house and broke into a run, no longer able to contain her fear. Her heartbeat pounded in her ears as her shoes sloshed into the wet leaves strewn across the grass. She headed directly for the deputy's car, not daring to look back at the house, feeling the chilling rain streak down her face.

Her pulse was pounding in her ears by the time she had reached the Sheriff's unit. She was bothered by the fact that the deputy still sat behind the wheel, but she reminded herself he didn't realize why she was running toward him so recklessly. However as soon as she approached the driver's side of the car, new fear stabbed at her insides. The deputy's head was lying across the steering wheel, a thick, dark mat of blood trickling down his neck. He had been knocked out! Maybe killed!

Then she heard the sound of running feet coming from the house. She looked up through the rain at the stocky man with the black curly beard. His evil face scowled as he ran toward her, a shiny steak knife gleaming out of his raised left hand.

Her heart pounded painfully as her brain urged her to find the deputy's gun. Her hand flew into the car across his body, but before it had gone far, she realized she didn't have time to extricate the gun—Robert Seaton would have already closed the distance between them and stabbed her to death.

The blood rushed to her ears as her feet pounded the wet earth. It was pouring in earnest now. She had no time for fear, no time to look back. Desperation gave unimagined strength to her legs and determination to her lungs. She ran for her life.

She could afford to think about nothing but the asphalt road in front of her. Two blocks away was her neighbor's house. If she could get there, she could get help. Her single-mindedness focused all her effort on fleeing. It wasn't until she was almost at her neighbor's house that she remembered the family was on vacation. Renewed despair and the wet soles of her shoes sent her slipping on the rain-drenched asphalt.

She fell sideways along the road, rolling over into the brush, the wind knocked from her. Her lungs ached as she gasped for air in a heavy wheeze while she tried to get up. It was no use. Her arms and legs wouldn't cooperate. She fell back exhausted. Then she felt a sharp pain in her thigh. It took her a moment before her brain processed the information that she had been kicked. She opened her eyes and felt her heart tighten in horror as she stared into the ruthless eyes of Robert Seaton towering over her, sweaty and gasping for breath, as the rain beat down on them both.

"Get up!"

Terror froze her limbs. He reached down and yanked at her left arm, dragging her to her feet. Her run for freedom had failed. He had caught her. And now he was raising the knife to her throat.

"Who knows about me and what do they know?"

His eyes gleamed eagerly, as though he was hoping she would refuse to answer. She could see he wanted to hurt her and considered her an easy victim. She had just one chance. She had to do something unexpected. In that split second when their eyes met, she felt the keys she still held in her right hand and with all her strength, she swerved away from the knife and chopped at his face.

The keys gouged into his bearded cheek, opening his eyes wide in surprise and pain. Claire dropped to a crouch, just dodging the thrust of the knife. While he was unbalanced from his ineffective swing, she kicked his shin and jerked her wet and slippery arm away from his grasp. Once free she turned tail and began running, this time back to her house.

She ignored the protests from her bruised and overtaxed muscles. She fled on sheer will alone, the foul cursing behind her spurring her on. She was terrified, but something determined inside her said that if she was to die today, she would not do so placidly. She would fight to her last breath.

That last breath did not seem far away. Her lungs burned from lack of oxygen, her arms and legs hurt beyond pain. She was just at her walkway when he tackled her legs, collapsing her like a glob of jelly onto the heady wet grass. She gasped hoarsely in defeat as his arm jerked her onto her back. Helpless, she looked up into his angry, evil face towering over her. His chest heaved in exertion as his eyes flared in a blood-lust and his left arm raised the knife.

He smiled as he began to plunge it toward her heart.

Chapter Sixteen

Wyatt knew something was wrong when he wasn't able to raise his deputy on watch in front of Claire's house on the car phone. He called for more backup and an ambulance as he pressed pedal to the metal, racing against time to Claire's.

But as he drove up, it appeared to be too late. He caught a glimpse of Claire running toward the front of her house and then collapsing at the edge of her walkway as Robert Seaton tackled her.

Wyatt jammed on the brakes, killing the engine. He jumped from the car and called out his warning, but he was aware the wind and rain might have drowned out his words as they had no doubt drowned out his car's approach. He couldn't afford a second warning or a second shot. Robert Seaton had raised the knife.

Wyatt aimed, blinking frantically to see through the blanket of rain. His gun cracked like nearby thunder in his ears. Seaton remained absolutely still for an instant, a stone statue with raised arm. Then in eerie slow motion he crumpled onto the sopping grass, as though his muscles and bones had suddenly liquefied. Before his body ceased to move, Wyatt had run the distance from his Chevy Blazer to Claire's side.

His heart lumped in his throat as he approached her still form. He was too late! Then suddenly her eyelids fluttered as her breath came in hoarse little gasps. She was alive!

He dropped to his knees. "Darling, can you hear me?"

He felt the soreness in his chest ease as she opened her eyes, her mouth smiling through its gasps.

"Wyatt...can't believe...you're here."

He cradled her to him then, rocking her back and forth, muttering foolish, silly things that he was only half-conscious of, as the pouring rain drenched them both to the bone. He knew then he had been wrong to think he could put restrictions on his love. In that moment when he thought he had lost her, he knew he could never willingly leave her, no matter what she held back.

Sometime later, three deputies and an ambulance arrived. The paramedics verified Robert Seaton was dead and hooked up an IV to the unconscious deputy whose vital signs were steady. All the time Wyatt remained kneeling next to Claire, holding her closely, protectively. Only when the paramedics insisted on checking her over did he reluctantly release her to their ministrations. He watched the ambulance drive away with her and the injured deputy inside, feeling a strong pull to follow.

When the flashing lights were completely out of sight, he turned to see Tom Watson studying him.

Wyatt coughed uneasily. "She'll want her brother with her. I'll go call him."

Tom rested his hand on Wyatt's arm. "She'll want you there, Wyatt. Why don't you let me call Alan Gillette?"

DESPITE ACHES in nearly every part of her body, Claire at least felt warm and dry an hour later as the nurse fitted the final dressing over a particularly nasty elbow abrasion she had gotten from falling on the asphalt. She was sitting in a treatment room, dressed only in a hospital bathrobe, and was beginning to feel like a mummy with all the bandages covering her arms and legs.

The nurse was jabbering about ointments and dressing changes, but Claire's mind kept remembering the feel of Wyatt's warm arms and the sound of his deep voice as the chilling summer storm soaked them in its fury. She had closed her eyes, expecting death; she had opened her eyes, delivered by his hand.

She looked up as the door swung open, hoping for Wyatt, and not disappointed at all when she saw it was both Wyatt and Alan. Alan reached her first with a hug, but it was Wyatt's smile she watched over Alan's shoulder that set fire to her heart.

"Wyatt's filled me in, Claire. Thank God you're all right. He's told me you two had figured out that our assassin was Robert Seaton. What else did you know about him?"

"Just that he was Robert Thayer's twin and Richard Quade's cousin. Have you any idea what caused him to kill?"

Alan hopped up next to Claire on the examining table. Wyatt made himself comfortable in a chair as Alan told them both about the military background of Robert Seaton and his tie-in with Barney Coffman's son, Larry, and their court martial for mutiny.

"So it was all for revenge?" Claire asked.

Alan nodded. "Seaton had a penchant for it."

Wyatt shook his head. "How could he kill his own twin?"

Alan shrugged. "Barney Coffman said Seaton talked about his twin brother and look-alike cousin with anger and resentment because he believed them to have had a better life than his."

"Do you know what Seaton's upbringing was like?" Claire asked.

Alan nodded. "Seaton's adoptive parents were very harsh, frequently beating him to ensure discipline. It warped him to the point that he only recognized violence as a resolution to conflict. His Navy record was replete with such incidences."

Claire nodded. "Yes, that can happen to abused children."

Alan shrugged. "His parents told him he was adopted. Seaton investigated and found out about his twin brother and traced his cousin when he broke in and stole his adoption records."

Wyatt nodded in understanding. "Now I know why the paper adoption records weren't there when we tried to subpoena them."

Alan nodded. "Seaton told Coffman he had been keeping tabs on a twin and a cousin look-alike for years. Coffman told us that's what brought Seaton to the Hood Canal last summer. He was trying to decide whether to steal Quade's wallet and driver's license."

"You mean he was there when Richard Quade died?" Claire asked.

Alan nodded. "He told Barney Coffman he'd been following Richard Quade when suddenly his twin appeared on the scene. He was shocked to see him since the last time he checked Roger Thayer was in jail in Nevada. He watched fascinated as the two men discovered each other. Just when he was trying to think how to use the situation to the best advantage, he saw Roger shoving Richard's body overboard."

"He actually saw it?" Claire asked.

"Oh yes. And he saw Thayer start the boat engine and take off. That's when Seaton fished the body out of the water and dumped it on the shore where he knew the authorities would find it."

"He wanted it found?"

"Yes," Wyatt said. "He later posed as the missing Canadian's brother so he could identify Richard Quade's body. The name John Luther was an alias Seaton used when he traveled through Canada. He was wanted there under that name for theft of explosive materials. By identifying Richard Quade as his alias, he was able to cover his own tracks. That was the reason the fingerprints looked close enough to fool the medical examiner."

"Yes, of course," Claire said. "The fingerprints of a cousin that genetically close would share many details. Only an expert would have been able to recognize the differences."

Alan nodded. "Coffman tells us that after identifying Quade's body as John Luther, Seaton followed his twin, Roger Thayer, and watched him take over their cousin's identity. That was when he decided to use the impersonation to his own advantage. He was only out of federal prison a short while himself at the time. Seeing the switch of his twin brother and cousin gave him the final basis for his plan of revenge and he began fitting each part into its place."

"And Barney Coffman?" Wyatt asked.

"Seaton added Coffman to his plan six months ago so he'd have the kind of intelligence he needed to pinpoint his targets. He scheduled everything to happen at the time the *Nimitz* would be coming in for refueling, knowing he could take over the identity of Richard Quade, just as his brother had, and gain access to the Shipyard. He probably also used his time to learn those rudimentary aspects of auto mechanics so he could pass for a few days."

"A very carefully thought-out scheme," Wyatt said. "It might have worked if a certain psychologist I know hadn't decided to drive to the store to get some fruit last Monday."

He looked over at her then, his eyes full of warmth. Claire felt her blood filling with a champagne-like intoxication. Then a nurse came in to call Alan to the phone.

BEFORE HE LEFT, Alan glanced back at Wyatt and Claire as they looked at each other. The glow of love on her face gladdened his heart and lifted the weight of guilt from his conscience.

She could never know about the classified file that accompanied her husband's death, the one that explained why his murder by a spy had been quickly accepted as suicide by NIS so that they could pretend not to know they had a mole dug into their organization. Even in his death, Jerry Boland was serving his country.

But Claire couldn't be told. The identified spy was too useful in passing on false information to the other side. National security demanded Alan's silence, even in the face of his sister's pain.

But he could see no pain on her face now—only love for this Sheriff's detective who had rescued her from both death and doubt.

And Alan knew then that Claire had healed. With a relieved smile he closed the door behind him.

WYATT SAT DOWN next to Claire on the examination table, taking her hand within his, feeling its warmth march through him like an invading army meeting no resistance.

"I've been talking to my Chief of Detectives. He thinks it would benefit the department to have a psychological consultant brought in on cases where normal law enforcement techniques might need a boost. So what do you say?"

Claire looked at his face in surprise. "Wyatt, are you offering me a job with the Kitsap County Sheriff's Department?"

His eyes looked searchingly into hers. "When cases lend themselves to psychological examination. Of course, I'm sure all my cases will qualify. You see, I've decided I'm willing to take whatever it is you can give, Claire. For as long as you can give it. I have no doubts about us. And I'll be around every day from now on to prove it."

Claire understood he was accepting her even with her previous doubts. Her voice caught as she felt the tears sting her eyes. "Wyatt, I love you, without a doubt in the world."

And then she was in his arms and he was kissing her, holding her close, whispering gently in her ear. "Claire, darling, I'm so glad. I love you so much. Every adorable, psychological inch of you. I want us to be married, to work together, to love together, to do everything together."

Claire smiled up into his eyes. "If that means I can get you on my couch, I think you should know from the beginning that I consider your case in need of a lifetime of therapy."

She kissed him slowly and passionately, savoring the taste and feel of him in her arms. When she finally pulled back, she could detect his reluctance to let the kiss end.

"If this is your special type of therapy, you're never going to be able to get me off your couch," he said, smiling happily.

She looked at him with excitement in her eyes and mischief in her voice. "There are more comfortable places."

Wyatt hopped off the examination table and in one quick swoop, picked up Claire and gently set her on her feet. As he looked down at her, her breath caught at the green-blue fire that lit his eyes. She felt her heart jolt happily as it answered the deep passion smoldering in his voice.

"Write up the commitment papers, Doc. This is one patient who can't wait to become your inmate."

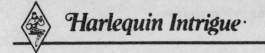

Harlequin Intrigue·

A SPAULDING & DARIEN MYSTERY

Make a date with Jenny Spaulding and Peter Darien when this engaging pair of amateur sleuths returns to solve their third puzzling mystery in Intrigue #171, ALL FALL DOWN (October 1991).

Coming in March from

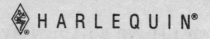

LaVyrle Spencer's unforgettable story of a
love that wouldn't die.

SWEET MEMORIES

She was as innocent as she was unsure . . . until a very special
man dared to unleash the butterfly wrapped in her cocoon and
open Teresa's eyes and heart to love.

SWEET MEMORIES is a love story to savor that will make you
laugh—and cry—as it brings warmth and magic into your
heart.

"Spencer's characters take on the richness of friends, relatives
and acquaintances."   —*Rocky Mountain News*

SWEET

HARLEQUIN
American Romance®

RELIVE THE MEMORIES....

All the way from turn-of-the-century Ellis Island to the future of the '90s...A CENTURY OF AMERICAN ROMANCE takes you on a nostalgic journey through the twentieth century.

Watch for all the A CENTURY OF AMERICAN ROMANCE titles coming to you one per month over the next two months in Harlequin American Romance, including #385 MY ONLY ONE by Eileen Nauman, in April.

Don't miss a day of A CENTURY OF AMERICAN ROMANCE.

The women...the men...the passions...the memories....

This April, don't miss #449, CHANCE OF A LIFETIME, Barbara Kaye's third and last book in the Harlequin Superromance miniseries

A powerful restaurant conglomerate draws the best and brightest to its executive ranks. Now almost eighty years old, Vanessa Hamilton, the founder of Hamilton House, must choose a successor. Who will it be?

Matt Logan: He's always been the company man, the quintessential team player. But tragedy in his daughter's life and a passionate love affair made him make some hard choices....

Paula Steele: Thoroughly accomplished, with a sharp mind, perfect breeding and looks to die for, Paula thrives on challenges and wants to have it all...but is this right for her?

Grady O'Connor: Working for Hamilton House was his salvation after Vietnam. The war had messed him up but good and had killed his storybook marriage. He's been given a second chance—only he doesn't know what the hell he's supposed to do with it....

Harlequin Superromance invites you to enjoy Barbara Kaye's dramatic and emotionally resonant miniseries about mature men and women making life-changing decisions.

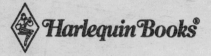 **Harlequin Books®**

GREAT NEWS...
HARLEQUIN UNVEILS NEW SHIPPING PLANS

For the convenience of customers, Harlequin has announced that Harlequin romances will now be available in stores at these convenient times each month*:

Harlequin Presents, American Romance, Historical, Intrigue:

> May titles: April 10
> June titles: May 8
> July titles: June 5
> August titles: July 10

Harlequin Romance, Superromance, Temptation, Regency Romance:

> May titles: April 24
> June titles: May 22
> July titles: June 19
> August titles: July 24

We hope this new schedule is convenient for you.

With only two trips each month to your local bookseller, you'll never miss any of your favorite authors!

*Please note: There may be slight variations in on-sale dates in your area due to differences in shipping and handling.

HDATES-R